The Little Life
of Richie Millipede

M. Reese Kennedy

SUNKEN GARDENS PRESS

www.sunkengardenspress.com

Cover Art: Elisabeth and Zoe Lawrence
Interior Art: Zoe Lawrence

Books by M. Reese Kennedy

The Plague of Dreamlessness (2012)

The Artist in the Pines (2014)

The Little Life of Richie Millipede (2017)

PART ONE

1. Jill

We dealt him an odd little life, from the moment of his highly optimized birth. Richie Millipede, we called him, fetus number seven from the Genesis Project. Picked offhandedly and signifying nothing, the name was an aberration in an otherwise controlled and sanitized environment. "Millipede" came from some video game the lab techs were playing at the time, though one particularly inane rumor would peg it to some fantastical notion of his leg count. "Richie" came from an old TV sitcom most of us had never seen. I tried calling him Richard for a while, thinking it a bit more dignified, but he never really took to it.

We'd had our first hint of him some years before he actually existed. It came at a Gathering – that was the BioSpore term for our all hands assemblies, though they weren't the backslapping forums or new product launches I imagined happening at other companies. Ours sat at the opposite end of the spectrum, strangely unbusinesslike, dreamy and disjointed. In spite of that, and in some part because of it, Gatherings were the uncontested centerpiece of the BioSpore culture. Beyond the peculiar stir they created in the moment, they had a vaguely prophetic air, something flighty that you'd dismiss until years later, when you'd recognize glimpses they'd given at any number of oncoming phenomena. Richie, as it happened, was one of those.

Gatherings popped up every two or three months, though always on insanely short notice – usually just an hour or two beforehand. This had a jarring effect on all of our schedules, for there was never any notion that attendance was optional. A Gathering was a summons, a corporate subpoena for every employee on campus, from the most senior science officer to the lowest maintenance worker. That's not to suggest any great resentment on our part. Gatherings were reliably engaging, and their fundamental weirdness was something that many of us, in our increasingly buttoned-up circles, found reassuring. People well beyond my own modest station considered them highly innovative and quite possibly brilliant – to the point that business schools were debating their merits well before we'd even begun our run on market share, back when academics and rueful investors were the only ones paying us any attention. Even our most revered in-house skeptics tempered their critiques with fond resignation. My colleague, Dr. Alton Falstaff, chalked one bit of quasi-formulaic commentary on a foyer blackboard, where it stood admired, or at least unerased, for the better part of a year: "Gatherings ≈ Grand menageries of quarter-baked utopioids ≈ Airy notions most executives wouldn't share with their closest confederates, let alone trumpet to the rank and file."

But Chuck Hansen, PhD and CEO, was no ordinary executive. He was quite happy to package such airy notions into fully choreographed spectacles, retaining a small staff of theater production people just for the purpose, and to pile the whole lot of us in for our famously abrupt matinees. They all had a bit of a raucous air, the product of the sudden break in our workaday routines, the oddly ethereal nature of the subject matter, and the mind-bending incongruity of the theatre that held them. That of course was the full-scale replica of The Globe from Shakespeare's London, time-warped into the center of our thoroughly postmodern Silicon Valley campus. As Falstaff would tell me, "Replicating the Globe is, perforce, a matter of some conjecture, since surprisingly little is really known of it." But we felt suitably transported when we streamed down the sunlit footpaths to converge at that theater, bottlenecking good-naturedly at the great wooden gates. Though many of the campus buildings were named, with varying degrees of reverence, for luminaries of the Renaissance – The Copernicus Center, The Kepler Complex, The Eye of Newton – the theater was officially untitled. But we all knew it as The Icosagon,[1] built as it was on the plan of a twenty-sided polyhedron.

Its whitewashed plaster walls, sectioned by dark oaken laths and staves, loomed at forty feet, and seemed all the taller for the stingy row of windows near the top. The roof was weather-blackened thatch, steeply pitched to raise its prominence. High-pointed gables at the four compass points bore flagpoles with pennants that flapped excitedly on Gathering days, even in the most windless conditions.[2] Inside, wooden benches filled three steeply graded tiers encircling an open-air pit and an apron stage. Scarred wooden posts and rough floorplanks capped the effect – it all seemed quite authentic but for a few small concessions, most notably a rafter-rattling sound system and excellent restroom facilities. Audience participation was boisterous, and Hansen would augment that with staff-members planted in the crowd to guffaw or to shout questions on cue. On occasion he'd let one of his prodigies take the lead – it mixed things up and promoted the company's egalitarian science-first approach. But more often than not it was Hansen himself on stage. The effect, as he saw it, was a glimpse into the mind of the highly visionary CEO he held himself to be. And the result, as he saw it, was nothing short of corporate rebirth, newly minted zeal and creativity through the workforce. Many of the topics were unashamedly and entirely unrelated to anything BioSpore was doing, or would ever do. But a critical few were more real than we might have thought,

---

1 I looked that up my first day on the job, wary of the stigma of having asked.
2 Those flagpoles marked a substantial upgrade on their medieval forbears. Activated by stagnation sensors, they generated their own air pressure and forced it through vertically linear vents, bringing life to drooping pennants. The product was deemed to have limited upside and was never released to the public.

windows into initiatives that would spawn new realms of research, massive reshufflings of personnel, and, eventually, product lines none of us had ever imagined.

Because I'd spent so much time in the field, I'd been on campus for just a handful of Gatherings over the prior few years. But this one, as it turned out, trumped all the many I'd missed. It began, as most of them did, with a video. Three gigantic screens shot up to an oddly Stonehengian effect through slots in the timber stage floor. An archive-stock black and white film leader flashed numbers from eight to one, each with a line segment spinning once from the midpoint. The main feature, also in black and white, began crisply at zero. A baby, far larger than life, gender unclear but very cute, lay supine on a plain white backdrop, wearing only a cotton diaper and a theatrically oversized safety pin. The camera pulled back, revealing a strange hybrid of a room, both nursery and laboratory, one part cuddly and two parts clinical. Right away the whole setup struck me as a little creepy, like we were supposed to believe the mother was just off camera, cooing from the fringes, while in fact she didn't exist at all, or had been coolly dispatched. A woman did appear, but her lab-coat suggested a role more clinical than maternal. Her face remained offscreen throughout, reinforcing the notion that she wasn't the mom, though the even creepier thought did occur to me, if only for a moment, that she *had* mothered the child, but strictly for scientific purposes. Looking back on it now, I see things a little more simply – she was a hand model, the consummate 1960's housewife from the wrist down, cinematically converted to the sciences. For all we knew, she was pockmarked in the face and pudgy at the hips, but her hands described something altogether different, something elegant, pristine, and perfect.[3] She pulled the baby up into a sitting position, then let it go. Not surprisingly, it toppled over.

---

3 I remember finding my own big-knuckled mitts tucked under my legs just then, a moment of subliminal shame.

I don't have any children myself, and at that point I had no particular expertise in childhood development. But I considered that response, or lack thereof, perfectly normal for a baby of that age – kind of cute, kind of funny. Given the overlarge head and the comparative skeletal-muscular deficiency, it was a matter of simple physics. As the faceless woman repeated the exercise, I noticed there'd been a silly sound effect dubbed in, an orchestra gone haywire like something from a Looney Tunes soundtrack, wind instruments falling sharply with a Doppler effect as if the whole horn section were leaping off a cliff with each drop of the baby's head. And when the camera zoomed in and she pulled the baby back up to topple for the third time, we'd all more than taken the point. But she kept at it, the baby going down for a fourth time, and a fifth, all to the same musical accompaniment. It became unsettling to watch.

"Consider one simple reality – the dimensions of the infant cranium." The voice oozed with competence, simultaneously provocative and reassuring, something out of a 1960s science reel. "The head is clearly outsized, to the point where this child, six months after its birth, can't even hold itself to sit upright. Endearing, perhaps even mildly comical, part of the baby's overall appeal – until you consider the asymmetry on its more practical levels. The most obvious problem is in relation to the birth canal..."

The video cut off, the screens dropped back through the floor, and out came Chuck Hansen, blonde hair and beach boy tan perfectly aglow, his whole figure enshrouded in a stage-light nimbus. The effect was somewhat diminished, as I recalled from earlier Gatherings, by his undersized mandible and his overconfident duck-footed stride. He twirled a microphone and kicked a pair of $900 Italian loafers under his tailored lab-coat, driving through the applause, right on the beat.

"We've all imagined, with some horror, the historical scenes of peasant women staggering into the fields, deep in the throes of labor.

Many were not old enough to hold learner's permits in today's world, but in those times they were old enough to suffer quite terribly, victims of a process so physiologically inefficient that it defies the very notion of evolution. An estimated one in five of those women, and more than one in five of their babies, would die in childbirth. Things were no better for the privileged, even for royalty – maybe worse, given the medical practitioners they relied on to prescribe toxic potions and drain blood by the pintful."

"And to charge them handsomely for the privilege," came a call from the upper tier.

Hanson paused for laughter, then added, "Some things never change."

And, "Those poor women would've been better off with a soggy poultice and a little bed rest."

He paused again. You could see he was already quite pleased with himself. He held comedy to be one of his many exceptional skills, and in an adolescent sort of way he actually was funny from time to time, a notion reliably validated by the lively and well-remunerated audience.

"Given such a poorly evolved mechanism for reproduction, it's a wonder the species moved forward at all. I don't have to tell the mothers here that this single and inexplicable design flaw – the size of the baby's head – plagues us even today. Childbirth remains an extremely taxing and risky enterprise, leaving a shocking percentage of mothers with some degree of permanent physical damage. Recovery times are long. Costs are staggering. And those are the least of the problems in our most underdeveloped countries, where maternal and neonatal mortality rates have improved just marginally since the Dark Ages.

"Now consider, for all this suffering, the best-case outcome, a healthy child. Six months of dedicated care, and he can't even sit up, as we've seen in the video, perhaps to excess." The Looney Tunes sample played for a moment, and Hansen paused for laughter that in this case was not forthcoming, a rare lapse.

"It's a full year before he can gather himself to walk. For all the intellectual firepower implied in that oversized head, it'll be another year and more before he can string together the most rudimentary sentence. And, as those of us with teenagers can attest, it'll be another twenty before he'll make the slightest bit of sense." Laughter here.

"Other animals can run, swim, crawl – do whatever they were destined to do, some directly from birth, some within hours thereafter. Some require no parental oversight whatsoever, propelling themselves and collecting their foodstuffs almost immediately. We, on the other hand, spend an inordinate amount of needlessly unpleasant time, and an unconscionable amount of physical resources, managing just one aspect of our children's functions. Defecation." Generous laughter here.

"This isn't the occasional indiscretion you might find from a puppy. As many or most of you know first hand, we're talking complete non-compliance, absolute incontinence spanning a period of years. Imagine again the medieval mother, fortunate enough to have survived her labor in the fields, rewarded now with the wailing infant's incessant soiling of its swaddling cloths and the unremitting stench in the family hovel. Take it back another several millennia, and you wonder how we avoided obliteration, extinction by infanticide, our young ones clubbed like seal pups. Credit to the Cro-Magnon and to others of the prehistoric ilk for a sensitivity and forbearance belying their barbarous appearance. And credit to our heroine of the less distant past, a solitary figure on the bank of some putrid creek, kneeling dutifully to scrub at the sludge of her progeny.

"Even in today's best-fitted homes this incontinence is a burden. The optimal output, or, should I say, the least egregious excretion, is solidly pressed, molded firmly to the buttocks as the child sits square on its treasure, witless as a dodo hen. The modern parent might feel

9

fortunate to simply peel away this rank mold, this gruesome plaster mask, this ill-favored breakfast cake. For she is all too aware of the alternative, the outflow that streams well beyond the confines of the wrap, soiling the dimpled thighs and all else in its putrescent path." Groans here from the audience.

"The arrangement is an unpleasant and unproductive one, for the parents, for the infants, and for the planet, given the diaper tonnage we add, day after day, to our mountainous landfills, or to the floating plastic islands in our oceans. We spend more time and more resources managing our children's defecation than most animals spend parenting in total. Our challenged infants require years to understand what cats and dogs grasp in days. Granted, no one presses our noses into the freshly soiled carpet while beating us about the hindquarters." Pause for more laughter.

"And who knows? Maybe they should. But I suspect the results would be disappointing."

2. Richie

Dawn at the compound. I'm awake just before the kookaburras blast reveille, lying on my back and staring into the wooden rafters as the darkness begins to slip. Jill carries on about my cathedral ceilings almost every time she visits, but even I can see they're more of a practicality than an architectural flourish. They're modestly scaled, nothing like the European basilicas we studied back at Genesis, or for that matter, nothing like the actual ceilings we had at Genesis. Even those dwarfed the ones I have here. But I'm always careful to tell Jill that I appreciate the cathedral effect, and my house in general. I know she went to a lot of trouble with it, and that appreciation is important to her.

And the truth is I do like my ceilings. There's something about their slope to the center beam that pulls your eye up and into the swirly patterns of the wood. It's like having enormous topographical maps pasted overhead, everywhere you go, any time of day. But first thing in the morning the world seems a bit dreamier, and it's then that I see the strata of great canyon walls, or a wind-rustled grassland, or ocean waves all in a row, each in tints of wooden orange. A knot becomes the sun sneaking up at land's edge, or a dwarf peeking over a drumlin. It's like the Rorschach tests we used to take, only now I don't have to answer on cue, and nobody's taking any notes.

Jill tells me the ceilings at her place are too low. She complains how hard it is to live any kind of an inspired life that way, with such a heaviness lurking just overhead. Besides a day or two in a travel carton, I don't have much experience with that. But I do try to acknowledge her discomfort. That seems important to her too.

3. Jill

In the words of the technology writer Ian Harding: "BioSpore's capitalization was a case study in itself. It fell neatly into one of those periodic wrinkles in financial time, the gap between a sudden vulnerability in the marketplace and the regulatory response that snuffs it. Bankers and academics had just begun to warn against such an unconventional public offering, the IPO gone viral, and now they pointed to BioSpore's astounding cash proceeds as the inevitable and entirely undesirable outcome. They condemned what they saw as an 'obscene windfall,' a 'gross excess,' and an 'unwarranted indulgence.' And the tough rhetoric held a certain logic, given how little the company had produced to that point, and how little it seemed compelled, or even inclined, to produce in the future. It all spoke to the brazen, even cynical vagueness of the BioSpore mission, the natural byproduct, it seemed, of the entitlement that pervaded its management core. The gray hairs of experience were conspicuously absent, usurped by coddled and callow youth running amok on an overly large custom-built campus. By nearly all accounts, once you'd stepped through those gates it was *Welcome to the Monkey House*.[4]

---

4 *Welcome to the Monkey House* was a popular internal catchphrase at BioSpore, though any link with the identically named collection of short stories by Kurt Vonnegut (1968), or the later album by The Dandy Warhols (2013), is unclear.

"But what the pundits hadn't considered, or not nearly enough, was that Chuck Hanson had pulled together a mob of the most brash and brilliant young minds in science. He'd plucked them domestically and globally, wherever they'd been stifled, from impotent academic programs, from underfunded start-ups, from big-cap high-techs grown cumbersome and unwieldy. He'd lured them in with salaries doubled and stock options granted, and with promises of generous autonomy, unsurpassed facilities, and lavish development support. It took years of percolation, and a corporate skin thick enough to brush off the legions of disgruntled shareholders. But something special did eventually spawn between the oversized war chest, the extraordinary collection of talent, and the alternative approach of the people behind it. And so began the madcap BioSpore run, spanning a range of disciplines and hitting the market like a set of big breakers on a fog-shrouded beach — you couldn't quite see them, but you had the idea there were plenty more on the way."

I was on the scene, at least peripherally, for a good deal of that. And, from my point of view, Harding has it mostly right. BioSpore was an amazing place in those halcyon days, and I could take pride in a lot of what it accomplished. But the Genesis Project, while just a ripple in the BioSpore tide, was never a good idea. It was never a good program. And it didn't get nearly the scrutiny it should have. I'm not a purist, or a fundamentalist — far from it. But on that project they'd messed with human DNA in ways it shouldn't be messed with, way beyond where most reasonable, thinking people would be comfortable. The target wasn't an occasional problem in the sequencing. They weren't after dyslexia, cleft palate, congenital deafness, that kind of thing. What they were after, as is now a matter of public record, was the universal acceleration of human development, with a special emphasis on gestation and infancy.

It's hard to say exactly why, but I didn't understand all that at the time. Or if I did understand it, I didn't especially care. I was coming off an assignment in San Francisco that had drifted into some pretty heavy stuff, street work, very hush-hush. I wanted something less stressful and more or less in-house, in a place where I'd actually be noticed. I wasn't the first person at BioSpore, or at any number of other companies, or in the military, who'd spent hard time in the field and wanted to consolidate that into something more stable, more secure, and substantially more lucrative.

Initially there'd been a big internal buzz around the Genesis Project, and while it seemed to have dissipated some by the time I was wrapping up in the city, I took that as the inevitable corporate shift to covertness. It was part of BioSpore's schizophrenic makeup, its normal spin cycle, its peculiar corporate ebb and flow – laying bare a range of airy initiatives in Gatherings that leaked, or rather, gushed into the social media; casting on the cloak of secrecy as they moved through the internal churn to oblivion or fruition; and launching the full public blitz as winning products emerged and readied for the marketplace.

I've mentioned that I was light on childhood development. And my law degree was probably more of a detriment than anything else. But my other credentials were solid: good schools, dual master's in zoology and public health, and several "well-comported" years in the field, by standards you'd find in any conventional personnel file and by others you definitely wouldn't. That is to say, I'd maintained a certain discretion, or rather, as they phrased it in one of my annual reviews, "an admirable air of corporate confidentiality." It was all just enough to land me the twelfth and final spot as a Development Staff Specialist.

Engineering, implantation and gestation were all wrapped up by then. Our job in Development was to manage the early phase of life with an emphasis on "fostering the accelerated acquisition of extraordinary skill sets." I'd had two full weeks of off-site orientation, but none of it was particularly useful for the simple reason that the subjects didn't actually exist, outside of their respective uteri, until the end of the second week. The surrogates, I'd learned, had all been implanted on the same day, February 14th – yes, Valentine's Day, the butt of many jokes around the Project. As expressly provided in their contracts, the surrogates had been on call throughout their pregnancies, so that when the first of them went into labor, the rest could be induced within a matter of hours. Not surprisingly then, all seven subjects shared the same birthday. This made for a happy occasion, most notably in the realm of operating efficiency. All seven tracking to the day meant uniform staging, fewer scientific variables, and better controls. My first shift fell on their fourth day, a Sunday, though at Genesis weekends were more or less irrelevant. Traditional day names were not even in the project vernacular. Time progressed in a straightforward numerical count from the common birth date. That Sunday, for example, was Postpartum 4, or P4.

Geographically, the job wasn't quite as "in-house" as I'd hoped. Genesis, as it turned out, wasn't housed on the BioSpore campus, but in an industrial park two exits up. The building had originally served as an indoor tennis center, and the only BioSpore modifications to the street-facing exterior had been the crude blocking up of the entry and the removal of the holdover signage.[5] The overall effect, an industrial barn of concrete block and corrugated metal, was no more or less hideous than the muddle of anonymous warehousing and light industry that surrounded it. The new entry was around the corner, on the shielded east side of the building, where the trappings of a more sophisticated operation were more apparent. I scanned my passkey, punched in my poor

---

5 A faint outline of crossing racquets persisted on the sun-bleached wall through the Genesis Project's occupancy.

pun of an alphanumeric security code, *madamecurious13*, and popped through two sets of very advanced-looking airlock doors. A huge man in a lab coat – I had him at six-foot-six, 250 pounds – stood just inside, fiddling with some cables. He dropped his bearded chin to consider me over the top of his glasses, a practice I associate with him to this day.

"Jill Edelman," I said.

"Alton Falstaff," he replied with an easy smile I couldn't help but admire. I think it's more genetic than conditioned – my life, on balance, has gone reasonably well – but I'm not a person of easy smiles. It remains a mystery to me how other women can flash with such impressive conviction, on demand, for any camera that pops out of someone's bag. Men, on the whole, seem less gifted in that way, but here was a giant of a man with a facility those women couldn't or wouldn't even aspire to, a completely natural and uncalculated affability.

"Nice doors," I said, looking somewhat awkwardly behind me.

"Shamelessly stolen from the plans for Soyuz spacecraft. We've got half a dozen of their guys now, holding forth on the main campus."

"I might have guessed," I said with a chuckle that was meant to be complicit but may have just missed the mark.

"You might see one or two of them giving me a hand here from time to time."

"Excellent. I was told to ask for Dr. Morben. Can you point me in his direction?"

Falstaff stepped to the side with the affected grace of a toreador, and indicated my pass with the sweep of an arm. "He's the tall guy. You can't miss him." Both the movement and the sudden dismissal struck me as strange, but then perhaps I'd been a bit brusque myself. Stranger still was his reference to "the tall guy," since he himself was one of the tallest people I'd ever met. But I took his instruction at face value and headed off in search of a giant in a lab coat.

The extraordinarily high ceilings were a reminder of the building's former incarnation, but the top-rate interior fitout quickly dispelled any notion of tennis ball fuzz gathered untidily behind the curtains. Just a few seconds inside gave the impression of next generation NASA and the Lyric Stage rolled into one. Technically, the facility exceeded ISO laboratory standard in every regard. I recognized the feel of the dynamic weight dispersion flooring just two or three steps in – this particular installation was also temperature-controlled, auto-hygienic, and overwhelmingly, disturbingly white. The air quality was sublime, the product, I thought, of particle filtering ventilation or of induction circulation, though I later learned that both systems were in place and working in tandem. Most interesting to me were the drone lighting units that floated overhead. I'd heard all the talk but had never actually seen one. I now counted seven hovering under this single roof. They supplemented multiple skylights set in receding trapezoids to optimize light quality at different hours and through all of the seasons, as I'd seen in another BioSpore facility not long before. Add multi-tiered banks of indirect, prismatic lighting, and I figured that would do it for the optics – until I got a better look at the main stage, or what they called the nursery.

Before I could manage that, Dr. Morben – Alfred Morben, Project Supervisor – lurched forward to make his introductions. I'd soon learn that everyone called him Dr. Moribund behind his back, though for the most part he seemed lively enough to me. Physically, I'd have to concede he fit the bill. As Falstaff had suggested, he was insanely tall – just an inch or two shy of seven feet. But he walked as if the ceiling were set at six and a half, his head ducked and stretched hideously forward, neck flexors straining through waxen flesh. This posture gave the impression of a great wading bird, a giant ebony-feathered heron with an ill-advised moustache. He was fiftyish, with jet-black hair cut short but left unchecked down the back of his neck and plunging rather horribly beneath his collar. He led me through the facility in a manner that placed me not beside him, but behind him, where I couldn't help but steal glances at his lofty nape and its vestigial plumage.

The main stage, or nursery, was raised uniformly at three feet and consumed about half the overall floorplan. It was cordoned on its three interior borders by glass walls running floor to ceiling. Outside the glass, along the main length, ran a line of twelve workstations, one of them earmarked for me, and several clusters of other more elaborate instrumentation. Overhead, staging catwalks bristled with automated theater lighting. Elevated observation stations hung on three sides, like private boxes in an opera house. At the near or eastern end of the nursery sat another concession to theater and an apparent deviation from clinical hygiene – a gilded birdcage on a slender stand in a ring of wrought-iron railing. I recognized the solitary occupant as a cockatiel, a mid-sized bird, gray through the body and wings but yellow in the face, with clownish rouge on both cheeks. Upright crown feathers suggested a tiny tribal chieftain.

We passed three workstations occupied by men whose green jackets marked them as lab techs. I noticed, to my mild surprise, that one of them was playing a video game, and, to my greater surprise, that he made no attempt to conceal it. He was muscled up like a comic book hero – perhaps he felt that exempted him from certain points of workplace protocol. Dr. Morben handed me off quite cordially to a Dr. Sloboth, whose legs, beneath her Genesis lab coat, were stuffed so heroically into denim as to suggest a pachyderm in blue panty hose. She had a lovely smile and a warm manner, but congeniality was not a strong suit for me in those days, and I can blame the fieldwork for only some of that. Bovine, porcine, elephantine – hippopotamine, that was the word. And once I had it I couldn't be rid of it, the lexical intruder tapping impishly at my shoulder as the woman plowed through her introduction, a blissful monologue that veered irretrievably to the trifling. Joining us at length were Doctors Dasher and Bitsen, names that sounded right off a team of reindeer, though I did resist sharing that particular observation. Dasher was a mid-thirtyish man, also above average in height, but most notable for his remarkably precise haircut.[6] Bitsen was a fortyish woman with glasses so thick I felt I was looking down the wrong end of a pair of binoculars. None of these people would have lasted a week in the field, I thought. When the conversation moved to children I quickly mentioned that I didn't have any, implying disinterest as politely as I could. But we made painstaking stops to admire family photos – eight children spread over three workstations. Through these extended pleasantries, all I truly yearned for, after two weeks of formal training and what seemed like months of speculation and anticipation, was one good, long, uninterrupted look through the glass. I deferred the formal introduction to my own workstation, reflecting, with a vague tinge of dread, how I'd always feared a desk job. Still, it took what seemed like forever to disengage without giving offense – didn't these people have work to do? At last I was unescorted, at the far end of the glass and free to take my first look.

I'd been briefed, but not nearly as well as I'd been led to believe. It was difficult to process what I was actually seeing. There through the glass was a cluster of seven very small people, exceptionally small, to the point where I had to step back to confirm that the glass wasn't having some distorting, refracting effect. But my view was clear – none of the seven were more than fifteen inches tall. That mightn't have been so strange if they'd been lying in incubated little cribs. But they weren't lying, or crawling, or even toddling. They were walking, on P4, like you or I would've walked in year four, slightly stiffer, but heel-to-toe and fully upright. Dr. Morben's notes from that day describe their collective

---

6 Over time I'd observe that Dasher's hair never grew the slightest bit longer, at least to the untrained eye. He had his hair cut on a strict ten-day cycle, which I calculated at roughly twelve times the frequency of my own.

postures as "vaguely suggestive of a military bearing." There's a good bit of truth to that. They were almost painfully erect, but pivoting and planting, ducking around corners, really getting around. And they seemed to nod to one another as they passed, as if life were already a quite manageable undertaking, and walking a particular point of satisfaction.

Chuck Hansen had ranted about babies' overlarge heads – I remembered that Gathering all too well. And now, just two years later, the problem seemed rectified. The heads on these seven were perfectly proportionate to their little bodies, not much larger than golf balls. And the bodies themselves were perfectly shaped, not as in perfectly cute little babies, but as in lithe little adults. Dimpled chins had given way to chiseled jaws, and fat diapered bottoms to tight little butts. The notion of fully ambulatory four-day-olds was strange enough, but they were sexy little things to boot. Tiny, yes. Innocent, you'd think, though whoever had dressed them in their skintight bodysuits hadn't done anything to encourage that line of thinking. The girls had Barbie Doll bodies – long legs, tiny waists, pert breasts. And the guys were comparably endowed, with broad-shoulders and lean-frames – GI Joes minus the machismo. All seven were sculpted and curvy, the kind of people you might see in open shirts and low-slung jeans through the windows of an Abercrombie & Fitch in, say, Lilliput. But no one on the Project seemed inclined to acknowledge the accelerated sexuality. I broached the point several times that afternoon, and the responses were so uniformly guarded you'd have thought its mere mention a dismissible offense. While such reserve may have been appropriate under normal circumstances, it seemed incongruous and impractical here. Even the irreverent Falstaff, when pressed, would only mutter his reply – "Yes, yes, nubile neonates" – peer at me over his glasses, and turn pointedly away.

The hair on these newborns added to the effect – not the wispy stuff of toddlers or the cute bowl cuts or ponytails of small children, but eye-catching, professionally rendered, full-bodied coiffures. Strangely enough, they were all styled for the square side of the 60s, with neat left-side parts for the guys and some bizarro puffy numbers for the girls,[7] with a single flip, or upcurl, traversing the shoulders. Just as I began to process all that, and as if on cue, a video clip popped up on the glass. It was a 60s-looking television sitcom, black and white, apparently chosen on the basis that its characters had the same out-landish haircuts as those I was seeing in the nursery. I noticed a bit of tittering around the facility. The clip didn't seem all that funny to me, but I may have been distracted by the fact that the glass I'd been look-ing through had suddenly morphed into a gigantic video screen. As it turned out, the longest of the three glass walls, the one facing our desks, held two All-Way PrismView units. Depending on the settings, they could function from either side as clear or shaded glass, or as clear glass from the outside while projecting video inside, or, as in this case, they could project on both sides. As with the drone lighting, I'd heard about PrismView, but had never actually seen it in action.[8] The intro-duction at this point was a bit startling, and I must have looked pretty foolish standing there trying to make sense of things while my several co-workers, I noticed a hair too late, watched and weighed my every move. It seemed the clip was airing at least partially, if not entirely, for my benefit, though I wasn't sure if I was supposed to be reacting to the Lilliputians, the PrismView, the video content, or all of the above.

A guy named Jerry, the muscle-bound tech I'd seen playing the video game, had dialed up that clip. It came from something called *The Dick Van Dyke Show*. The coif on the lead woman, a comely if slightly cal-orie-deficient brunette — Mary Tyler Moore playing Laura Petrie — was a particularly obvious match, although, if possible, that hairstyle was

---

7 Or at least for the white girls. One of the subjects, Gamma Girl, was black. She wore a tight Afro at that time.

8 BioSpore's release of PrismView would be tied up in the courts for the better part of a decade.

even more freakish on her than on the little girls[9] in the nursery. I'm all for humor – in projects like this it's sometimes what holds everything together. But shocked as I was with the appearance and abilities of the little people, the PrismView, and the uncanny match of the haircuts in the video, I was just as surprised that a guy like Jerry, on his own volition, could play something so frivolous as that video, in full view not only of the entire staff, but of the subjects themselves, every one of whom was taking full notice. I took a quick look at Doctor Morben, but he seemed as amused, in his uniquely leaden way, as the rest. The whole crew had a good chuckle, and apparently not for the first time. From what I could tell, they'd adopted that clip as a sort of theme for the project.

At this point what I really needed was a good stiff drink, or, failing that, a bit of private time, a minute or two to regroup. But I was still under the observation, or, rather, the assessment of my co-workers. I needed to say something, anything, even if slightly inane, to check a box, to demonstrate a certain unflappability. I turned to Dr. Sloboth, who, with the others, was still wiping the laughter from her eyes.

"Who did those haircuts?"

She regarded me for a moment, her laughter subsiding just ahead of its natural course. "They found a microstylist, if you can believe it," she managed to say. "Media relations tracked her down in LA. They flew her in just yesterday."

Impressive as it may have been to source an expert in mini-coiffure, bringing *anyone* in from the outside at this stage seemed a pretty flagrant security breach to me. But I'd learn soon enough that on the Genesis Project, management would sometimes push cutesiness at the expense of both security and science, as if we were producing a line

9 Terms such as "little girls," "little boys," and "children" are not to be construed here in the conventional sense, but in the miniaturized nuance specific to the Genesis Project.

of playtoys for the mass market. The bits of informality I'd already observed in the operation were hard to reconcile with the contentious nature of the research, and with the windowless highly secured facility, the dual passkey access, the round-the-clock video surveillance, and the ongoing gag order on all staff, complete with a perfectly fictional employment narrative for each of us. As far as my friends and family were aware, I was working in assisted reproduction.

4. Richie

When the kookaburras pound out their second call, that's my cue to get up for the day. If you'd never heard what I describe to Jill as the din at dawn, you'd think I was sharing the grounds with a troop of howler monkeys. But the more you hear it, the more you get used to it, and the more you begin to appreciate its finer points. I haven't found much information about kookaburra calls in other parts of Australia, but here in East Central they do it in two or three parts – not in harmony per se, at least not as musical theorists might define it, but in distinct bits that seem to work together nonetheless. The syncopation is complex, each bird rotating on the underbeat while the others run variations over the top – half notes, quarter notes, sixteenths – all within the same highly pronounced pulse. I don't have the equipment to make recordings I can break into separate tracks. I've made the request to Jill three or four times now, but it doesn't seem forthcoming. Not in the budget, apparently.

I've listened to those kookaburra calls, twice at dawn, twice at dusk, and occasionally in the afternoons, each of the four hundred days I've lived here. It works to more than two thousand performances. But since they generally set up beyond my walking range, I've actually only *seen* them do it once. It was a perfectly normal day, just as I was headed in, and there they were, just overhead, all in a line in one of my great eucalyptus trees, craning their heads and stiffening their bodies into three feathered coach horns, their throats and chests pulsating like bellows. As a matter of policy I don't linger outdoors, but in this case I couldn't help but stand in admiration. It's a wonder they don't fall right off the branch the way they go at it. I still don't have much idea what gets them so worked up, but, as Jill put it when we were sitting through one particularly raucous sundown sendoff, they practically blow their brains out up there.

Only a simpleton would equate the kookaburra call with laughter. It's territorial and highly threatening, and I imagine that ground creatures any smaller than I am would quite rightly cower at the sound of it. But the kookaburras never really scared me, except when I first got here and pretty much everything did. They've got big nasty beaks, for sure, and huge heads and strong necks, all perfectly designed for throttling prey. I've seen them knock the daylights out of all kinds of crawly things, whacking them on stout branches with more violence and repetition than might seem necessary. Birds don't have the range of facial expressions that humans do, with their stony beaks and feathered-over faces. But their eyes can be expressive, and they look plenty ferocious at those moments, what might even be called murderous. As Jill says, it's hard to remain completely detached from one's line of work. But overall I've come to know the kookaburras for a demeanor I consider forthright, the implication being that they won't bother me if I don't bother them – which, of course, is about the last thing I'd ever do.

5. Jill

I settled in watching PrismView West, the screen that filled the daytime hours when the subjects were not engaged directly with staff. The program streamed the latest in educational video, with animated letters and dancing numbers and a woman's voice chirping inane little sentences so cheerfully that I already wanted to strangle her. The little people sat before the screen like miniature kindergarteners, some cross-legged and attentive, some fidgeting and distracted.

I was scheduled first inside, and as 09:00 approached I scrubbed up and headed to the west entry chamber, where another set of airlock doors awaited me. With a quiet swish, the door behind me slid shut and the door in front of me slid open. The PrismView programming faded out, as was the default mode with any staff entry. I stepped forward, and my maiden shift was underway.

As part of the daytime protocol, Dr. Falstaff had dropped the nursery temperature, and the subjects had been changed out of their skin-tight sleeping numbers. They now wore cream-colored karate suits with brown sashes at the waist. This gave me the impression, just a few steps in, of being surrounded by half a dozen Jedi action figures. But they weren't moving like toys, or even quite as mechanically as I'd seen them earlier that morning. They were living, breathing little animals, swarming me like kittens. And, despite their persistently "military bearings" and the rather serious expressions projected in most of the early photos, that's what their earliest behavior actually suggested, a bunch of little kittens – cute, needy, and born with a nose for mischief. Right away a pair of them hopped onto my surgical booties as if boarding trolley cars from opposite sides of the street, one on my left foot, one on my right, each grabbing a leg of my scrub pants with the practiced air of a commuter. I stopped in my tracks, horrified I might crush one underfoot, a sub-optimal outcome, surely, for my first day on the job. I recognized Alpha Girl – she was the only blonde of the seven – but I was too new on the Project to identify the boy from that sharp overhead angle, at least while distracted with the very real prospect of trampling him to death. Both of them tugged at my pant legs and peered up at me with expressions I read as *get going, dumbass,* or something similar.

I took a quick look to the nearest observation booth, OB2, where I got an emphatic nod from Dr. Dasher, whose hair didn't move in the least. Dasher didn't outrank me on paper, but his three days of nursery experience certainly trumped my three minutes. So I allowed myself some reassurance, and took one stiff step, then another, a Godzilla blimp in the Macy's Thanksgiving Day Parade, inching my haughty booty-top passengers forward while the others squealed and kept pace alongside.

"You don't have to walk on eggshells," came the voice in my headset. It was Dr. Morben, perched, as he nearly always was, in OB1. "They do this a fair bit. And we've found them to be quite robust."

Apparently I needed to get past my instinctive caution. Dr. Morben was, after all, the Project Super. And since the system recorded every comment from the observation booths, I considered myself suitably indemnified. I picked up my pace, moving across the dynamic weight dispersion floor in something resembling a more natural stride. The little blonde girl, if you could call her that – her breasts were particularly assertive, even under the karate suit – rode my left foot, clucking and giggling every time one foot passed the other, or, rather, every time she passed her male cohort riding on my right. He, for his part, had released one hand and was peering ahead like a sailor beating upwind into choppy seas. They weren't anywhere near verbal on P4, but their vocalizations were far more developed, more complex and directed, than those of normal and much older babies. This was in keeping with virtually all the result curves to date. The little people had been out-performing normal babies, decisively and across the board, from early gestation.

After first trimesters that had been unusually draining on the sur-rogates, the pregnancies had leveled off to become remarkably untaxing in their later stages. The surrogates acquired much less bulk than might normally have been projected. Those who'd carried previously – five of the seven[10] – all reported less third trimester discomfort and greater ranges of maintained activity than in their prior pregnancies. And the deliveries themselves, on cue at forty weeks,[11] were pristine, seamless. I saw a few of the surrogate birthing videos, and they reminded me of clips we'd seen in zoology school, with sea mammals whose offspring seemed to shoot right out, perfectly streamlined for the purpose.

Our subjects were far smaller than normal babies, by length and particularly by weight. All seven were born at 870 to 900 grams, or just under two pounds. But when they went right to solid foods we figured they'd be catching up in a hurry. Breastfeeding had never been in the plans, but neither had the complete bypassing of formula. They didn't seem to have a taste for it, and there was no reason to bother with bottles since they'd entered the world with full sets of teeth. They'd been feed-ing themselves since P2 – I'd watched that video too – eschewing pap

---

10 Genesis had originally contracted with eight surrogates, one of whom was released when her fetus did not survive the first trimester.

11 Or, rather, the uninduced surrogate was on cue at forty weeks. For what it's worth, consensus around the building was that the others weren't far behind.

for small bits of solids, which they'd grasped, moved to their mouths, chewed and swallowed. The initial hand-eye and hand-to-mouth coordination had been a pleasant surprise, way above Project expectations. Happily absent was the normal mealtime inefficiency, the appalling mess, the waste, the smashing of food against the face, all of which I'd seen far more often than I'd liked with my seven nieces and nephews.

And while it may seem a bit off-color, I'd be remiss here not to mention defecation. Don't think I didn't remember that little sequence from Hansen's presentation. From what I'd read in the logs, the staff had initially wrapped the subjects in tiny custom-made diapers. Toilet training was a category marked for fast-tracking, but no one had foreseen what happened early on P3, when the subjects, led by Alpha Boy, undid their tiny adhesive tabs, peeled off their diapers, and wrapped themselves instead in makeshift swaddling cloths they'd pulled from the shelves. Given the incubated conditions within the glass, warmth was not a factor, so the self-swaddling seemed to indicate some measure of inborn modesty or refinement. The boys were already standing to urinate, and were doing so exclusively in the corners. No one had anticipated their being so directed in their excretions this early. Certainly no one had sourced the diminutive toilet fixtures circumstances now demanded. It was actually one of the techs who came up with the short-term solution, a shallow plastic box filled with commercial kitty litter and set in the corner. All of them took to it at once. The girls, who'd begun gathering to urinate in groups – "We only used to do that in the clubs," cracked Dr. Bitsen through her coke-bottle glasses – showed a proclivity to kick their litter in unison.

As I've mentioned, I've never had a baby myself, but the literature, anecdotally verified by each of my three sisters, describes a tarry substance in the earliest days, followed by an output visually analogous to Grey Poupon. Our subjects, however, were straight to a more advanced, solid fecal matter. They'd cover it meticulously – not like kittens kicking backwards with little care or effect, but like you'd expect a reasonably fastidious human adult might do without the benefit of plumbing or a shovel, facing the feces directly, plowing litter with the inside edges of their feet, and persevering for thorough coverage. They observed what seemed an innate sense of decorum through all stages of defecation, turning from each other's labors in a timely and tasteful fashion.

I found myself back where I'd begun, in front of PrismView West, slightly out of breath and considering my options. The impromptu foot-riding had run its course. A second subject pair had taken a turn on my booties, the others had demurely declined, and I'd managed, happily enough, not to crush anyone underfoot. The episode had cost me fifteen minutes of my allocated hour, and I resented the lack of warning from any of my co-workers. But the unexpected introduction had shown me how far along the subjects really were, and had saved me the embarrassment of rolling out my original and absurdly rudimentary plan with cameras rolling and co-workers smirking. I needed an alternative approach for the balance of the hour, and preferably one that set me up for at least the next few days as well. I was new on the job, the last one in, and this was a critical opportunity to flounder. But time in the field had whittled away at my panic impulse, or at least I liked to think so. Just in front of me was a whole wall of shelves, each of them teeming with playthings.[12] My eye ran to the several boxes of Brio.

As a young girl, I'd had a proclivity for those Swedish-made tracks and trains, though they'd always been in relatively short supply at our family home on the shores of Lake Ontario.[13] This was on account of

---

12 The San Francisco Chronicle would later report that the Genesis Project had a toy budget exceeding that of all the county's kindergarten programs combined.

13 The Edelman family home was actually several blocks off the lake, in Oswego, NY.

Brio's inexplicably high pricing and its poorly perceived suitability for girls. Here now was a collection more extravagant than anything I'd ever imagined, enough track, with accompanying switches, bridges, stations and roundabouts for each of the seven children to build individual railways and, in aggregate, to network the entire expanse of nursery. I grabbed a box and settled calmly to the floor, as if this had been my plan from the start.

The feel of the wooden tracks had a nostalgic and briefly soothing effect, but I couldn't help the disjointed sensation of leading a children's play group while clad in scrubs, cap and surgical mask, and while caged in glass with drone lights floating in silent menace overhead. I felt like a test pilot fingering some tic-tac-toe on the frosted cockpit glass at eighty thousand feet, or a moonwalker breaking out some hopscotch in the lunar dust. On the other hand, the little people showed no indication that anything was out of the ordinary. They had, after all, no reference point to the contrary. They settled around me like the most well-behaved of all possible children. Their interest was so immediate and so touchingly naïve that I initially suspected it all to be a ruse, that everyone, staff and subjects together, were in on some elaborate hazing scheme at my expense. The whole thing must have been catching up with me just then. When I realized that their curiosity was genuine, and that they were truly "very nearly enthralled," as my notes from that day would describe them, I shifted directly from paranoia to a suffocating bout of self-consciousness. I was a Julie Andrews wannabe playing Maria with miniature children Von Trapp. I needed a complete personal makeover – hair, body, face, teeth, singing voice – and to swap the scrubs and Jedi garb for dirndls and lederhosen. But I snapped past it. I was back in the moment, with unlimited Brio and seven very advanced little children.

They seemed to grasp the peg and hole system innately. Several of them pieced together sections of track before I'd even begun my instruction. Others anticipated the pinch for space and began lugging their stacks of track into open areas. Their strength surprised me, but I reined them back for fear of slipped discs and neonatal hernias and introduced them to proper lifting technique, backs straight and knees bent. Their eyes bored into mine, a function of both their curious natures and my surgical mask – they had little beyond my eyes to take in. I directed them each to specific areas of operation, and in short order they were hoisting the tracks like proper railway coolies and setting them in their assigned places.

I'd doled out the track with the most basic pattern in mind, and now I clacked my own eight curves into a circle. This drew something like the chirping of gerbils – laughter perhaps, though I couldn't really be sure. They'd nearly completed their own matching circles when Beta Girl, with a little squeal, broke into non-conforming S patterns. The others followed her lead. I was unsure whether this was mischief or regression – I now lean to the former – but recalling my several peers watching through the glass, I insisted on the circular orientation. I stole a look at OB1, where Dr. Morben simply nodded, continuously and rhythmically, as if he had marching music going in his booth.

Ten minutes later I was glad I'd pressed the point. It was astounding to me that on the morning of P4, on their first exposure to Brio, all seven sat in circles of their own making. I cooed their praises, and moved directly to engines and boxcars, setting them onto the grooved wooden tracks, connecting them with their magnetized couplers, and rolling them to and fro. They were quick studies here too -- by the end of the session, with only forty-five minutes devoted to Brio, we had eight trains in motion, eight of us crawling at the perimeter of eight wooden circles. As if there'd been any doubt, these children were truly exceptional. There was an air of laughter and general delight.

The glass was generally tinted from the inside, but Falstaff dropped that setting for a moment, and I got a quick look out. I hadn't noticed Morben slipping out of OB1, but he stood just behind the desks with a woman in a pricey business suit tapered snugly at the hips and chest. I recognized her as Marcia Tompkins, an in-house media person I'd seen flitting around a few Gatherings over the years, and in our own facility earlier that morning, chatting with Jerry of all people. Her tablet pressed firmly to one breast, more bustier than office tool. She had a photographer in tow, clad so strangely in jungle khaki, and slung so heavily with lenses at the waist, that he seemed a caricature of himself. She didn't pay him the slightest attention, but spoke only with Morben, pointing officiously to a few of the overhead cameras. I figured that the untold hours of footage, beyond aiding our work, were compiling a story for a later telling to a vast public. I began to wonder if and how my Brio work might play into that.

In one improvised session I'd compiled a fine set of learning sequences and displays of physical strength, manual dexterity, and pattern recognition. And as I watched the children pushing their trains around their circular tracks I began to think about less obvious benchmarks. From P1, for example, they'd bypassed all forms of crawling – standard, military, and bear. The precocious little creatures had begun life like little fawns, directly on their feet. Here, I hoped, was our first proof that they were perfectly capable of elementary hand-and-knee locomotion. I considered whether this had any practical significance – beyond pushing a toy along a track, when was crawling preferable to walking upright? – advancing in a war zone, escaping a smoke-filled room, retrieving something from under a table...

"What's happening with Delta Boy?" came the voice through my headset.

I saw that he was stricken with a convulsive little shaking. Just my luck to have a medical disaster my first shift inside.

"Looks like some kind of seizure."

"Can you make out any lachrymation?"

I recognized the voice as that of Dr. Hayes, one of two staff pediatricians. And on closer inspection I realized she was right -- this was likely as simple as weeping, or its laboratory equivalent. I could just make out the tiny tears. None of the subjects had manifested that behavior before, and we had no protocol on the point. I kicked into weep-response mode, as I'd have done with any of my nieces or nephews – I picked him up and held him to my shoulder. He stiffened and kicked, this also consistent with my experience as a beleaguered aunt. I held him out for what I hoped would be some soothing eye contact. "There, there," I said, a phrase I still employed despite its having proven so thoroughly ineffective over the years. Compressed by the surgical mask, the effect was even worse. I was The Bride of Vader giving succor. Delta Boy rolled back his head, turned an alarming shade of puce, and gasped for breath.

Normally, at such a point, my policy is to pass the child back to the nearest parent in the firmest possible manner. With that option unavailable, I pressed him again to my shoulder. He gripped the neckline of my scrubs, burrowed his head and worked his feet into my chest pocket. After a moment, he crouched as best he could – an awkward fit at best -- and went silent. I had the other children box up their Brio while I picked up Delta Boy's myself, kneeling with my upper body upright to preclude his tumbling out, and resolving to sew deeper pockets into my lab coats. When I set him back at the end of the hour, he scampered off to join the others, apparently no worse for wear. Dr. Hayes would run him through a few tests late that afternoon, but for now she was content to stand down.

6. Richie

I scrabble down the roping and touch briefly on the cold wooden floor. I've positioned my slippers so I can step into them now without delay. The way this place is set up, it's a long haul down to the kitchen, and in the cold season I don't want to lose that kind of heat through my feet. I still don't know why they put me in such a gigantic house. You'd think a far smaller floor plan would have suited just fine, and saved them a lot on materials. Instead, they've got me in a place nearly sixty meters long, a good bit larger than what all seven of us shared at Genesis. It's clearly been designed with an eye to utility over grace. If you shoved six Monopoly houses into one contiguous row, you'd have a good idea of its shape.

The walls are mostly glass. Jill seemed especially happy about that, saying I'd be used to it from Genesis. And while I am pleased with the glass, it's not from any nostalgic predilection. On the contrary, it's for what this glass looks out on, specifically in contrast to the glass at Genesis. For as nice as things mostly were there, the view could get a little depressing. The glass was tinted so dark we had to strain to see through it, for the dubious reward of desks and the big blank wall behind. Besides the coming and going of the staff, nothing much changed from day to day. And as tiresome as their staring got for us toward the end, a solid wall would have suited us just fine. But through the glass here I've got all outdoors – the sky and the clouds, always moving and taking on the different colors of the day, the morning sun poking through the trees, acres of grass waving in the breeze, fog on the double-humped mountain just behind. The fact is, Jill was right. I can hardly imagine life here without the view.

The only heat is the stone fireplace in the kitchen. I can't set the fire before bed because the tiniest leftover coal can ignite it while I'm sleeping. So that's my first job on winter mornings, and I'm usually shivering by the time I get it lit. I sit as close as I can until my circulation begins to run. I don't need it for long, just something to take the edge off until the sun clears the tree line and starts working through the glass.

My fires have a distinctly eucalyptus composition, with bark strips for tinder and crackly sticks for fuel. As far as I can tell, eucalypts – gums informally – are the dominant trees in this part of the world. They stand in a few varieties on both sides of the house, tall and widely dispersed, as if each holds an exclusive claim to land by the terms of some ancient arboreal accord. Some are pale and paper-smooth, so I can watch the dawn drape them with its colors, then double back for an equally spectacular show at sunset. Others are dark and furrowed, with bark hanging in straggly strips like the unkempt beards and ruined robes of timeworn kings, or broken off and caught in their wooden crotches, unsightly tufts grayed and drooping. Their soaring crowns are gapped and gouged as if with the scars of battle, the stubs of their many severed limbs marking ruinous voids in their otherwise majestic canopies. But over time those gaps seem less like disfigurements from where I sit, filled as they so often are with clouds passing through in endless shapes and textures. Many of the surviving branches heave out on strange, desperate tangents, as if offering alliances to distant and more resilient monarchs. But as you could easily infer, the heavier winds can set them all writhing to the lash and their great limbs crashing to the earth. You see the raw, orange-tinted carnage, the torn branch-ends, and you appreciate just how rough it can get out there. Many of the downed limbs are gigantic and immovable, some as thick as I am tall. Shorn bark lies everywhere, sometimes fifty meters from the tree. I scurry along to gather it, and what sticks I can handle, with a steady mind to my morning woodfires.

All of these great gums are shedding at what I hold to be an unsustainable rate. Their loss of wood mass far exceeds any conceivable model of growth. I have to conclude that they're well into decline, likely into their final few decades. At first I thought it all very messy, and more than a little sad, but now I've come to appreciate their largesse, nature's gift to her most unnatural creature. Without their droppings I'd be shivering all winter.

7. *Jill*

My orientation had been a barrage of pre-kindergarten learning theory, much of which I recognized now in the children's video. Delivered in relentless doses not feasible in standard residential or educational environments, that programming would accelerate the ABCs, early language, and the introduction to numbers. Dr. Henderson, a compulsive runner whose delayed showers prolonged her gamey air, had particular expertise in the field and ran that side of the operation.

Beyond Henderson, the staff included the two pediatricians, Drs. Hayes and Manly; the dietician, Dr. Bitsen; the language acquisition specialist, Dr. Sloboth; and the technical director, Dr. Falstaff. That left six of us, Dr. Dasher and myself included, charged with socialization and the acquisition of physical skills. Anything that accelerated benchmarks in those areas was understood to be encouraged, but strange as it sounds, we had very few procedural directives. Many of us had seen this before -- it was the nature of business with the more speculative projects, the first generation initiatives. There were no blueprints to consult, no operating guides with help screens or working indices. We had well-articulated objectives – BioSpore was ever proficient there – and a few rules governing direct engagement, hygiene and safety. Beyond that, what instructions we had were purposely hedged, more suggestive than prescriptive. So I'd anticipated our doing a lot on the fly, executing a collective, consensus-based progression. What I didn't expect was the degree of ongoing individual autonomy. We were improvising, playing it by ear, free to pursue and establish our own interactive approaches, so long as they were sensible, consistent, and extremely well documented.

Once I'd dumped my scrubs in the barrel, I sat at my workstation and cued up the video of my first shift inside. There I was entering the nursery, there the two pairs taking their foot-riding turns, and there the third pair declining. Only now did I notice the absence of the seventh child. Of the procedural directives I mentioned above, the one emphasized every day of my orientation, was "consistently and actively engaging" all seven subjects. The video rolled minute after damaging minute, with Delta Boy adrift -- unseen, unengaged, and unaccounted. Any of my co-workers could have alerted me if they'd chosen. But in testament to our sorry collegiality, they'd left me to dangle.

Delta Boy had tucked himself at the back of the birdcage. That was a bit of a blind spot from most vantage points in the nursery, and for most of the cameras. Several of them caught him slipping from the pack when I'd come through the entry, but only one picked him up at the cage. Once he'd settled there he'd barely seemed to move. He'd leaned with his elbows on a rail, shifting his legs only occasionally while steadily watching the bird. But as I zoomed and watched a second time, and then a third, I could pick up slight alterations in his expression, little puckerings of his face, as if he were cooing at or clucking with the bird, though none of the mikes had picked up much sound from either party. He'd rejoined us only when I'd brought out the Brio, and by the time I'd noticed him, with a hint of misgiving I'd somehow managed to suppress, he was sitting comfortably with the group.

The way I saw it, that equanimity, sustained for half an hour, eliminated my neglect as the cause of his lachrymation. But it didn't exonerate me entirely, even on my first shift. When Dr. Morben passed by the workstations on a bathroom break from OB1, I thought I'd inject a preemptive mea culpa and, with any luck, put it to bed.

"Dr. Morben, excuse me, I was just reviewing my session and realize I ignored one of the subjects for the first fifteen minutes."

I'd startled him, and his momentary silence had me hoping he had no idea what I was talking about. He did.

"Yes, it was Delta Boy you overlooked."

"I apologize for that. It won't happen again."

He seemed not to acknowledge or even hear the apology, staring right through me, completely without expression, as if waiting for me to get to the point, which I thought I already had.

"He, uh, Delta Boy, seemed very interested in the bird," I ventured, and I think it's likely we'll see that behavior again." More awkward silence. "We might learn something if we shift another camera over there. And I was thinking we could maybe drop a mike over the cage."

It was presumptuous to suggest monitoring adjustments after just one shift inside, and such a flawed shift at that. I regretted it immediately. But his unruffled response surprised me more than my impertinence, apparently, had surprised him.

"You can do that sort of thing yourself," he said, "right from your own workstation. That's how we're set up here, though the media people seem to have their own ideas on camera and microphone placement. You're due your systems tutorial, and that'll all be covered. Dr. Falstaff will be happy to run you through it."

"Great, thank you." There followed another lull in the conversation, and still he made no motion to continue along. I looked into the nursery, where the children had been herded into quasi-casual, photographically appealing positions near the glass. The khaki-clad photographer stood just outside, his back to us, briskly at his work. "Why doesn't that guy scrub up and go inside rather than shooting through the glass? Is it an authorization issue, or is he a little gun-shy? Or is he just too lazy to scrub?"

Dr. Morben took a moment before answering. "I'm afraid scrubs might appear a bit too sterile. What they're really filming is the photo shoot itself. Any pictures he takes are secondary, quite possibly irrelevant. He may even be shooting blanks. The important thing is how it all comes off, how he looks doing it, and how they look having it done."

"I assume the hairstylist had to scrub yesterday. Hard to cut hair through glass. Even with PrismView." The attempt at humor appeared to fall just short.

"Oh yes, we walked her through a vigorous scrubbing. Though I did come into a bit of grief on the point."

With a rueful look to end the conversation, he turned and resumed his trek. I was beginning to see how *Dr. Moribund* might have been a fit. But as I watched him down the corridor I realized there was something soothing about his running the Project. His frame and his gait were so fundamentally off kilter that they offset our tightly engineered environment in a way I was finding oddly therapeutic. Watching him had an almost mantric effect for me as I contemplated the strange incongruities in this workplace. The Project was held to be confidential. We maintained quarantine-equivalent standards. We referenced the children with rigid scientific detachment, by order of birth weight and gender – Alpha, Beta, and Gamma Girls; Alpha, Beta, Gamma, and Delta Boys. And all the while, the media team had them sitting for beauty appointments and photo shoots.

Falstaff had a visitor at his desk, but I hovered until I had his attention.

"Excuse me, Dr. Falstaff. I need to get on your schedule for my systems tutorial."

"Ah, yes, Dr. Edelman,"[14] he said, considering me over his glasses as if for the first time. "We could do it now, if that suits. By the way, do I understand you hail from Buffalo?"

"Oswego actually, and now would suit perfectly."

"Ah, snow country. The romantic wintry childhood – that gives you something very much in common with my good friend, Dmitri Larionov." He turned to make the introduction. "Dmitri hails from the great city of Omsk, in southwestern Siberia."

"As opposed to the more culturally renowned southeastern Siberia," he said with a smile, reaching for my hand.

"I was going to say," I quipped. He had the shoulders, and the hands, and the square jaw of an athlete, and his fluid movements furthered the impression.

"I imagine what we actually have in common are childhoods spent far too much indoors."

"What about the clack of pucks on the frozen lakes?" said Falstaff. "The ice fishing. The dogsledding. The great outdoor life in Omsk. Or in Oswego, as it were."

"I don't recall a lot of dogsledding," I said.

"Nor do I," said Dmitri.

"Humor me, people. I'm from LA. Ten lane freeways, heat waves, water restrictions."

"We did do some ice fishing," I said. "And my father played a lot of hockey in rinks. Personally, I was more of a barroom player. A fair body of work says I was the best female bubble hockey player in all of Upstate New York."

---

14 I have a JD and two Master's Degrees, but no PhD or MD. I didn't take the trouble to correct him.

"Unique qualifications for this line of work," said Falstaff. Both men had a good laugh, and I found myself joining in. "Let's make it official," he said, extending his hand. "Welcome to the Monkey House."

Dmitri chuckled again on his way out.

"You're a Vonnegut fan?" I asked Falstaff.

"I read a lot of him when I was younger. My great-grandfather was friendly with him. They grew up together in Indianapolis. So it goes."

"I'm sure they'd both have appreciated our little nursery," I said. "The drone lighting in particular," I added for no particular reason, looking plaintively upward.

"Yes, yes, seven units tracking seven subjects. Personal little suns, if you will, though they don't throw much heat – not that we need any more of it in our oversized incubator. In this application the drones are basically dedicated, unmanned spotlights. They throw a tempered blue light that enhances the night video. But I'd say their most notable contribution is to add just a little more creepiness to the operation."

A moment of silence followed, not an awkward one, for a change, but one that seemed to establish some solidarity between us. We settled into the tutorial and spent the better part of an hour navigating through the system. Everything was automated, intuitive, and remotely operable, a clever setup that I suspected had Falstaff's fingerprints all over it. He guided me through moving unrestricted mikes and cameras for better coverage around the birdcage. Every ten minutes or so we'd find ourselves looking through the glass, watching Dasher running the little people through some music and pattern recognition.

"You see those two, Beta Boy and Gamma Girl?" I said. "They're not sitting together, but their shoulders are swaying in sync. And look at the two bobbing their heads – they're making a lot of eye contact. I think they were the first two who rode my feet."

"Yes, they were. Alpha Girl and Gamma Boy. Interesting. Signs of early socialization, maybe even preliminary pairing."

"Have you noticed it before?"

"Not the pairing, no. You're the first to mention it."

"Actually you're the one who mentioned it."

"Yes, but you're the one who observed it."

"I might look for more in the video."

"If you find it, that's exactly the sort of thing you might track in your talks. No one else is on that path."

He was referring to our daily 07:00 briefings. Dr. Morben called them "our Little Gatherings," quite wittily I thought, though I seemed to be alone in that regard. They occurred in our own little amphitheater, a room strange in its compactness but somehow perfect for its purpose. Eight of the twelve staff specialists would attend, the other four allocated to the night shift or scheduled days off. Morben was a fixture as facilitator. He didn't take days off. Though he'd duck out for an occasional afternoon, he never missed a single Little Gathering for the duration of Project Genesis.

The format was well established and precise. We'd each give three-minute video briefings,[15] showing selected clips from the prior day's shift, explaining what we'd tried to accomplish and what we'd actually observed. Then we'd accept a question or two and some quick bits of feedback before Morben sounded the five-minute buzzer. Thirty-five minutes of briefings, five for general matters, and out like clockwork.

Each briefing was recorded for the review of Senior Science Officers. This imposed a quality imperative beyond the norms of peer pressure. A self-referential sub-context soon emerged – in time we were reviewing not only our one-hour nursery shifts, but our five-minute performances at the podium, hoping to correct annoying hand gestures and glitches in speech, or worse, any gaps in logic that our peers

---

15 Neither Dr. Morben nor Dr. Falstaff had scheduled nursery shifts, and they would not generally present.

may or may not have pointed out. But the real idea was a much larger one. With each of us developing and tracking our own approaches, the Project had an assortment of petri dishes to observe and assess, diversifying the approach and maximizing the experiential data. In time they could cull the underperforming methodologies, accelerate the successes, and set new hybrid courses. From a management point of view, it was a brilliant setup – twelve highly trained people working independently but constantly pushing each other and reviewing and refining each other's work.

For now, with my first report lurking, I was naturally inclined to prepare somewhat thoroughly – that is to say, to work late. BioSpore was brilliant at supporting "extended hours." Our facility had a work-out room, small but superbly ventilated, complete with lockers and showers. Caterers arrived every day with breakfast, lunch and dinner, all of a quality surpassing what I could have made myself or picked up on the way home. Very few of us went out to lunch, and very few of us turned down the dinner. And given all the extra hours they got out of us, it all made perfect fiscal sense.

This time through the video, dining at my desk, I focused on the subject pairings. The pairs that had ridden my shoes and the pair that had declined had all shown signs of bonding throughout the day. Beyond the foot-riding, the coupling was not overt. The physical contact was unexceptional, and the pairs weren't exclusive to the point of not mingling with the larger group. It was all more subtle than that – synchronized movements and directed eye contact during Dr. Dasher's musical session, and meaningful little glances when Dr. Sloboth reviewed basic word association or when they all sat together to watch the screen. The impression wasn't so much of flirtation as of reassurance, like a young child having a first try at something on his own and looking back periodically at his mother.

As to Delta Boy, the one outside the pairings, he was a little tougher to read. He was perfectly sociable, but in a distracted kind of way. Only with the cockatiel did he seem fully engaged. He'd circled back to the cage several times during the day, and both he and the cockatiel seemed more animated with each visit. Even in the group I could see him repeating bits of the imitative behavior, trace formations of clucks and coos on his lips.

I had plenty of positive takeaways for my video presentation the next morning. I expounded on the general Brio proficiency, Delta Boy's bird bonding, and the early pairings among the other six – and all with some proficiency given the fiercely enforced time restrictions. But I couldn't in good faith exclude the crying. And that bit is exactly what my co-workers picked up on.

"There, there," said Dr. Dasher when the video cut off, affecting a singsong, parroting voice.

From a protocol standpoint this was a bit of shock. I didn't know yet that the Q&A portions of the Little Gatherings, while recorded, were not shared with the Senior Science Officers. I was unaware that Dr. Morben preferred we speak "without inhibition" during those few minutes. Nor did I recognize what's so obvious to me now, that Dasher was joking. His kidding manner was a form of welcome, an introduction to the group. But at that point I didn't really know him. And, as a rule, I'm not all that jovial at 07:00. We went right at it.[16]

Me: What the hell am I supposed to say? The kid's got only a lab name. I'm holding him in rubber gloves and talking through a surgical mask. 'There, there, Delta Boy?' Would that have been better?

Dasher: Maybe if you worked on the inflection.

---

16 To ensure accuracy, this exchange, and several others that follow, have been transcribed directly from Genesis Project audio files.

Me: Maybe if we worked on some real names we could actually start communicating with these kids.

Dasher: They're not kids.

Me: Excuse me. Children.

Dasher: No, not children either.

Me: Well, they seem a bit advanced to be called babies.

Dasher: They seem a bit advanced to be called people.

Brief silence.

Sloboth: In a way, they look more like people than real babies do.

Dasher: That's absurd. By definition, real babies are exactly what people look like.

Bitsen: Only at the beginning.

Dasher: Well of course only at the beginning. If we still looked like babies I'd have a head the size of a medicine ball.

Falstaff: You pretty much do.

Everyone laughed, including Dasher. He did have a big head. I was appalled at his attitude toward the little people, but I couldn't help but think this crew might turn out to be a decent bunch after all. I snuck a look at Dr. Morben. He rarely spoke at the Little Gatherings, barely registered any change in expression. He seemed to like letting things play out.

Bitsen: Do we have any idea why Delta Boy was crying?

Me: Nothing particular showed up in the video. No obvious episode of physical pain, frustration, anger – nothing along those lines.

Hayes: I'd be surprised if he isn't picking up on the pairings as well as you are, Dr. Edelman. I imagine he might feel a bit left out.

Falstaff: I wouldn't rule out a random moment of metaphysical anguish.

Longer silence.

Dasher: Are you joking?

Falstaff: No, I'm not. We have a unique situation here – intelligent beings self-aware at the earliest stage of life. They're perfectly positioned to be asking the big questions.

Dasher: Like what?

Falstaff: Like, what is this place? Who am I? Why am I here?

More silence.

Me: That might be a little too much for us to take on just now. Can we at least get some consensus on the names? I know this is only my second day here, and I don't mean to overstep, but I can't help but push on this. Today is P5, and we're still going by Alpha Boy and Beta Girl. If corporate isn't supplying real names – and the surrogates definitely aren't – then we need to do it ourselves. Surely we can agree we're not breeding lab rats here.

Silence yet again.

Bitsen: You know, it's actually not that uncommon for people to take a week or two after birth to settle on names. Some people do the John Doe thing for a while. They like to experience their children and get to know them a bit before committing to a real name. I know a couple who did exactly that with both of their kids. It actually makes some sense when you stop to think about it.

Dasher: And it's not like we've got family heirlooms to work with here. We're not really in a position to name one of these things after its uncle.

Me: They're not things.

Falstaff: And it's not heirlooms we'd be after. Heirlooms are objects, not names. You mean we don't have family namesakes to work with.

Dasher: No, I don't mean namesake. Namesake refers to the newer entity. The offspring, not the progenitor. The heir, not the forebear.

Groans throughout the room.

Me: Well, put it this way. How many kids don't have names by the time they're walking around and playing with early elementary school toys?

Dasher: Again, they're not kids. And besides, who wouldn't like a cool name like Beta Boy?

Falstaff: He's got a point there.

Morben sounded the five-minute buzzer.

8. Richie

It's only after I've warmed my exterior at the fire and my interior with some breakfast that I head outdoors for my morning discharges. I'd much rather do things the other way around, as I always did at Genesis, but circumstances here in East Central dictate otherwise. For reasons of personal preservation I just can't go out there cold and creaky. I need to be energized and ready to move.

I've mentioned that I'm more or less comfortable with the kooka-burras, but that doesn't mean I'm the undersized victor sitting on top of the local food chain. Technically, I'm an interloper, an outlier, an independent observer, and not a part of the food chain at all. And my primary objective, each and every day, is to keep it that way. Just this morning I carved the hashmark marking four hundred days in East Central, and the magpies, among a few of the other locals, still scare the hell out of me. You can't help but notice their devilish eyes – crazy, fiery, reddish-orange. It's obvious that they're a different kind of bird, and in all the wrong ways. They're smart, and they carry a particular brand of hostility, premeditated and relentless.

Through a piece of horrible luck my transfer over here came in the heart of magpie breeding season, exactly when they're the most aggres-sive. I guess nobody at Genesis knew anything about that, and I doubt they'd have done anything differently if they had, other than including it as part of my reassignment briefing, unhelpful as that was. The trip over had been pretty miserable. While I'd slept much of the way, I'd still been in the travel carton for more than twenty hours, spanning the overseas flight and the multi-hour ordeal at special customs. And by the time I climbed out of the travel carton – Jill hadn't mentioned that she'd unlocked it – I was stuck in the back of a van. The carpet floor smelled like urine, and a steel screen separated me from where Jill sat to drive. She apologized – the screen was meant for dogs, she said. I could have squeezed through, but she didn't want me up front. I couldn't really see out from the floor back there. And while that was something I was more or less used to from Genesis, it was definitely not helpful on this occasion. The van was bouncing me around, and I'd begun to feel sick to my stomach. When I mentioned this to Jill, she said "Yeah, sorry. This thing's got shit for suspension." I didn't know what she meant by that, but I was too sick to press the point.

We didn't say much more until we got to the compound some three or four hours later. She seemed more interested than I was to see the place, even though, as it turned out, I'd be the one living there. The grounds were gorgeous – I'd never seen nature anything like that apart from pictures. But the house was hideous, the roof particularly so, corrugated metal running the whole length on both sides, peeling and faded where it hadn't gone to rust. I was a little down just then, but Jill has a way of mustering enough enthusiasm, even over the most mundane things, to keep you going. She walked me inside and toured me around the place like she'd built it herself, taking special delight in pointing out the bits meant just for me. She loved the "cat door," a smallish rubberized flap hinged from the top and opening at floor level with a push in either direction. She carried on about the cathedral ceilings and the views – the place had more glass than any house she'd ever seen. And she raved about the security. Excellent fencing, she said, ran along the entire perimeter. She left me after an hour or so with a cheery promise to return in the morning.

I couldn't help but notice that there was still plenty of light, and it was of a kind I'd never seen before. I still marvel at it most afternoons. It filters through the mountains at the acute angle of late day and pours into the valley in a way that makes every leaf seem to glow, hundreds of thousands of them in curious focus all at once. I suppose it's no wonder I had the notion to stroll the grounds. It seemed the perfect antidote to the travel carton. A bit of exercise would help me stay awake until dark, which Jill had said was the first step in getting acclimated to this far side of the world. And I'd taken her praise of the security fencing as subtle encouragement to venture out.

For all that, it was a terrible idea. Never mind my complete ignorance of the local airborne threats, I'd never been on an unattended outdoor excursion in my life. I'd always been indoors, or in outdoor situations that were brief, heavily restricted, and amply supervised. I was jittery enough just on that basis, and with the heavy dose of jet lag on top I was in a dismal state to be making my first pass into the wild.

The grass here is up to my shoulders, and I realized right away I wasn't all that comfortable moving through it. There's an uneven bunching near the roots that's not easy to gauge, and it makes for a constant tripping hazard. I stumbled twice in the first ten or fifteen meters. Keeping my knees high seemed to help, and I'd just settled into an adjusted stride when a whoosh exploded in my ear. I jerked in terror, a half-jump, half-duck, with my hands shooting over my head like a marionette's. I can still hear my pathetic little shriek — it's embarrassing to even think about. And from a tactical standpoint, the response, if you could call it that, was utterly inept, absurdly late. I'd been the easiest possible game.

I remember a feeling of gratitude that this new place wasn't set up like Genesis, teeming with video cameras and driven by performance assessment. But it was just that conditioning to performance, along with the stunted reason of a jet-lagged half-wit, that pushed me to press on. I had no idea what had hit me, but I continued forward, steeling myself against another possible attack, which meant that as I high-stepped though the tangle I tried to look tough rather than frightened half to death, and that I glanced periodically over both shoulders to monitor my perimeter. Another swoop cuffed me hard on the head and shoulders – this one sent me sprawling. I gathered myself on hands and knees and pulled myself upright just in time for another whack, and, an anguished few seconds later, another. Each attack had come from behind, unseen and unheard until the clap of wings had detonated in my ears and the talons had delivered their blow. Another cuff knocked me hard off my feet – this time I saw the blur of black feathers, the wings of a dark demon.

I was, of course, familiar with the notion of death. But until that moment I hadn't understood how it might actually pertain to me. Now it was as clear as could be. At the conclusion of this systematic thrashing, I, little Richie Millipede, defenseless and alone, would be skewered, shredded, and swallowed in bits, twenty meters from my designated safe house. I ran then, gasping and weeping and skittering through the grass like a field mouse. The difference, I thought bitterly, was that the mouse, running on all fours, would not be at risk of the deadly trip and fall as I was, running upright. A conscious commitment to high knees was the only thing that kept me on my feet. I hit the cat door at full speed, jamming my shoulder in the process, piled through and rolled two full revolutions on the floor. I lay there panting for an indefinite time, the fog of shock broken in turns by the amber of sunset and the throbbing of my shoulders on the hard wood floor. As night settled in, my heart was still going rat-a-tat-tat – I swear I could hear it. I'm a strictly diurnal creature, and there I was in a strange dark place, with death at the door and my sleepmates, for all I knew, half a world away. I longed for the calming blue of my overhead drone. Even now, the memory is unnerving.

9. Jill

On many BioSpore projects the lead Senior Science Officers would be right in the mix, spending time on site, making friendly with the staff, engaging in the kind of hands-on management you might expect. On others it'd be clear they were juggling other commitments, dropping in from time to time and interacting mostly with the Project Supervisors. But at Genesis we didn't even know who our lead officer was, or if we had one at all. Dr. Morben seemed to report to more than one person, but whether that was a formal group or a shuffling of interested and high-ranking parties, we couldn't say.

Even in my first few days I'd picked up on a lot of speculation within the staff. But I took it at face value, and still do, that Hansen and his group were chasing something that was not, by their standards, completely outrageous. Simply put, they wanted a solution for busy couples looking to ease the earliest stages of parenting. For all the innuendo to the contrary, I believe their goals were simply to lessen the difficulties of childbirth and to expedite early postnatal development. It wasn't like anyone was trying to develop some super genome, or master race, or any of that malarkey.[17] While the donors had been selected on some criteria of intelligence, good looks, and

---

17 Personally, I'm opposed to all the engineering, more so now than ever. And as I've said, the Project should have come under more scrutiny than it eventually did.

athleticism, they were hardly alpha specimens. As I understood it, they were people who'd fallen just short in athletics or the arts and were well in need of a few bucks — washed-up ballplayers, failed writers, idling actors, sore-kneed dancers. In any event, editing genomes is an uncertain science. We were all in uncharted terrain.

Dr. Morben surprised us with two announcements at the P7 Little Gathering. The scrubs and masks mandate had been abruptly suspended. And we'd been given new names for the children. The scrubs decision was the more surprising of the two — we still had no evidence that the subject children were any more or less susceptible to infection than normal children. And with so many staff children spending long hours in day care — eight of them just between Dasher, Sloboth and Bitsen — there was plenty of infection to go around. But given the robust physicality the subject children, however undersized, had displayed in the early going, the thought of the Senior Science Officers, whoever they were, was apparently to downplay clinical precaution in favor of more human contact. So the scrubs and masks were out, and with them went the Greek alphabet lab names.

I didn't flatter myself that my complaints from the bottom of the totem pole had been instrumental in either change. We'd all been assured that the Q&A segments of the Little Gatherings weren't shared with senior people. No one higher than Dr. Morben would have even heard them. And Morben didn't seem like a man who'd drop the scrubbing protocol on a hunch and a hope, even if, as seemed unlikely, he had the authority to do so. While I'd found the surgical masks offputting, the public health side of me was a bit alarmed at their sudden removal. But it'd been clear from the onset that the media relations people, Marcia Tompkins and her crowd, had a lot of clout on certain matters, and these two issues were right in their sweet spot. I'd already imagined the short video clips and the longer documentary treatments they'd roll out when the time was right. The benefit of presenting a more appealing and nurturing upbringing was obvious, and homey names and unmasked mentors would make an excellent start. And yet the names suggested that someone, somewhere, was paying attention to my pairing hypothesis, and giving it more credence than it could possibly have deserved at such an early stage. Even I knew enough about 1960s television to recognize Kirk and Uhura, and Samantha and Darrin.[18] And, thanks to Jerry's frequent video clips, I'd had plenty of on-the-job exposure to Rob and Laura.

Dasher: OK, first question. What extremely clever person christened our seven little amigos?

Morben: That's not being disclosed at this stage. It was thought best to keep the process at some remove from the group here.

Dasher: Ah, the telling passive voice from our Project Super.

Dasher was pretty brash, but there was never any question of Morben's taking offense. He'd just smile his wooden smile and say nothing. The two of them had worked together on previous projects, and Morben seemed to appreciate the disarming atmosphere Dasher brought to a given group.

Bitsen: Why keep the process "at some remove" from the people working directly with the subjects? You'd think we'd be better positioned than anyone to assign appropriate names.

Morben: I suppose that's really the point. Scientific neutrality and some measure of detachment are, after all, critical to our work.

Dasher: So what, we're like farmers' children, forbidden to name the livestock?

---

18 Character names from the television series *Star Trek* and *Bewitched*, respectively.

Morben: Livestock is a bit dramatic. The subjects at hand, as you're perfectly aware, are not being raised for the abattoir. Quite to the contrary.

Falstaff: We're apparently to provide warm and nurturing mentorships, but in a measured and overridingly academic manner.

We mulled this over for a moment, as we did with many of Falstaff's observations.

Sloboth: Those names sound a lot like Jerry's doing.

Me: He does seem to like his classic TV.

Bitsen: And he's awfully friendly with Marcia Tompkins.

Dasher: Though you wouldn't think he'd be in a pay grade she'd acknowledge.

Morben: If the names came from Jerry I wasn't made aware of it. You can ask him, but I doubt he'd tell you one way or the other.

Dasher: You have remarkable insight into third party responses to hypothetical questions.

Me: I'm concerned about the pairing references. I know I've been the one documenting the behavior, but what we've seen is all very early stage. Whereas, Kirk and Uhura, Darrin and Samantha, Rob and Laura... I take it these names are meant to be permanent?

Dasher: To be clear, Dr. Edelman, we have no evidence that Kirk and Uhura were ever paired, in the biblical sense.

Falstaff: Though most fans would insist it's implied.

Sloboth: Understood to have occurred.

Bitsen: Though in a purely fictional construct.

Dasher: Ah, the steamy sixties. It makes you wonder about Mary Poppins and Bert.

Me: Whatever the relationship between Kirk and Uhura, they're obviously linked. It's not like anyone's going to miss the reference. As far as I know, that character is the only Uhura in the history of Western pop culture.

Henderson: Why not "James" or "Jim"? The others go by first names.

Henderson was still pink in the cheeks and wet around the hairline from her early run. She had the nose of someone wearing her workout clothes more than once between washes.

Me: Because they're way less recognizable than Kirk as part of that idiom. There's not even a question as to the relationship of the other two couples. Darrin and Samantha, Rob and Laura – definitively married.

Sloboth: Though I seem to remember twin beds in at least one of those cases.

Bitsen: Maybe both.

Me: All of which begs the obvious question. Are we in the business of arranging cutesy little marriages here? And if so, what we're doing doesn't seem all that different than raising animals, for the abattoir or otherwise.

Dasher: Well said, Dr. Edelman!

Henderson: To be fair, the children won't understand those nuances for quite some time.

Me: They're pre-lingual, for god's sake. They wouldn't understand *Dumbass* right now either, but you wouldn't name them that, would you?

Bitsen: I think that may be one of those names the state doesn't allow.

Sloboth: Well, naming someone after Darrin is almost as bad. The guy was whiny and obnoxious, not to mention ugly.

I agreed with whiny and obnoxious, but it surprised me for a moment that someone like Dr. Sloboth, aswim in her own adipose, would consider someone like Darrin to be ugly. I don't know why – he was a perfectly homely character, and she had every right to her opinion. I guess I'd just never considered it.

Dasher: Yeah, nobody with access to a television has a clue why Samantha would ever have hooked up with him.

This drew a series of affirmatives from around the room.

Falstaff: Here at last is something we can all agree upon.

Me: Well, our particular Darrin doesn't seem all that bad.

Bitsen: No, no, he's a little studmuffin.

Dasher: Did you just say "studmuffin?"

Sloboth: And what's with "Richie?" Am I missing something, or is he the only non-obvious reference to 1960s television?

Dasher: Good question. *Happy Days* had a Richie, but that show came later. Mid '70s, I think.

Falstaff: And I'm guessing the relevant surname in that case wasn't Millipede.

Bitsen: No doubt. So why here?

Me: Why the surname at all? None of the others got one.

Dasher: I thought we'd established that Kirk got only a surname.

Henderson: I just did a search on Richie Millipede. Nothing comes up.

Dasher: Isn't Millipede the game the techs are always playing in lieu of their real duties?

Sloboth: So it was Jerry!

Jerry never did let on. A half-nod to a slightly mistaken genre, or not even that, Delta Boy's redesignation was more or less random. That is, a person with no particular connection or affinity just thought it had a certain ring. But as much as I'd complained about the Greek lab names, I couldn't feasibly boycott the new ones. And as it happened, my nursery shift was the first on that day's docket, so I'd be the one making the introductions, the first to address the children by their new names. With the new mask-free policy I'd also be the first specialist to show her face inside the glass.

I should mention that, to this point, there'd been no interaction with the children *through* the glass. The practice was discouraged to prevent any compromise of the controlled work within the nursery, which is why Falstaff generally dialed up the one-way shading. On that background, the impact of my maskless entry was immediate and tangible. The sound of my unmuffled voice – I'd summoned my cheeriest "Good morning!" – was an immediate show-stopper, pulling all the children's attention to my face. And their reactions, to my great surprise, were expressions of wonder, of admiration, and possibly even of affection. I was thoroughly unaccustomed to any of it.

I began by calling a name, pointing to the appropriate child, and prodding for an arm raised in response. I hadn't bothered with a list or any other kind of a prop. The names just came pretty naturally for me, as they did for all the specialists who followed. Loathe as we were to admit it, they were pretty good fits. When all seven children could respond without my pointing – and this took just a matter of minutes – I shifted into our regular Brio operations. Richie was prone to a certain dreaminess – he might lie on his belly rolling a couple cars back and forth just to watch the action of the wheels. But by this point, my fourth shift in the nursery, they were all seeing complex track designs in their little heads, and executing them without much difficulty. The simple circle was long passé, as was the standard figure eight with the bridge in the middle. A few of the latest designs had elaborate switch networks, and two of them incorporated repair sheds with multiple approaches. I admired that particular accessory with a tinge of envy. I'd never had one as a kid. Either it didn't exist yet, or it hadn't hit Oswego, or my parents had been too cheap to get me one.

Ten minutes in, Rob and Laura, formerly Beta Boy and Gamma Girl, merged their rail grids into one integrated line. I reflected that while this overt pairing made me look good, my interests on the point were aligned, very much against my wishes, with Jerry, or with Marcia Tompkins, whoever had originated and authorized the paired names. Kirk took a linear approach that day, running a long straightaway to the far east end of the nursery. I sat there with him as he banged his train into the glass wall, backed it off, and banged it again. Jerry was in my headset — "Looks like you've got yourself a regular Bam-Bam Rubble in there!" — but I did my best to ignore him. Kirk displayed all the signs of delight you might expect of a small child with a new trick, but I was unprepared when he looked to me for validation. I found myself smiling and nodding like an idiot — for a moment I actually missed the surgical mask. The hum of an overhead drone alerted me to another child's approach. Uhura had left her own grid and walked the length of Kirk's to join him at the glass. He grinned and banged all the more.

In view of Richie's scientifically relevant dynamic with The Chief, we'd formally waived the requirement for "consistently and actively engaging" him. He was in his happy place at the birdcage, elbows on a rail, feet spread to shoulder width, chin up, peering up through the bars. He'd become quite good at mimicking the cockatiel. I'd actually spent most of my morning's briefing on that particular acuity. The bird, which we'd cleverly taken to calling "The Chief," still seemed to enjoy the boy's company, or at least to take an interest. It was markedly more animated when the boy was at hand, maintaining a steady stream of staccato chirps and short melody runs, climbing the bars of its cage or sidling in little hop-steps across its swing bar.

The science is still fuzzy on how it is that we can sense other creatures looking at us. I know BioSpore has a group that's spent time on it, as have a few other companies and academic groups, though I'm not aware of any breakthroughs on the topic. But while completely absorbed in the cockatiel's hop-steps, I definitely felt the stare. Richie had broken his bird-watch and turned his attention to me. I met his eyes, and as we regarded each other it became clear that the only point of this exercise, his only intent in so purposely drawing me in, was the conveyance of a smile. It was a smile of sheer happiness, completely devoid of agenda, and so cute that it actually startled me. I'd spend some time after my shift reviewing that moment on video, searching multiple cameras, isolating and zooming for the best look. But his face was so small that sufficient magnification produced only an irritating graininess. I felt like a Kennedy assassination buff belaboring the Zapruder film, and gave up after an hour of floundering. What was I going to do with a picture anyway? Tack it up over my desk? Hang it at home with a fridge magnet? Send it to my mother?

To that point I hadn't really warmed up to the children in that way. They were reasonably endearing, once you'd spent a certain amount of time with them, and there was something poignant about them in their sterilized and unparented environment. With their faces so small, you really had to bore in just to read their expressions. Maybe after a few days I was just getting a little better. I returned his smile as best I could, which I'm afraid was not very convincing, though perhaps an improvement on what I'd managed for Kirk. I held his glance, as we'd all been trained to do, until he turned, happily enough it seemed, back to the bird. Accompanied by Uhura and her dedicated drone, I walked back to the west end, where the other four children were running their Brios. Uhura resumed operations at her own grid, which, that day's distracted effort notwithstanding, was generally the most intricate and accomplished of any in the group.

Kirk was still banging his train on the wall near the end of the hour, an unusually repetitive exercise for such a curious and creative little creature. At this point the action was intermittent and listless, and attended with a certain grimness of face. It called to mind a zoo trip I'd made years prior in the dead of an upstate winter. Attendance was sparse. I'd been the only visitor in the primate facility for at least an hour. The animals were in the indoor sections of their enclosures. For the solitary male silverback, this meant cement floors, cinderblock walls, cold fluorescent lighting, and the obligatory tree trunk laid flat. He'd lurched back and forth along the glass, banging it with an open palm and eyeing me with increasing malevolence. Just as I considered my exit, he stopped short, reached behind himself, and shat in his hand. He held it toward me in the crude serving dish of his stubby black fingers, looked me square in the eye, and splattered it on the glass. Kirk, of course, did nothing of the sort, and I filed the memory under the heading of random, unpleasant, and hopefully irrelevant recollections.

10. Richie

By the next morning my initial catharsis had more or less subsided. Granted, I was nearly frozen after a few hours sleeping on the wooden floor, and this worsened the aftereffects of the bludgeoning I'd taken to the head, neck, and shoulders. But once I got my blood flowing I was able to move pretty well again, and to reflect more rationally on the attack. I'd been helpless out there, unprepared and unequipped, outflanked and outnumbered. I didn't know just yet how well those magpies worked in groups, but already something told me that if they'd been in a truly murderous mindset I wouldn't have lasted more than a minute. I suspected I'd been as much a surprise to them as they'd been to me. The next time they'd be ready. They could finish me then, or at any later date of their choosing. At a minimum, they'd established that security fencing didn't pertain to them in any way, shape or form; that they didn't like my type; and that they wouldn't hesitate to make my life an ongoing misery.

Jill downplayed the affair when she arrived a few hours later. "A few songbirds aren't going to take you down, Richie."

"Magpies aren't your typical songbirds."

"Maybe not, but you're way too big for them. The only conceivable threat from the air would be one of the larger owls, but they only hunt at night when you're indoors sleeping."

"I'll try not to stray from my natural cycles."

She sighed to signal her annoyance. She'd done her research, and now began, with an air of aggrieved patience, to run through the various forms of wildlife I might encounter. Just that morning I'd seen my first kangaroos. I had to admit they were splendid to look at.

"They'd have been eastern greys," said Jill. "Bigger than I am, right?"

"Yup. And a lot more athletic."

"I beg your pardon?"

"Nothing personal."

"Well, lucky for you, they're strictly herbivorous."

Brushtail possums were next. I had no familiarity with them, so she pulled up some images on my tablet. They were bulgy-eyed, grim-looking marsupials with surprisingly nasty teeth. "Primarily herbivorous," she assured me.

"With certain exceptions."

"They'll raid nests for eggs and chicks, but that's about as carnivorous as they get. They're slow afoot, and mostly nocturnal."

"And equipped, I see, with some savage-looking claws."

"Well evolved for climbing."

"And, I'm guessing, for grasping and tearing."

"Again, they're not predatory threats, except to bird chicks a fraction of your size. The alpha predators in this part of the world are dingos, but they've all been fenced out."

"What are dingos?"

"Wild dogs."

"Oh, terrific!"

"What's with all the sarcasm this morning?"

We knew a few dog breeds from the Genesis videos. I remembered one clip that I think was meant to be cute, an adolescent Staffordshire terrier – a Staffie, they called it – playing with an Andean doll toy. In reality, he was shaking the hell out of it. I suppose that was well enough since Andean doll toys aren't built around brittle little endoskeletons with brittle little necks. But watching that video gave me the sensation of my own neck snapping like a celery stick. I remember feeling an involuntary tightening in my sphincter. From that point on I was more afraid of dogs than of anything else I could imagine. When I started explaining this to Jill she quickly interrupted.

"You're obviously not aware of the Great Dingo Fence."

I allowed that I wasn't.

"It's the longest fence in the world, 5,600 kilometers, built specifically to keep dingos out of this part of Australia. It's regularly patrolled and professionally maintained."

She paused to let that sink in.

"If there was any significant human population around here you might have to worry about the occasional domesticated stray. But as a practical matter, there isn't. And in the unlikely event that some outlier dog does wander by, you've got your own personal fence to boot. I just walked the whole perimeter, as a matter of fact. Every foot of it. Secure the whole way."

"I didn't know that was in question. You seemed pretty sure of that last night."

"I was. But way more so now. Agricultural barbed wire, weather-treated wooden posts, all in good repair, just like they told me. It'll definitely keep the bigger dogs out, and even a smaller dog would have to be pretty motivated to work through."

She must have overestimated the amount of reassurance that provided. Even a small dog could outweigh me by a factor of eight or ten, which from Jill's perspective would make it a Great White on four legs. But there wasn't much use belaboring the point. "No one's forcing you to enjoy the outdoors," she said, "but I think you'd be crazy not to. You've got a beautiful place here." At least on the latter point, I couldn't disagree with her.

She'd arrived dressed like I'd never seen her, in workboots and jeans. She'd brought a number of things, the largest of which were a cardboard box and a heavy-duty plastic case. The latter had me worried — I didn't want back in a travel box — but it turned out to be the housing for a heavy hand tool she called a tacking gun. She sliced the cardboard box with a retractable blade and started pulling out lengths of nylon mesh netting in garish blue. "Sorry about the color," she said. "It's all they had."

She fiddled and fussed, loading up the tacking gun, stretching the mesh as if gauging its tautness, walking around the house, sizing things up. At some point she caught me staring. "You have to think things through, you know," she said.

"I wasn't criticizing."

"I know that, Richie."

She straightened up after a bit, finally ready to work.

"Did you sleep on the bed last night?"

"No, as I think I mentioned, I ended up on the floor."

"That doesn't seem very intelligent. The floors here aren't warm and forgiving like the ones at Genesis. Weren't you cold and stiff in the morning?"

"Yes, very much so."

"Well, maybe if it's easier to get up and down you'll be more inclined to use the bed. That's what I'm doing here with the mesh."

She knows that I can jump up onto things pretty well but don't like jumping too far down. On hard surfaces like the wooden floors here, the landings hurt my feet. I jumped onto the bed, bounced around a bit, and lay down.

"Not bad," I said.

"I thought you might use these dish towels as blankets. They're a nice quality cotton." She draped one over me, then a second, and a third. "Beats the floor, right?"

"Yes, much better," I said, snuggling in.

She knelt, placed the mesh, and fired the gun. I shrieked at the sound of it.

"Sorry about that. You understand I'm just trying to make things a little more comfortable for you."

"Yes, I appreciate that. It's all built for big people."

"Cover your ears."

She fired the gun twice more, then walked around the bed, carrying the loose end of the mesh with her. She draped it over the bed and pulled it tight.

"I assume the tighter it is, the easier it is to climb. Why don't you give it a try?"

She held her end, while I climbed down to the tacked end.

"Yes," I said from the floor. "The tighter the better."

She fired the gun several more times and cut the excess mesh with shears. A section of blue mesh now straddled the bed, and I could climb up or down easily on either side. We worked our way around the house, tacking the mesh at strategic points, at counters and shelves, at the windowsill, anywhere I might want to go. After an hour or so we had things pretty well covered.

"OK," she said, surveying her work. "You should be able to get around pretty well in here now. I've brought you plenty of food. Do you think you'll be warm enough with those blankets?"

"Yes. The problem will be when I get up. It's pretty cold here in the mornings."

"Do you want me to try to shut that window?"

Walled mostly in glass, the house had just one window that actually opened and closed. It was set in the slant of the roof and made the only break in the entire roofline. On that angle and at that elevation it looked difficult even for Jill to operate. It was a big heavy thing, a wooden frame holding a single glass pane five feet high by three wide, and opened out like a trapdoor. The opening, fortunately, was screened, or I'd have been vulnerable to any number of carnivorous intruders.

"I think we can leave it open," I said, quite possibly staking my life on the integrity of a decades-old screen installation.

"I think that's the right call. You need the ventilation. Let's get you comfortable with your fireplace so you can get rid of the chill when you need to. I've been told it's in good working order. Are you up for that?"

"Sure."

"The first thing to do is to gather your fuel, which shouldn't be any problem around here."

We went outside, where I half hoped that a swarm of magpies would assault me in her presence. But cagey beasts that they are, they stayed well out of view. We collected our respective armloads of bark and sticks, carried them inside, and dropped them near the fireplace. Jill knelt to build what I think of now as a sort of reverse nest, with soft bark strips on the bottom, smaller branches on top of them, and bigger branches on those. She tugged at a handle and something clanked into place. "That's the flue," she said. "We'll just keep it open for you and you won't have to mess with it." She handed me a box of wooden matches. "OK, now you can light it."

I'd never even seen fire, let alone struck a match. I had to hold the match with two hands, which meant I couldn't secure the striking surface. Jill solved the problem by disassembling the matchbox and stapling the striking surface to the wall at my waist level, where it remains to this day. I managed to light the match, and then, to my astonishment, the larger fire. We watched the flames grow, and I experimented with standing at various distances and turning around as needed to warm myself without overheating.

"People have been doing this since the days of the cavemen," Jill said.

"Are you going to build fires where you live?"

"No, my place has central heat."

"Where is your place?"

"In the city."

"You mean back by the airport?"

"More or less."

"Isn't that a long drive from here?"

"Yes, it is. But we'll see plenty of each other."

"You'll be driving here every day?"

"Probably more like every other day."

We watched the fire for a minute or two.

"You can throw more fuel on if you want to keep it going."

I heaved on a couple sticks, and they caught nicely.

"That's good. You should have access to all the bark and sticks you need. Keep a couple days' supply on hand in case it rains. It won't burn if it's wet. Just be careful to keep your pile far enough away from the fire that it doesn't catch."

I nodded.

"OK, I've got a lot to do," she said, "so I'd better be going. I'll see you again the day after tomorrow."

I followed her out.

"By the way," she said, reaching into the van, "the sun can be pretty harsh out here. Too much exposure can burn your skin. So I got you this for some cover." She pulled out an umbrella, bright red and just my size. "A real novelty item. I picked it up in the States before we left. I thought it'd be perfect for you."

She made me open it, carry it around, and close it. She was right – it was something I could definitely handle. Still, it was all a little perplexing. I didn't know the sun could burn you, and I'd thought umbrellas were for rain. But even if an umbrella for sun protection made sense, why that when there were so many more useful things she'd neglected? I had my reading and writing tablet, a case of clothing, a toothbrush, a paring knife, three blankets, and an umbrella. Period. I made a few jokes about how a few combat-oriented items might have been useful. I may have mentioned a small shotgun and a little suit of armor. But the fact is I didn't have any books, or linens, or a table, a chair, or plates, or any cutlery in my size. Not even a litter box.

We'd had no discussion of sanitation strategies to that point, and, as it turned out, we never would. At Genesis it'd always been one of the techs who'd changed our litter. Jill had cleaned up after The Chief, but I wouldn't say she'd ever been very happy about it. Apparently, she wasn't volunteering to resume those duties here. And to tell you the truth, I didn't want her on that job. In the group setting there'd been a certain anonymity, a given dropping untraceable to a given individual. But the thought of her in my own personal litter was a little too demeaning, no matter how well I covered. Her assumption, as far as I could tell, was that I'd do my business outdoors. And I was happy enough with that, in theory. But the magpies had made that a problem, whether she'd acknowledge it or not.

11. Jill

Beyond my pioneering maskless entry, my P7 nursery shift had show-cased the two most telling instances of preliminary pairing to date. Rob and Laura had merged their systems, and Uhura had followed Kirk to the far edge of their environment. But I had the sense that none of my peers were paying me the slightest bit of attention. As best I could see through the darkened glass, the whole staff was crowded down with the techs. I couldn't make out what they were discussing – the glass walls were virtually soundproof – but it was apparently a lot more interesting than any scientific progress I was making. None of them even noticed when I exited the nursery, but at last I could identify the cause of the excitement.

A shipment of small clothing had arrived. Jerry was already calling it "the collection." I was mortified at the way he cooed and fawned – he called to mind a grotesquely muscled Coco Chanel in ugly green paja-mas. There were four identical silver cases about the size of briefcases, but thicker, like small valises, with heavy-duty locking latches. One sat on the floor, unopened, looking like it might hold the detonator to a weapons system. The three others stood upright on a desk, swung open like little closets. They were perfect little clothes lockers, a straight-bar on each side, each with tiny garments swaying appealingly on tiny hangers. Drs. Sloboth and Bitsen had begun to lay the outfits on a table like ginger men in a row. The two of them looked like museum curators setting a miniature exhibit of 1960s fashion designs. There was hippie stuff — turtlenecks and vests, bellbottoms and miniskirts, florals and tie-dyes. And there was square stuff — blue and gray slim-cut suits, white shirts, and skinny ties for the guys; slacks and sweater tops, or pastel suits with gloves and matching hats, for the girls.

"Here's the suit Jackie wore in Dallas," cried Bitsen, holding a short, pink, double-breasted jacket with a navy collar and oversized navy buttons in one hand, and a matching skirt and pillbox hat in the other. That outfit may have been in questionable taste, but I know something about clothing, and it was authentic woolen boucle, fully lined. Nothing in that shipment came in the cheap materials you'd expect in doll-sized garments. Every piece was cut from fine fabrics and quality-stitched.

"Here's a whole Star Trek collection," said Dr. Sloboth, now into the fourth case at another desk. This brought everyone shuffling over for a peek. The case was stuffed with enough uniforms to outfit everyone on the bridge of our hypothetical little starship. There were tight long-sleeve velour shirts in golds, reds, and blues; and black pants cut and flared at mid-calf. And there were similarly tight long-sleeve velour mini-dresses, these only in red. All were shameless knockoffs, with Genesis Project chest logos in lieu of the classic Federation icons.

A video popped up on the PrismView just then, as if to commemorate fashion's introduction to the nursery. Leggy models lit up the big screens, working a runway that seemed to straddle a void — the event was bereft of photographers or an audience of any kind. The outfits replicated what we'd just seen in the valises. Down the catwalk went a lithesome brunette in the Jackie suit with the pillbox hat. Two others followed in tight slacks and sweater tops, then some men in gray suits and thin ties, a co-ed march of hippies, and finally, a strange little Star Trek procession. Falstaff shifted the PrismView setting so we could get a real-time look at the little people's reaction. The one-way effect was particularly disturbing in cases like this when the children were spellbound by the screen, staring in our direction as if right through us. Falstaff shifted back to the video just as it segued backstage for a behind-the-scenes action sequence in which the hurried models popped out of skirts and slacks to haul on whatever outfit came next.

Bitsen: Wow, corporate's really gone to town on this whole wardrobe thing.

Sloboth: Pretty racy show. I never knew runway models don't bother with underwear.

Dasher: It's not that they don't bother. It's a tactical imperative. They have to make quick changes, and they can't show any lines.

Sloboth: But this is obviously a staged production. There's no audience. It's not a real fashion show. So what's the rush?

Bitsen: It's an excuse to obviate the undergarments.

Dasher: Of course it's not a real fashion show. It was shot in some studio somewhere as the clothing designer's pitch to media relations. They weren't going to put up a runway in the Icosagon.

Me: Too bad. We'd have had Marcia Tompkins up there modeling one of her whorish business suits.

Sloboth: And her matching harlot's heels.

Bitsen: Sans her sluttish underwear.

Dasher: Ladies, ladies. Strike those comments from the record. I, for one, support underwear's obviation in these settings. As I'm sure did Chuck Hansen if he had a look at the video, which I'm guessing he did. I also support screening it here in our own modest facility. From a strictly professional standpoint, dressing is one of the basic skill sets we're meant to instill, and this would seem an effective visual tutorial. Certainly the little people have taken a keen interest. Would you agree Dr. Henderson?

Henderson: To a point. I'm hoping there's more to it than "sex sells."

Sloboth: Don't count on it. Seems to me we're watching a fully-sanctioned corporate peep show.

Dasher: Such cynicism does not become you, Doctors. Perhaps underwear is just not in the cards for our little people. Have you considered that? I don't recall seeing any in the shipment. Does anyone else?

Silence.

Me: Hmm. So... Who gets to wear what? Did we get some protocol on the point?

Bitsen: I think it's pretty clear what corporate is after. Uhura in the red velour mini. Laura in above-the-ankle house slacks, slim fit.

Dasher: Seems like a safe bet.

Me: Things are definitely going to hell around here. I say we stick it to media relations and let the children choose their own outfits. Sizing shouldn't be much of a factor. They're all pretty close by height and weight.

Dasher: What if Kirk puts on the miniskirt? Are you going to be OK with that, Dr. Edelman? And if so, do you think corporate is going to play along?

Henderson: He makes a good point. Normal children get parental guidance on clothing, with complete parental control in the early years. It's not appropriate for our little people to be making those choices on their own. Beyond our own attire – and lab coats aren't being offered here – they have no concept of basic gender conventions. They're missing all the reference points, societal, cultural, familial.

Me: The video seems to be making up for that pretty quickly.

We all stopped for another look. The camera cut close to a sultry black woman in the Uhura mini. And before it cut to a blonde in slim-fit slacks and a sweater top I could have sworn I saw a half-second cut of Samantha Stevens herself, holding forth in her black and white living room.

Me: Did anybody else just see that bit of Samantha? Are they actually going subliminal on us?

Falstaff: Since you had conscious recognition, then, technically, it's short of subliminal. But, yes, I've noticed a few of them. And the whole thing seems to be on master key mode. I can't override it.

12. Richie

That day and the next I peed strictly through the cat door. From a hygienic standpoint it was an unsustainable approach. Even here in East Central the urine would eventually puddle and fester. But the ever more pressing point was defecation, which, by its nature, didn't lend itself to the cat door perch. I'd not been long on this earth, but even I knew not to protrude my naked blind side into a swarm of ill-disposed raptors, abdominal discomfort notwithstanding.

Extended exposure to the magpies has confirmed my earliest impression that their primary rule of attack is to never come straight on. That's the unsettling thing about them, the fact that they're always coming out of your blind spot. It's the fear of the unknown, or rather the fear of the indefinite certainty. You know it's coming, but you don't know just when. When you brace yourself for the attack, you've only made things worse. The whack on the back of the head is bound to startle you no matter how diligently you've maintained your wretched little anticipation. And when you're all tensed up you don't roll with it as well as you might.

When I see a magpie on a branch, he'll have his head turned idly to the side, like some two-bit actor playing it casual. But then someone else in his gang will fly across my field of vision, stealing my attention so the first one can shoot off somewhere else, working his way behind me. It's tough to catch sight of him again – they vary their vertical vantage points, perching high or low so you don't know what plane to look along, even if you happen to be looking in the right direction. And that's exactly where the game is won and lost, with field of vision, or the lack of it. They can see how we're built. They can see the set of our eyes, fixed as they are to the narrow frontal view. It's a deadly flaw, and they never tire of exploiting it.

To say I've been battling them for four hundred days is not quite accurate. Battling requires the ability to inflict injury as well as to suffer it. And while I've suffered countless bruises, and the occasional gouge, and immeasurable distress, I've yet to inflict the slightest injury in return. Nor have I even much endeavored to. The best I can hope for is to conduct my outdoor business and return to my quarters unscathed. If that can be considered a form of victory, inglorious as it may be, then I suppose I've not done too badly.

A plan came to me somewhere between uneasy sleep and regretful waking, at dawn on the third day. It was predicated on the umbrella, and seems obvious in retrospect – I'd leap through the cat door, pop it open, stay low, and proceed under its cover. When I practiced that sequence in the glow of the morning woodfire, the immediate effect was to bring my intestinal distress to a crisis. But in the end, that was a good thing. Physical urgency overwhelmed fear and indecision. I sprinted to the cat door, pushed through, and launched.

The jump was fueled with adrenalin, longer and higher than the few I'd practiced, and by mistake I popped open the umbrella while still in the air. I felt an immediate updraft and a swing to the left. For all my ruminations on the wind, it'd never occurred to me I could be borne away with it. But the drift was mercifully short-lived. I landed and crouched, not quite where I'd expected, but duly shielded. I held that position and gripped the handle against the hit I knew was coming.

But it didn't come – for ten, fifteen, twenty seconds. The umbrella seemed to be having some deterring or confusing effect. I began a stooped walk that was particularly difficult in my condition. Fearing the avian bludgeon at every step, I passed into a sort of trance, lifting one leg after the other and proceeding steadily from the house. In time, I sensed I'd ventured far enough and crouched once again. And on its first test, the umbrella fulfilled more functions than I might ever have imagined, repelling magpies, shading me from the elements, and providing at least some illusion of privacy.

From the moment of my relief, I was taken with the expanse of grass undulating in the breeze, and with the stirring of the well-spaced eucalyptus trees. A pair of eastern greys thundered by, unaware of me or indifferent. I took a long look at the house, my first from this vantage point. It nestled almost agreeably among the small cluster of trees on one side, with the crowns of greater trees peeking over the roofline on the other, and, past them all, distant mountains in receding shades of purplish-green. In that early light, the eyesore of a roof seemed a little less hideous. The fading and rusting suggested a return to the earth, its own path to oblivion in its own particular time.

13. Jill

We thought ourselves rather daring, even righteous, when at the next morning's Little Gathering we resolved to let the children pick their own outfits. Dr. Dasher, for all his jibes the day before, surprised us by supporting free choice. Dr. Morben was silent on the point, a position indecipherable as either support or dissent. Dr. Bitsen, as it happened, was the lone holdout. While nothing in our charter required unanimity, we tended to operate that way. We hounded her like a jury looking to get home for supper, and she capitulated in time for Morben's buzzer.

The children always slept in their skin-tight black bodysuits, and the techs had always dressed them for the day while we were in the Little Gathering. But now things were going to be a little different. Falstaff dimmed all the lights in the building. The techs collapsed the table legs and, under the cover of darkness, moved the clothing display to the nursery floor. When they'd exited, Falstaff used the spotlights to pull the children straight to it.[19] They gathered around the well-lit clothing, picking at certain items and growing in agitation until they jostled like Christmas shoppers at a bargain

---

19 This was a way we had of controlling their attentions, directing them to or from certain things with lighting or dimming. Falstaff would also enhance the sunsets, supplementing the skylights with light-washes of orange and pink. The children seemed to enjoy this, and it made them more amenable to the bedtime proceedings.

table. Falstaff popped the nursery lights back on. Bodysuits littered the floor as the children tugged on outfits and paraded before the glass. The darkened view to the outside had a mirroring effect for them, and, in this instance, a bit of a discomfiting peep show effect for us. They were impressive little specimens. After several outfit changes each, they seemed to settle on their choices. I half-expected them to line up at some unseen checkout stand. Uhura, as we feared and more or less expected, walked away in the red velour miniskirt and black boots to the knees. Kirk followed with a blue velour top and black pants flared at the calves. Darrin and Rob were in gray suits, struggling with their neckties – Henderson would help them with those a little later. Samantha and Laura wore sweater tops with sleeves pushed to the elbows, slim-fitting cotton slacks cut above the ankles, and flat shoes.

Falstaff: What we've just seen is the defeat of so-called free choice. A sobering affirmation of pre-determination. Fatalism, if you will.

Bitsen: Well at least nobody picked the pink Jackie suit. I don't think I could handle that.

Sloboth: Yeah, I don't know what corporate was thinking on that one.

Me: You never know, one of the girls might go for it tomorrow.

Dasher: In that case I may have to organize a small motorcade.

Sloboth: Richie's still deciding.

There he stood, the last of the seven, buck naked, his little backside pressed to the glass, contemplating the clothing arrayed on the flattened tabletop before him. His hair, which I'd always pegged as auburn, looked a brighter orange in contrast with the peachy-cream tone of his body.

Henderson: Imagine the pressure. We make our way to self-awareness and position ourselves in the world over a period of many years. He's making a choice eight days in, insulated and uninformed, that could define him for life.

Me: I don't know about that. He could pick one thing today and something entirely different tomorrow.

Bitsen: I have a hunch that's not going to be the case with these people.

Sloboth: I think he's going flower child.

Dasher: Business casual.

Unaware of his role in the ongoing drama, Richie made his selection. Based on criteria none of us would fully understand, he pulled a striped cotton tee shirt over his head, struggling some with his arms before poking them through. After another few seconds, he stepped into a pair of cuffed bluejeans.

Sloboth: Ugh!

Bitsen: Happy Days.

Dasher: Two trekkies, four 60s suburbanites, and a 50s dipshit.

Henderson: For the first time, I begin to see the value in school uniforms.

Morben: Alright people, show's over. Let's get on with the day.

Beyond the Little Gathering buzzers, that was one of the few displays of discipline I ever saw from our supervisor.

Dasher: Aye, sir. We now return you to the regularly scheduled events of P8, further adventures in the acquisition of exceptional skill sets.

At the risk of seeming egotistical, I should mention that among those charged with the aforementioned acquisition of exceptional skill sets, Dasher and I were the clear leaders. Academically, my work was head and shoulders above everyone's, including Dasher's. My Brio sessions were both creative and technically demanding, and Brio's unique compatibility with quantitative analysis allowed for compelling, data-based mapping of each child's acquisition rate. Overall track count was the simplest metric – how much track was each child setting in the given time. But track density – how much track in a given area – quickly struck me as the more telling indicator. It implied a complexity of design, switchbacks, overpasses and so on, a level of engineering sophistication. At the end of each session, Falstaff would project four-meter laser circles onto the points of maximum density in each of the seven children's grids, then snap overhead still shots from which I'd glean the track counts. I had this methodology in place by my third session and was stockpiling data before the rest of the staff, all of whom had a head start of several days, knew what had hit them. Not only was I tracking and graphing the two numerical counts, total track and four-meter density, but I was also compiling the photos in a library of aesthetic maturation, the design pattern progression for each child. I couldn't help but notice that the Brio sessions had the attention of at least a couple up-and-ups, people in expensive suits who dropped in a time or two to have a look.

I was also documenting the pairing behaviors of the three couples and Richie's developing rapport with the cockatiel. These, I admit, were intrinsically more interesting than the Brio, although socialization was generally considered a lesser priority than skill acquisition. Like some high-tech Catholic school nun, I spliced together video documenting every meaningful exchange between Kirk and Uhura, every longing look between Rob and Laura, every come hither glance between Darrin and Samantha. I quantified them as best I could – frequency of interaction, intensity of interaction – though it was all a bit subjective for my liking. Richie's banter with the bird didn't even qualify as socialization, at least as defined in our charter, but I was able to quantify his vocalizations as a percentage of the "total chirp," giving me a basis to measure any progress he might make going forward. For all their shortcomings, even these secondary pursuits made for better science than anything anyone else was doing.

But for all that, Dasher's enterprise was flashier. And even in the science business, maybe especially in the science business, flash matters. His early musical recognition exercises had evolved into simple dance steps, and then on to elementary line dancing. At the beginning it was really just seven kids standing there with their hands on their hips, kicking out the occasional tentative foot. But it quickly evolved into something compelling, even entertaining. Soon the whole staff was stopping to watch – country music pumping on both sides of the glass, the little people facing us in two staggered lines, three fronting four, hands on hips, sidling left, sidling right, rotating one heel then the other, stepping over, stepping back, pivoting ninety, kicking out, slapping heels. There was not only a precision to the movement, but a uniform stillness of the upper body, thumbs hooked into imaginary hip pockets, and an utter lack of facial expression. Dasher had belabored these points above all others.

So endearing were these performances that Bitsen lodged a formal request for a line of tiny western wear, there being something fundamentally askew in a line dance of trekkies, 60s suburbanites, and, heaven forbid, Jackie in pink. Despite some unavoidable competitive resentment, I couldn't help but lead the cheers. The shaded and more or less soundproof glass was unfortunate, muffling our hoots and hollers and the rhythmic pounding on our desks. But over the next few days, Falstaff dialed back the shading and began to pipe our crowd noise inside.

More executives, only a few of whom I could identify, began to drop in during Dasher's shifts. These groups were bigger, more frequent, and more enthusiastic than any I'd had for Brio. On occasion they threw in a few hoots and hollers of their own. Marcia Tompkins became a regular attendee, though all the while affecting an absurd indifference. Dmitri was also there more often than not, huddling with

Falstaff as a production mate. Early on, those two had added some effective theatrics by dimming the house lights in favor of spots. Those operated manually, however, and tracking the seven dancers thrust the two into an extreme desktop sport of their own, grimacing and lurching to maneuver multiple joysticks at once. They soon hit upon an easier approach, killing both the house lights and the spots and leaving only the bluish cylinders from the overhead drones. The effect was pleasingly sinister, turning the dancers' hair into manes of blue fire and their quick little feet into tiny rhythmic strobes. And it cast the rest of their smooth-stepping frames into dramatic shadow – they appeared now as throbbing, pulsing, fifteen-inch specters. As Dasher's choreography became more complex with the passing of the days, the drones were forced to an eerie little dance of their own, weaving amongst themselves in an airborne frenzy to track their charges beneath.

I was as big a fan of that line dance as anyone, but I was also competing with it. I knew that sooner or later I'd have to reconsider my commitment to Brio. Railroading has its merits, but it's not much of a spectator sport. And after every shift we were obliged to leave the nursery as we'd found it, which meant returning the track to its boxes and starting from scratch the next day. We could improve our efficiencies and marginally improve our designs, but there was no chance for staged progress, no chance to build the ultimate Brio network over the many days it would require. I could see that ripping up the tracks at the end of every session was discouraging not only to me, but to the little people. I used the overhead photos not just to document the science, but to bolster our morale with a permanent record of our work. Like a proud but somewhat desperate schoolmarm, I taped them up on the back wall, printing each designer's name in thick ink letters in the bottom right hand corner – Laura, Rob, Uhura, Kirk, and so on.

One downside of displaying everyone's work was that Richie's paled a bit by comparison. It was numerically sub-par and aesthetically monotonous – his track generally ran to the birdcage and circled it like a storybook zoo train. In my view, this didn't reflect a lack of aptitude so much as a lack of interest, along with some spotty attendance. Don't get me wrong – he was there every day. None of them had a choice in the matter. But some days he just looked so forlorn that I'd give him the nod, and he'd leave his track work and scamper off to join The Chief at the rail. His exchanges there were becoming ever more interactive and loquacious. His percentage of the total chirp had jumped from ten percent to nearly twenty-five. And his vocalizations were becoming more complex, although I couldn't take the time to quantify the acquired avian voicings. In retrospect, I wish I had.

Birds had never been my zoological strong suit, and for all the skill sets within our staff, nobody else knew them nearly as well as I did. It was a mystery how The Chief had gotten to us in the first place. He'd just seemed to come with the building. I'd had to look things up to confirm that he was even a male. Dr. Bitsen had ordered in some seed, and when it became apparent that no one else would do it, I became the one to clean the cage every third day. I'd always take Richie with me, and he'd watch from the railing while I gathered the soiled newspaper and wood shavings and set the fresh stock in place. The bird would sulk on the far end of his perch, complaining incessantly. "Grump," I'd say, and "ingrate," enunciating and repeating and trying to induce Richie, with his squeaky little voice, to mimic my words between his vocalizations of the bird sounds. I can't say he showed much interest. Good sport that I am, I always offered The Chief a finger, but he didn't show much interest either. On one occasion he did hop aboard for ten or fifteen seconds, but he refused my offers thereafter.

Somewhere along the line, and for reasons I've never understood, The Chief's affections for Richie began regressing. I felt bad for the little guy when he'd squeak out a few rudimentary phrases of cockatiel jabber and The Chief would interrupt with an air of savage contempt, ripping off a furious sequence of chirping and squawking that would run for minutes at a time. It felt a bit like the banjo scene in *Deliverance,* with Richie picking out a few tentative guitar notes and the albino boy blowing him away. And like the albino boy, when The Chief had had his say, he'd sidle dismissively to the side or turn completely away, suffering no further interaction. But if Richie was ever discouraged, he never let on. He'd stand and stare for just a minute, then walk back to his Brio station, where he'd set to the admittedly uninspiring business of laying track that'd be pulled back up within the hour.

I was beginning to relate to Richie, at least on that point. Each day made it more evident that Brio was a dead end. The children's improvement curves were flattening badly. But abandoning it would put me back where I'd started, at the bottom of the specialist heap. And I was having a tough time coming up with an alternative.

If I were a certain kind of person, I'd have taken consolation in the fact that at least one of my associates, Dr. Bitsen, had a more pressing problem. She was the nutritionist in the group, specifically a pediatric nutritionist, and prominent enough in her field to have been hired, as we all had been, over dozens of highly qualified applicants. She'd been dealt a strange opening hand when the newborns had bypassed formula and moved directly to solids. In retrospect, she and the two pediatricians, Drs. Hayes and Manly, might have anticipated that from the advanced dentistry in the prenatal scans. Failing that, her reaction to the rejected formula was immediate and decisive – she trucked baby food in by the caseload. But after two full days of trying nearly all of it – jars and tubes, fruit and vegetables, meat, mush and pap – she hadn't found a thing they'd eat. Dasher, who had four kids of his own, acting on a blind hunch and with Bitsen's reluctant approval, cut servings of his own catered meal into the tiniest possible bites and set them on a large communal plate on the nursery floor. Video shows the children circling at first, like a wolfpack investigating an abandoned kill. To their credit, they didn't jostle and didn't feed directly from the plate, but settled in Indian style and, after some initial hesitation, began to feed themselves in the most civilized manner that bare hands would allow. Not only were they eating, they were doing so with a physical coordination and a civilized manner no one could have imagined. Bitsen swallowed her pride and adopted Dasher's approach going forward, small pre-cut bites of our own meals served communally for breakfast, lunch and dinner.[20]

As part of her original regimen, Bitsen had conducted minutely calibrated measurements of height, weight, and head circumference for each child twice daily. All seven had avoided the initial weight loss of normal newborns, an early positive. But despite what seemed like robust intake, none of them gained anything over the next many days. Any tiny victories in the morning, a gram here, a gram there, were wiped away by dusk. As for height, not a child had a millimeter's change. Even the normal margin for posture was missing, given the military bearings in play. These children didn't slouch.

By the P10 Little Gathering this had become a point of concern. Manly suggested testing for growth hormone levels, but Hayes and Morben thought this premature. Bitsen reassured us that "most babies are just getting back to their birth weights at seven or ten days, and many normal babies take even longer." But by P14, Dr. Sloboth, her closest confidant at the Project, whispered that Bitsen herself was the one most needing reassurance.

---

20 Dasher lorded this over Bitsen incessantly, if not cruelly. He took to walking around the building spooning himself little bites from a jar of the abandoned baby food. "Delicious," he'd say every time he passed her workstation. And, "I don't know why we all don't eat this stuff. It's super nutritious, and God knows we've got a supply for several lifetimes."

14. Richie

I've been up for hours, and still so much of the day lies ahead. At Genesis, chunks of days flew by almost unnoticed. We didn't get a lot of "idle time," as they called it. But East Central presents a whole new construct. Time has expanded. Idling, in the sense of time spent quietly, is not only permissible, it's compulsory.

I climb onto the pantry shelf and grab some seeds and fruit for the midday meal. Within a few days of arriving I'd gotten pretty good at scrambling up and down the netting, and now, four hundred days in, it's as natural as breathing. In her better moods Jill might say I'm "as nimble as an able seaman." Some days she'll poke her head in the door and say, "Permission to come aboard?" And when she sees me it's, "And how is the old salt?" It took me a while to have any idea what she was talking about.

She dropped in late yesterday afternoon with a good batch of supplies. Among other things, she left me a pomegranate, a particular favorite of mine that she says can be difficult to source in Australia. I roll it down the netting and onto the floor so when I've taken my meal I can wrestle the remainder into the fridge. Cutting into it isn't an easy chore, but I've developed some skill with the knife. I have enough fruit and other staples to cover all my meals until her next visit. Those visits have dropped to every six or seven days now and tend to come late in the day. I'd like to stay up after dark to extend my time with her, but, as I've mentioned, my kind are strictly diurnal. At Genesis, apparently, we all went out within moments of each other, and from that point almost nothing could stir us. I'm reliably asleep just after dark here too, though I find myself awake a little later when the rain comes heavy and pounds on the metal roof. Jill was surprised to hear even that can keep me up.

I had just that kind of rain on the afternoon of my seventh day here, harder than I'd ever thought rain could fall. Watching such a torrent through the glass didn't seem to do it justice, so I climbed to the sill of the trapdoor window. There's a cluster of trees running from that window – jacarandas, tulipwoods, and a blend of smaller varieties – and I had an immediate feeling of being up in them. The acoustics were better, and I had the surprising pleasures of smelling the rain and feeling its mist through the screen. The window itself, as I've mentioned, is opened into a horizontal position and supported by a wooden bracing near its outer edge. That bracing has a crossbar just low enough for birds to perch under the shelter of the glass. A single bird settled there to wait out the weather, four feet from my position. I sat as quietly as I could.

After my rude introduction to the magpies I'd done what research I could on the local avifauna. There's no internet here, but Jill had loaded my tablet with some Wiki reference drives, and I could tentatively identify this one from behind as a butcherbird. I say "tentatively" because the butcherbird does look a lot like the magpie, alarmingly so at first glance – same shape, same beak, same basic colors. They're actually in the same genus, *Cracticus*. The principle difference is that the butcherbird is white-plumed in the body, whereas the magpie is entirely black in the body – "The avian Darth Vader," Jill used to crack in a way that wasn't all that humorous, or all that accurate. When I looked up Darth Vader he didn't have any white on him at all, whereas magpies have white napes, some white wing feathers, and chalky beaks.

With a flyscreen between us the distinction was more or less moot, but it should be said that the butcherbird isn't as crazy in the eyes, and I've found its disposition far more pleasant than that of its blacker cousin. In the interest of full disclosure, its name does derive from the distinctive practice of skewering prey on sharp branches and leaving it there to dangle. It would seem a clever if unkind way to save a meal for later, or to show it off among peers or potential mates, or to hold one part while devouring another. Jill calls this bird the "Feathered Vlad" or the "Avian Impaler."

The butcherbird was calling out a short two-note volley, over and over, while cocking her head at something just out of my view. I took her to be chirping to another of her kind, and doing so in a matter we might call insistent, though I've since learned to be careful drawing any particular intention from repetitive calls. Birds love hearing themselves, and, frankly, the less intelligent of them will drone out the same dull-witted phrase for an hour at a time. Given how little I knew of the different birds and their chatter when I first got here, I'd made nothing more than a "wild-ass guess," as Jill would say. But I was proven right when the male flew in and took his place beside his partner on the beam. He shook himself out a few times, and she sidled testily a step or two away. But eventually they settled in, facing away from me and watching the storm in what seemed, after the ruffled beginning, a surprisingly perfect unison. I could hear their muffled chatter through the screens. The butcherbirds are a particularly musical bunch, and distinctly conversational – this was way more complex than anything I was used to with The Chief. In retrospect, either The Chief had suffered a stunted development, presumably from the lack of stimulating mentors or peers, or his kind has a lesser acuity than the birds of *Cracticus*. I suspect a bit of both.

Neither bird seemed to notice me through the flyscreen – I can be pretty quiet when I need to. And since I have nothing if not time

here in East Central, I decided to ride out the storm sitting on the sill
with my back against the side jamb, picking up whatever bits of the birdsong I could. The rain kept on for several hours, and the three of us
hardly budged. I can't say I learned much or understood anything. But I
picked up some distinct phrasings, beautiful things I was dying to mimic
out loud. Given the complexity, I knew I needed repetitions. For now
though, I felt I was better off holding my quiet profile. I kept the mimicking just under my breath, tucked away for later.

I suppose I'd gotten a little too comfortable by the time the storm
cleared and I ventured out at the end of the day. A small river flowed
where it hadn't before – rainwater draining from the mountain face
and rushing through a channel in the grounds. Dark clouds ran off
to the east, and the sky shone the startling blue that so often follows
such an outburst. I was taking all this in, holding the umbrella pretty
casually, when a hard thump knocked it clean out of my hands, not
fifteen feet from the house. There I was, sprawled in the grass, while a
magpie gripped one of the metal ribs in his beak, taking quick hopsteps
away. I dove for the handle and pulled back. This was my first face-
to-face encounter with a magpie buck. He was a few inches shorter
than I, but that wasn't the dimension that had my attention. It was his
wingspan, which was nearly twice my height. Every flap of those wings
produced a surge of energy pulling against me, my feet sliding away in
matching increments. I let him catch my eye just then, another mistake
on my part, a play into his strong suit, as if he'd been waiting to pull me
in. Now I was locked there. The glare was terrifying, and at the same
time almost conversational, to the point where I felt my grip actually
beginning to loosen. This finally jarred me to my senses – I shook off
the stare and fought with new resolve. The grip of the magpie beak
is better suited for soft tissues than for metal, and once I'd focused
it was no match for my own opposable thumbs and the full leverage
of my legs. My feet locked in a cluster of grass roots, and after a few

dedicated jerks I'd wrestled the umbrella back. Now we were both in hop-steps, I hopping backwards with the umbrella held before me, and the magpie hopping in measured pursuit while calling to his mates for mobbing support. Within seconds there were three of them, but by that time I was too close to the house for what would likely have been a disastrous attack from the rear. My bottom hit the cat door, and I was never so grateful for anything in my life. I pushed my way in, still gripping the umbrella on the outside. Even at the risk of damage to my hands, I couldn't afford to lose it. While I labored to fold it down it weathered several heavy thumps and the first tear in its fabric. I felt the last savage clack of a beak on the metal tip, and pulled it in.

Three hundred and ninety-three days later, that umbrella is unrecognizable, a metal skeleton with a battered wooden handle. To its credit, it still opens and closes, but there's no trace of the original fabric. That's been pulled to pieces and dispersed over untold acres, along with the dozens of jury-rigged replacement strips I've tied into place. But while any benefits of privacy and sun protection have long expired, the skeleton is still effective against the magpies, with its sharp edges and pokey points. It's still one of the most important things I own.

15. Jill

As it turned out, Dr. Dasher was in a jam as thick as mine. He knew his line dancing, I had to give him that. He'd grown up in Oklahoma, in some town along the Red River where line dancing, to hear him describe it, was a way of life, a pleasing amalgamation of community, cadence, beer, and western wear, not too grubby and not too new. While Dasher was a clever man, and never shy to tell you so himself, he was neither a trained choreographer nor so naturally gifted as to conjure up a whole new production every couple of days. Once he'd gotten that initial routine to a certain level he was at a loss for his next act, and it all fell around him within a matter of days. His high-profile audience stood through the same show, with what minor adjustments he could effect, for a second time, and for part of a third. After that they just stopped coming.

Of course, if we hadn't been hamstrung with security considerations and could have catered to the entire BioSpore workforce or to the general public, that show would have pulled raucous crowds for months or years on end. But only Genesis insiders and a certain executive group had access to the building, or, for that matter, any awareness of it. And while that latter group in particular constituted a highly desirable demographic, they weren't going to "keep the barn full," as Dasher put it. The executives were the first to drop out, and one dance without them was enough to scatter Marcia Tompkins and her crowd for the duration. Just like that we were back to the core group – project staff and Dmitri. For our part, we remained a warm and faithful audience. We all looked forward to the afternoon show, and in a way we liked having it back to ourselves. Falstaff cut the shading entirely and restored some light to the stage, and we made a game out of trying to draw some eye contact from the stone-faced dancers, maybe even draw a smile or two from the easier targets like Richie and Laura. Dasher feigned outrage at these antics, but deep down I think he appreciated our enthusiasm.

In a way, he and I were both victims of the children's insanely quick learning. If we'd been training elephants, or apes, or parrots, we'd have been graded on an animal handler's curve. But we were working with little people, and from what we could tell management already considered them less neonates than optimized little adults, with minds as clear as blank canvasses and lives stripped of worry and distraction. There was some truth to that, though as I saw it, students without language, however gifted, were hardly optimal.

Dasher and I were also victims of our mutual proficiency. The other skill facilitators, our *so-called peers,*[21] hadn't brought all that much to the table, some torpid efforts at playing Monopoly perhaps the most notable effort. Had I not rather dramatically demonstrated the children's facility with engineering, Dasher's achievement would have shone far brighter. And if Dasher hadn't wowed everyone with his little lords of the dance, then the Brio would have stood far prouder. In combination, the children's feats said

---

21 I'm not proud of it, but as we grew friendlier Dasher and I began to refer to the other four skill facilitators as SCPs. For all Ian Harding's raving about BioSpore's "mob of the most brash and brilliant young minds in science," those people don't generally hold the day-to-day jobs at the project execution level.

more about their own innate abilities than about their lab-coated mentors.

No one could say that Dasher didn't do his homework. Several nights running, long after the children were deep in sleep and most of the staff had gone home, he'd taken late dinners at his terminal and studied line dance choreography. Sometimes he'd jump out of his seat to try a few moves, and we'd both get a good laugh out of it. He didn't lose that zeal even later, when he'd resigned to moving on. He channeled that energy, those untold hours, into researching the area's top instructors and choreographers in tap, ballet, and modern dance, people he could bring in to supplement his work, to introduce whole new domains of movement. He lobbied tirelessly up the chain for clearance to do that, but was denied on every count. Security, for once, took priority – and properly so in my opinion, though I kept that view to myself. The dance card had been played. Our dog and pony show needed entirely new tricks.

But the next trick, as it turned out, wasn't conjured by Dasher, or myself, or any of our SCPs. It was Richie's doing. If I hadn't put that second camera over the birdcage we might never have known what he'd really pulled off. Nobody saw it in real time. We were all huddled in a Little Gathering, and as we filed out, we heard a squawk and saw a bird flying overhead, well above the drones, up near the skylights. At first I thought it was an interloper from the outside. But our physical plant was much too secure for that. It was The Chief, sprung from his cage, on the loose and flying free.

I was the only one with any idea how to clip a wing, and the only one who'd even considered the need. But I'd had little inclination to actually do it. And right or wrong, it was water under the bridge with The Chief in his loops, squawking like a lunatic at forty feet. I saw through the glass that Richie was beside himself in panic, even though our later video review would show him to be the sole enabler of the escape. He'd calmly approached the railing, gathered himself, and leapt straight to the top bar – twice his body height! None of us had seen anything like it. He'd pulled himself to a standing position, perched there for a moment, and leapt across to the cage bars. From there he'd sidled to the door and sprung the latch. I had to watch it twice to even believe what I'd seen, and we'd all watch that tape dozens of times over the next few days. But for all his superhero antics, Richie had never actually seen a bird in flight, and it must have come as quite a shock to him when The Chief exploded from the cage and shot up to the skylights.

While the rest of the staff gawked and pointed, I went inside to try to settle Richie. "There, there," I cooed moronically. He nestled deeply into my lab coat chest pocket -- by then I'd hand-sewn the deeper version -- but he wouldn't go quiet. I could feel him shaking as he wept. I caught Falstaff's eye, and motioned for him to join me. After a few more forays around the perimeter, The Chief settled on the truss that held the uppermost bank of spotlights. With all eyes on him, and possibly in response to that, he loosed a generous glop of excreta. It made a long dramatic drop through the stage lighting and splatted onto the pristine nursery floor, near where the other six children were gathered to watch. They tittered with delight. The Chief took off again, circling at the building's upper reaches.

"We'd better reel that bird in before this one's heart rate goes through the roof," I said, pointing to my chest pocket.

"I don't know if you're personally inclined to do that, or how you'd actually go about it," said Falstaff, "but you can get up there." He pointed to the ladder running up the back wall to the catwalk. Speaking in as soothing tones as I could muster, I fished Richie out of my pocket and turned him over to Falstaff. He'd never held any of the children and acted as if I'd handed him a small explosive. The Chief, meanwhile, settled again on the truss.

Like the rungs on a utility pole, or a New York City fire escape, the ladder stopped a good nine feet above the ground. I used a stool to reach the bottom rung with one hand, then took a little skip step to get my second hand latched on. I was pretty self conscious about that little jump – all of an inch or two – and in a particularly undignified follow-up, I began to walk up the wall, my butt sticking further out with each step. I felt the many sets of eyes tracking my contortions as I worked my hands up one notch, and then another until my feet could find the bottom rung. I hoped to redeem myself by appearing both athletic and nonchalant through the rest of the climb. But one of the lights was positioned in such a way as to burn my retinas every time I looked up, twice halting my progress while I rubbed with one hand. It was a relief to step at last onto the catwalk. The Chief hadn't moved, facing away on the truss. I inched ahead, hoping not to startle him, but as I drew within ten feet, he turned to regard me, not with the least bit of surprise, but with the air that he'd known what I'd been up to all along and was just now bothering to acknowledge it. He cocked his head to one side, his headfeathers tilting like a party hat held only by its rubber string, sizing me up as if he'd never seen me before.

"Come on, Chief. Let's get you back down."

I leaned out slowly, extending my forefinger as far as I could. He took two steps further away, leaving my reach a foot short of him. I craned further out and, for the first time, snuck a quick look down. The desks appeared in a tidy little row, with a huddle of my co-workers just behind them, staring up. From my elevated vantage point they looked a bit like Samantha and Darrin riding my feet back on P4.

"Ms. Edelman," came Dr. Morben's voice over the PA. "Please come down at once." The instruction was clear enough, but the intonation was muted, almost whispered, as if Morben was tacitly aligned with me in not wishing to startle The Chief, and therefore, I reasoned, holding out some hope for a last-gasp success. I gave it one more lean, straining out as far as I could. The Chief responded by giving me a good smart peck on the finger – I've seen slightly larger birds of the parrot family take substantial chunks out of two-by-fours – but with a cringe and a deep swallow I kept it in place for one last moment. He surprised me by hopping aboard, though he made it a point to show his displeasure.

"There, there," I said to soothe the ruffled bird as I moved back along the catwalk. I'm no bird psychologist, though I understand they do exist, but as odd as it sounds, I sensed that his agitation owed less to the excitement of the flight than to the indignity of riding my finger. It also occurred to me, later than it probably should have, that I couldn't go down the ladder one-handed. I could never have stuffed him in a bag, even if someone had brought me one. In a desperate longshot, I moved him toward my shoulder, and he surprised me again by taking right to it, shifting into place like Captain Jack's parrot. He was immediately more at ease – the shoulder seemed less demeaning. I continued to the ladder, declining use of the handrails to keep my shoulders as steady as possible. Keeping a fixed head position seemed paramount, but I couldn't help a few sidelong glances at The Chief during my descent, hoping desperately that he wouldn't fly away or bite off a piece of my ear.

Someone had replaced the stool with a stepladder, smoothing my transition to the weight dispersion flooring. I felt oddly like Neil Armstong -- if I'd been wearing a headset I might have endeavoured at something witty. Instead I snuck a quick look at Falstaff and headed directly to the cage, afraid to give The Chief any time to reconsider. Falstaff had a hand to his heart, like a schoolboy at his Pledge of

Allegiance. Only after a moment did I realize it was there to support Richie standing upright in his standard-depth chest pocket. I declined any further eye contact, putting my mind to holding a steady gait and preventing any swing in the shoulders. At the cage I again offered The Chief my finger, and again he accepted – as if we did this kind of thing every day! – and I moved him gently inside. He hopped to his perch, and I latched the door shut.

Someone clapped, others joined and, and within moments applause sounded through the building. To my horror, I thought I might actually have blushed.[22] "Well done, Dr. Edelman," called a voice I recognized as Dr. Dasher's. I couldn't see very well through the shaded glass, but I gave a little bow to what looked like a cluster of people on the other side. Falstaff bent down to put Richie on the floor, and I had my first glimpse at just how fast the little people really were. I couldn't actually differentiate the movement in real time, but he was at the cage in a flash. He and the bird began at once to jabber like a couple of old hens.

I'll never know why The Chief hopped onto that finger and cooperated so fully in his own re-incarceration. Perhaps he'd never been out of a cage, and was simply terrified. Perhaps he didn't see all that much upside to flying around in an ugly old tennis center. But that decision, that single resolution in his little birdbrain, proved itself a watershed event, a turning point in the dynamics between the three of us – Richie, The Chief, and me.

From that moment on, Richie and The Chief were in constant jabber mode. Richie was near the cage at every unstructured moment, and The Chief, for his part, abandoned his condescension and irritability, presumably in appreciation for Richie's having

---

22 Later video review confirmed a slight reddening in the face.

sprung the cage door. The two of them began to connect more or less as equals, engaging each other with mutual energy and enthusiasm. Richie's percentage of the birdspeak approached forty percent during this period, but that tells only part of the story. Without having catalogued his whistles and coos, and without formal training as a linguist, I can offer only a novice's opinion, though one gleaned from direct observation, that Richie's vocabulary grew exponentially from the moment of the cagebreak. In a period of about a week, far less time than he'd previously required to compile a few tentative whistles and a few halting singsong phrases, he mastered a full musical compendium, sufficiently complex, at least in my mind, to be considered a form of language. The Chief would cock his head to listen while Richie puffed his cheeks and screwed up his eyes to make his concentrated little whistles and calls. When Richie had finished, The Chief would consider for a moment and respond in earnest.

As for me, from that day forward The Chief accepted every finger I offered. He sat calmly on my shoulder when I cleaned his cage, and I, in turn, stopped calling him "ingrate." I even took to carrying him around during my formal nursery shifts. Having The Chief at large on my shoulder was a delight to the children, though a frequent distraction as he and Richie would often jabber out of turn like little miscreants. I stopped walking on eggshells, as Dr. Morben used to say, but began instead to stand, sit, and bend over without making any particular accommodations. The Chief took care of his own positioning, shuffling his feet to find the level point, or, failing that, pinching into my lab coat and clamping hold. I found the perfection of his feathering all the more admirable when viewed so closely. But at the intimate proximity of my shoulder he also exuded a musty scent, the sort I associated with barns, or with pet stores. It wasn't necessarily offputting – grounding is the term I would use – like walking into a dressing room of post-performance ballerinas and realizing that even the most graceful creatures exude their earthy scents.

I never did clip his wings, and certainly no one else did either. Beyond my briefings, none of the other specialists paid him the slightest bit of attention, before or after the cagebreak, except to make note of ill-placed excretions. He would occasionally fly from my shoulder to the lip of the PrismView, where he'd perch and dribble. I endured the occasional jibe on his account – "Hey, Bird Woman, can you clean that shit off the glass?" – and various catty remarks about some droppings on my shoulder. But fresh lab coats were always at the ready. And the jibes were in good fun, except for the occasional intimation from Dr. Manly that I was pandering more to the bird than the children. I admit I'd grown fond of The Chief, but I didn't need to apologize to anyone – Dr. Manly in particular, the surly bastard – about my attention to the children.

None of the staffers had a closer relationship with any of them than I did with Richie. After the rescue he seemed to regard me as something of a hero, his little features speaking clearly of gratitude and respect. He stopped cutting my nursery sessions, sitting patiently for the duration rather than jockeying for permission to break away. He even took to sitting on my shoulder, the one opposite The Chief, where he'd pull lightly at my collar, or at my ear, or stroke my hair. I took special care to spread my attentions to the other children, and logistics alone would keep any dependence in check. My daytime in the nursery was limited by the schedule, and there was no socializing with the little Rip Van Winkles at night.

They slept huddled together on a double yoga mat, which caused a nightly consternation among the seven drones, programmed as they were to hold positions directly above their respective wards.

At bedtime they'd jockey at twenty feet, battling for vertical vantage points in a silent mechanized frenzy, bobbing and weaving at speeds our naked eyes could barely process. It was a spectacle of fine engineering, and a regular piece of entertainment for the group of us who tended to work late. "An automated, aerial shell game," Falstaff called it, "with seven cups instead of three for those extra few gears of mayhem." The children were oddly oblivious to the antics of the drones, but when they settled into sleep, which they did nearly in unison, the drones went still right with them, floating like tranquil moons and casting their blue cylinders of light on the tangle of bodies below. It had the effect of the last act of some futuristic stage tragedy.

Like a ship's mate running autopilot, the main objective on nightwatch was simply to stay awake. The specialist on duty had to log in at least hourly or get called out by the system and face Morben's censure in the morning. Morben was uncharacteristically animated on the point, as we'd learned watching him dress down the sinfully somnolent Dr. Henderson to open one Little Gathering. In my informal poll of co-workers, some spent their nightshift hours catching up on paperwork or personal correspondence. Others worked out, did some gaming, or streamed television, with a pervasive emphasis on 60s sitcoms. Dasher liked to settle in with popcorn and Coke and watch three movies. He insisted that was the optimal number. "Imagine an overseas flight with unlimited leg room, no lines at the bathroom, and no customs to clear at the end," he said. "Not too bad really, but for the very regrettable lack of alcohol."

By the time my first nightshift got underway I couldn't muster much enthusiasm for any of those pastimes. I'd always found all-nighters unsettling, and university libraries were never as eerie as this place. Not that there was anything I couldn't handle. The children slept so soundly there was virtually no chance of any nocturnal drama. And one of our two pediatricians was always on call in the remote event of a medical problem.

I'd often wondered what it was like in the nursery after dark. While I'd never heard of anyone going in after hours, I'd never heard any rules forbidding it. Now, almost on impulse, I popped through the airlock doors. The warmth hit me at once, somehow more incongruous by night. And the stillness was disorienting after the liveliness of our day shifts. Eerie optics competed in the glass, shadowy reflections from within and the LED glows from workstations without. I took a turn or two along the perimeter, playing the beat cop while trying to ignore myself in the glass. Then I stood hovering until I began to feel like a creep, staring at sleeping children with no parental or professional purpose. It struck me then to look for signs of nocturnal pairing – I wondered why I hadn't thought of it before. They were all in a tangle, but if you looked closely enough, Kirk had an arm over Uhura, Laura and Rob were in a semi-spoon, and Samantha, oddly enough, had slung her leg over Darrin's throat – I wondered how he could even maintain his airway. Richie lay on his back, his legs splayed and draped over a few of his peers, his face turned toward mine. I wondered if I could get some overhead photographs in this light, but as I began to consider the logistics I suddenly lost interest. I sat down, clasping my arms over my knees and breathing the particle-filtered air, oxygen-rich and fresh as pre-industrial Earth. They snored ever so softly, like little kittens – the effect was one collective purr. They were the picture of content, piled and draped over each other so nicely. For a moment I actually envied them.

I dropped flat on the mat and put my face as close to Richie's as I dared. I made myself go quiet, let my breathing go still. Only then could I feel his little exhalations, sweet and feathery on my cheek. I lay there motionless for a good while. When my back seized up I lurched to a stand and headed to the airlocks.

16. Richie

As often as I ask about the others, Jill answers that she doesn't really know. She says that they're almost certainly not in Australia, and that I'll have to do without them for the foreseeable future. None of the other staff specialists seem to be here either. Jill's the only one I have any contact with, and these days I don't even see a lot of her. I mention all this only to reiterate that I've got a lot of time on my hands, a situation not only conducive to learning the birdsong, but more or less requiring it.

Three species are steady enough here to give me the exposure I need. I've already mentioned the magpies and the butcherbirds, whose dialects I've found, as expected, to be closely related. You may be surprised that I've engaged with the magpies at all. But in the words of Sun Tzu, one must strive to "know thy enemy," especially when tucked safely behind a screen. The third species is the ever-present and aptly named Noisy Miner. The Miner is a notch smaller than the other two, a particularly gregarious member of the honeyeater family. Gray with faint white scallops, it'd be visually unremarkable but for the bright yellow flap it carries behind each eye. The first impression is unsettling, that of a big, amorphous yellow eye oddly displaced to the cranial posterior. But on closer inspection, the eye is beady black and right where it belongs, and the flap sweeps behind it like a coat of garish eyeshadow, its yellow a studied match with the beak.

All three of these species are obsessively territorial, but seem to live in a perpetual uneasy truce. A good sampling of each are based in the cluster of trees near my window. This keeps them all in my earshot. And for all the inherent hostility, they're a chatty bunch. Those two factors, proximity and volubility, have proven ideal for my learning. There are plenty of other birds around here, but for the most part they fall into one of two categories. Either they're prone to unintelligible grunting, or they're on the premises too sporadically to study. The former seem to be those who spend a lot of time on the ground – the ibis, the bush turkey, the purple swamphen and others. The latter are primarily in the parrot group – the lorikeet, the cockatoo, the galah and others. Even if they were around more steadily, I've pretty much written them off, to coin another of Jill's phrases, as "batshit crazy." As to the kookaburras, I think they've written me off on basically the same grounds. That's okay with me – they're pretty quiet outside of their showy coach horn routines, and, as I've mentioned, there's just something there that tells me not to mess with them.

After that first thunderstorm I started spending a lot of time up on the windowsill. I had each of the three greeting calls – the magpie's, the butcherbird's, and the miner's – down pretty quickly. For all of these birds, greeting calls are synonymous with beckoning calls – "hello" is basically the same as "come here." I didn't quite understand that at the time, but it suited my purposes perfectly – I managed to attract a few individuals for quick, fidgety visits to the beam. Rather than hiding quietly in the dark as I'd done that first afternoon, I'd resolved to show myself up front so I'd be free to mimic them and imprint their song patterns in my head. As I'd feared, my recall of the more complex calls from my first session on the sill had been dismal. Without recording equipment I didn't have much choice – I needed the benefit of call and answer, essentially the routine I'd had with The Chief, to progress at any kind of a pace. One risk was that I'd drive them away from the sill, leaving me to listen from a tougher distance. Another was that I'd irritate them enough that they'd maul me to death the next time I ventured out. But my overriding hope was to pick up some birdsong and parlay that into improved avian relations, and ultimately into better odds of mid-term survival.

I wasn't surprised that my open mimicking was poorly received. They strained to look through the screen, much as we had at Genesis, and it's safe to say they were disgusted at the sight of me. In the hot afternoons I often wear little or no clothing – to them I must have appeared horribly diseased or brutally plucked. They recoiled, flying in place or drifting slightly backwards before darting off altogether. They seemed outraged that I dared to sound their calls. Or outraged that I actually *could* sound their calls, with at least a passable inflection. Or outraged that I was out of thrashing reach behind the screen. Or, in all probability, all of the above. There was quite a bit of chatter among them in the branches around that window. And for the better part of that day none of them would revisit the beam, despite my persistent entreaties. But toward dusk they did begin to rotate through, first the butcherbirds, then the miners, then the magpies, each of them circling back for one last look before dark. Surprise and outrage were the principle reactions – "It's still there!" or something to that effect – but less pronounced than before.

Within a day or two they'd grown more accustomed to me. But every time I lured one in I hit the same dead end. I could start a conversation, but I couldn't carry it on. They'd settle on a nearby branch and give me a quick look or two through the screen, scanning their perimeters all the while as if they weren't to be seen with me. They'd squawk some command or other, and when they saw that I either didn't understand or wouldn't comply, they'd shudder with disgust. I'd seen that act plenty of times from The Chief – it was practically his signature move for a while there. Then they'd fly off.

But just as I'd stumbled into the worst possible time for the assaults of lunatic, hyper-aggressive males, I'd also come into the best time for more civilized maternal attentions, however misplaced they might have been. For hatchlings in multiple nests had begun to call out within my earshot, and I was easily able to pick up their simple and plaintive cries. To this day I don't know if those peeps signify exclusively that "I'm hungry," or if slight variations within them can alter the meaning to "I'm lonely," or "I'm afraid," or "I'm cold." After a while they were just plain irritating, from my point of view and presumably from that of their parents. But once I had them down they were far superior to the calls I'd been using before. They attracted only a favorable class of respondents, the females of all three species without broods of their own. Most of their energies were spent fulfilling their duties, giving succor and nurture to the hatchlings of other more successful females. But I had a feeling that, secretly, each of them wished for something more. And I might have been some distorted version of that something for a select few of them. I was oversized, dimwitted, and grossly deformed. But for all that, I had a certain appeal, stranded, abandoned, and extremely needy.

17. Jill

By turns, Dr. Bitsen had added second breakfast, afternoon tea, and early evening snack. And for all that, none of the children had gained any height or weight. The pediatricians, with their well-developed political acumen, positioned the problem as an unsolved nutritional riddle, which left the ever-upstanding Bitsen on an island. Her daily presentations struck all the right chords, sounding a composed, professional concern and a steady, logical and inclusive approach.

But by P20, the children's growth curve — or lack of it — had reached enough of a crisis point to preclude the calm facade. In the course of her three minutes, she reviewed the gloomy trail of flat-line data and the equally gloomy trail of her failed initiatives, offered her resignation, rescinded it, and offered it again.

For all the enthusiasm around line dancing, Brio, defecation protocol, and dozens of other areas of encouragement, this was a sobering moment. We all liked and respected Bitsen, and we supported her as best we could.[23] Physiological stasis was certainly alarming,

---

23 The pediatricians were less supportive. Hayes was a nice enough woman, but guarded in her remarks. Manly said nothing whatsoever. A tall, smug man with a sunken chest and a pronounced Adam's apple, he was erudite in his own pediatric briefings, but had offered hardly a word of feedback, let alone encouragement, to anyone else for as long as I'd been there.

we conceded, but the other vital signs were excellent. The children were brimming with energy and progressing beyond expectations on virtually every aspect of socialization and skill acquisition. Beyond that, there wasn't a lot to say. The one time we seemed to have talked ourselves out, Dr. Morben made an unprecedented break from Little Gathering protocol. He waived the time limit.

Morben: We need ideas, people. Anything that comes to mind. Remember, there's no senior review here. No thought is too vapid.

Dasher: Hah, an excellent framework for this group.

Morben: Dr. Manly, what are your thoughts?

I was thrilled to hear him called out.

Manly (seeming a bit put upon): The data tells us that they're eating sufficient quantities by normal standards. With the communal plate approach we don't have individual numbers, but as a group they're ingesting more joules as a percentage of their body weight than normal babies. But still, we have no way of knowing if it's the right quantity for them. Or the right mix. Those are Dr. Bitsen's big challenges.

Dasher: Hard to believe quantity is the issue. We can't realistically hope to feed them any more often than we are. We're already up to, what, six meals a day?

Bitsen: Personally, I haven't ruled out increased frequency.

Dasher: What are you thinking, an all-day buffet?

Bitsen: Actually, I'm thinking about night feeds.

Dasher: They're comatose after dark. You can hardly stir them, let alone get them to chew and swallow.

Hayes: *Comatose* may be overstated, but he's essentially correct. As you all know, we've measured extraordinary drops in nocturnal heart rate and breathing rate during sleep. The effect is nearly hibernatory.

Bitsen: But we may have to push the point.

Dasher: What are we going to do, midnight force feeds? Feeding tubes?

Falstaff: In the foie gras industry the term is *gavage*.

Dasher: Yes, let's order some tiny feedbags and tie them around their muzzles until their bellies bloat.

Henderson: We could think about adding some appetite stimulation content in the video presentation.

Dasher: What, like Applebee's commercials?

Sloboth: I'd go Red Lobster.

Me: Maybe we need to think outside of food. It's possible these children require specific conditions that we're not providing.

Bitsen: Like what?

Me: Higher ambient temperatures. Direct sunlight. Breast milk. More sleep. Some semblance of privacy. Mothers. Fathers. Families. The possibilities are endless. Maybe we just need to cut the burn rate. I don't want to put a damper on the line dancing, but we might need to back that off a bit, just to see what happens.

All eyes turned to Dasher.

Dasher (after some pause, and appearing offended): I should probably recuse myself on the point, but I will say that within the hierarchy of dance, line dancing is among the very least demanding, from a purely physical standpoint. I would also make the observation that the rest of the subjects' day is fairly restful. I mean, physically unchallenging. Other than the ongoing railroad labor, of course.

He gave me a wink. I flipped him off as covertly as I could. He seemed to enjoy the exchange.

Bitsen: I've thought about this, and I tend to agree with Dr. Dasher. I can't make a case that they're being pushed too aggressively. A rational amount of exercise should promote both appetite and growth, not inhibit them.

Dasher: It's not like we're pushing extreme endurance activities. Distance running, ironman – none of that stuff.

Sloboth: Of course not.

Me: It's possible they're just wired to have their growth kick in later, after a longer period of stasis than we're used to. We may just have to wait.

Falstaff: It's also possible this is as big as they're going to get.

Silence.

Manly: My guess here is a genetic pituitary dysfunction. As I said some time ago, we need those growth hormone tests.

Hayes: At this point I'd have to agree with you.

Morben: I'd like to hold off on that.

Manly: On what basis?

Morben: That in this particular case, the unknown may be preferable to the definitive. For everyone concerned.

With such a deliberately cryptic response, the conversation was as good as over. He didn't actually sound the buzzer, but he might as well have.

18. Richie

One thing I've learned watching the birdlife from my sill, or from other vantage points through the house, is that here in East Central the smallest birds rule. Traditional notions of size and dominance are upside down. While the noisy miner can hover with the control of a hummingbird to take a moth from the air, it can also veer and shift and dive and lift at astounding speeds. Unimposing as it may appear at rest, it's the fastest and the shiftiest fighter jet in the sky. And at least around here, that more than trumps any edge in physical strength or weaponry.

I was astounded when I first saw the miners chasing larger and seemingly more ferocious birds. Many of those are amazing fliers in their own right who can zig and zag at the very edge of control without gaining the slightest separation. Grim in their pursuit, the miners hold the tiniest clearance at the fringe of the tail feathers, and with a composure suggesting another gear in reserve. From what I've seen, they're born to the chase, forever after something. They harass the ground birds, who dash quickly off to cover. Even those capable of flight don't presume to take wing, but simply bend their heads to a hurried walk, like city pedestrians in a driving rain. The miners work well in groups, but it's the solitary chase of the better fliers that they live for, the suicide spitfire runs on the tails of certain magpies and butcherbirds, their closest rivals in aeronautic mastery, by the terms of some territorial code I still haven't cracked. And failing all else, they chase each other, particularly at dusk, in keeping with another cryptic code, the one that governs their evening cliques and the night's roost.

The inverse law of dominance seems ingrained in all of them, as if settled through millennia of their forbears. The miners are fearless and unshakable, and the larger birds acquiesce without shame, resistance, or resentment. It can become a formality at times, a miner escorting a kookaburra, for example, out of a certain zone, holding its customary position just inches off the tail feathers with neither bird in any particular hurry.

I enjoyed watching the occasional magpie on the receiving end of the aerial assaults. The bully was getting his due, as it were, though my feelings on the point were more mixed than you might have guessed. By that time I had a number of acquaintances, magpies among them, friendly enough females who'd respond to my calls with regular visits to the sill. With the screen in place they'd figured out pretty quickly there wasn't much they could do for me. By their standards I was so grossly deformed they may quite rightly have preferred that I simply go quiet, curl up, and die – on more than one occasion I got the impression they were surprised that I hadn't. But I'd picked up just enough language to sprinkle their monologues with the occasional interjection, and that seemed sufficient to hold their interest. In time I began to identify them as individuals, which allowed me to customize those interjections, limited as they were, to maximize their impact. Some of them began to chat quite openly, principally the magpies and butcherbirds. The miners, I was finding, were a little too high-strung for that, much as they jabbered among themselves. In the case of the magpies, these chats took tones I found increasingly disarming, even beguiling. A breathtaking run of notes, a pause, a repeat at softer volume, and I'd drift off into something trance-like, just short of sleep. Only a last-second glance at the beady red eyes, or the sudden memory of them as my own eyes fell shut, would keep me in check.

For all I knew, I was the one being played. I was currying their favor, but it seemed just as likely they were currying mine, luring me off my guard toward a fatal lapse, a moment of lethal vulnerability. Not that I was about to drop the screen or head outdoors for a leisurely mid-day stroll among them. But from my windows it all looked so nice, everything so green and lovely, that I couldn't help but to long for it.

19. Jill

Our resident linguist, Dr. Sloboth, would never credit the point, but Richie's progress with the cockatiel jabber was a big factor in the group's assimilation of English. His dialogue with The Chief had been of great interest not only to me and to the rest of the staff, but to his peers as well. The six of them had taken to following him over to the cage and eavesdropping from a respectful distance of about two body lengths. They would jabber quietly among themselves, in emulation perhaps of his conversational demeanor, though they did so in the squeaky tones that seemed natural to them rather than mimicking the birdsong. Their jabber struck me as a sort of primitive language in itself, and it held more urgency and purpose now than it had before. But Sloboth, who had a lot more at stake in the matter, took only moderate interest. Sub-linguistic voicings, after all, weren't going to improve her performance marks. English was required, the King's English. And, to date, none of our otherwise gifted subjects had spoken a word of it. To be fair, no one would have expected speech anywhere near this early. But with the prodigious progress in so many other areas, expectations had been steadily creeping. In that context, speechlessness was curious, even perplexing.

Late one afternoon with no one in session, Dr. Henderson gave the video a long overdue rest. Most of us were sitting at our desks, reviewing our sessions and prepping for the next morning's Little

Gathering. Falstaff had the audio on open mike, which picked up the sounds from the nursery and ran them through the system. I'm not a country person, but the place felt suddenly bucolic, perfectly still but for the chirping of The Chief and the sporadic squeaking of the children.

And then, with startling clarity: "Brunji."

We all looked up. It was Richie, standing at the cage and holding half a cracker. I pulled Camera 22, the birdcage unit, up on my screen. Brunji, of course, is nonsensical in isolation. But in this highly scrutinized environment it sounded like the makings of a word, the first reasonably enunciated multi-syllabic phrase any of them had ever uttered. It was less squeaky than usual, slightly deeper in tone, and spoken clearly enough that afterwards we could all agree on the transcription. Brunji.

Dr. Sloboth responded decisively. "Birdie," she prodded, her voice sounding through the nursery.

She exchanged glances with a few of us. We all knew what was at stake for her. I backed up the video twenty seconds. The Chief had snapped off a bite of the cracker, sidled into the corner and shown Richie his backside. It was surly behavior, uncharacteristic of The Chief since the cagebreak.

"Ingrate," I said, half under my breath, though my mike carried it inside.

"Birdie," Dr. Sloboth repeated.

Richie glanced dismissively toward the glass and returned his attentions to The Chief, who now turned to face him.

"Brunji ingrate," he squeaked, in a tone I interpreted as both triumphant and indignant.

"Birdie is an ingrate," Dr. Sloboth enunciated.

Uhura was the first to respond, a lone voice from the crowd. "Birdie ingrate," she repeated. "Birdie ingrate." The others followed in a chorus of just decipherable utterings interspersed with odd little whistles. Even The Chief had to turn and take notice.

Embryonic English came in waves for the rest of P21. And it picked right up the following morning, not as with a normal child venturing a few half-formed grunts and partial phrases over the course of several months, but as with an adult emerging from a coma, recalling the language of her past in great swaths of vocabulary and grammar. The words had been incubating, building inside them, and some unknown trigger mechanism had brought them gushing out. Two days later they were speaking in complete sentences. By P32 they were sprinkling in subordinate clauses, hypotheticals, knowing little asides, idiomatic constructs, nuances of adult speech. In that short period, Dr. Sloboth's standing was completely transformed. She was giddy with excitement, as to some degree we all were. To hear her tell it, which I did with some frequency sitting at the adjacent desk, the children's vocabulary had already surpassed that of most incoming college freshman. In her view, their mastery of the verb forms, regular and irregular, was particularly astounding.

Dr. Henderson probably deserves some credit here. For nearly three weeks she'd had her video programming on Sesame Street cruise control, taking her leisurely runs and heading home promptly at 17:00. But from the first coherent phrase out of that nursery she'd kicked into high gear, rolling out a language acceleration program so compelling that we often found ourselves paying more attention to the screens than to the children. The grammar module, which classified the parts of speech and parsed out sentence structure, held our attention more than any of us would have imagined. Extremely proper usage became a running gag around the facility. As the days went by we became a group of regular Henry Jamesians, dropping little bits of "by which" and "to whom" into our most mundane conversations. "The coffee machine, by which I achieve my daily equilibrium, is not currently functional," Dr. Bitsen deadpanned into the sound system. "To whom shall I address this matter?"[24]

Language and comprehension were moving at such a pace that Sesame Street gave way to full documentary features from the BBC and National Geographic[25] – wartime biopics, snippets from space, sharks and cheetahs on the hunt. I considered some of it a bit harsh for the young people, but it again proved captivating for the staff. Citing productivity issues, Dr. Morben took the extraordinary step of ordering the PrismView temporarily darkened on the side facing us.

If there's a downside to the rapid and auspicious developments at that time, it was Richie's acquisition of the strange head movements that would stay with him for the rest of his life. He began by cocking his head at any moment of concentrated listening. I noticed it first as he watched the videos, and it quickly migrated to moments of direct interaction with peers and staffers. Still more disconcerting was his acquired approach to situational observation. For a visual scan he'd rotate his head in twenty or more ten-degree ticks, like a windup toy clicking through its calibrations. Sometimes his head would double back in the other direction. Other times it would return to face-forward and settle. His face was blank, almost stony, throughout – I joked half-heartedly we had Dasher's dance regimen to blame for that. I found these behaviors more irritating than distressing. They suggested movements easily observed in The Chief. Others may have disagreed, but in Richie I considered them affectations rather than dysfunctions, though I was never able to confirm that one way or the other.

---

24 Bitsen, whose own career was sinking by the day, took Sloboth's good fortune with remarkable grace and humor.

25 I had writing credits on a few of them, traces of my life before BioSpore. Dr. Henderson was kind enough to point them out.

The acquisition of language seemed to benefit our SCPs more than Dasher or myself. Jasper Scott, the only other non-PhD on staff and the man behind the Monopoly initiative, enjoyed the most substantial windfall. Before the onset of language, his sessions, to be charitable, were reliably listless. In fairness, the children had developed some basic skills relative to the game. They could link themselves to a particular metal token.[26] They could roll the dice, though only one die at a time, gripping the cube with two hands between their legs and heaving it in Scottish log toss fashion. They could read and add the rolled numbers, and move their pieces accordingly. After some time they could even count money, something Scott trumpeted ad nauseam, as if he'd just uncovered some great scientific treasure. But the rest of the game was beyond them, or perhaps just unappealing enough that they wouldn't engage. They hadn't the slightest interest in buying property, and steadfastly declined to do so despite Scott's extremely unprofessional badgering. They preferred a simple and uncluttered perambulation of the board, rejecting the very notion of private ownership. Falstaff viewed the behavior as classically Marxist, with the clear effect of fostering the common wealth. By fours and sevens they'd make their rent-free rounds, collecting $200 at every pass by GO, and accumulating copious cash reserves with the steady passage of time. They took apparent pleasure in heaving the dice for height and distance, but the game was otherwise uneventful for them. And it was certainly a snoozefest for the rest of us, obliged as we were to at least minimally monitor the proceedings. This version lacked the core emotions of Monopoly, the greed and ambition, the triumph and despair, all the things we'd experienced playing the game as children.

---

26 The thimble, the top hat, and the race car were the consensus favorites for reasons that couldn't possibly be understood, though Scott belabored the point beyond all reason, floating vacuous theories in several Little Gatherings for want of anything more substantial to discuss.

Instead, Scott would heave a sigh of resignation at the end of each session, bundle up their little wads of cash, and make note of their positions on the board so that, beyond the daily reassignment of the tokens, play would resume each day as it ended the day before. The game was a continuum dating to the early days of the Project, but the board was pristine, free of any speculation or development. Scott, as the banker, had to break open a second game set – we had half a dozen of them – to honor his growing cash commitments.

But that all seemed to change with the onset of language. The children loved sounding out all the property names – Richie was particularly endearing with his "Mahvin Gahdins" – and that led to an interest in the deeds themselves, with the color-coded bands on top and the rental tables, or "the actuary tables," as Scott mistakenly called them, and persisted in calling them even after being corrected by at least two of us. The children began to hoard their deeds with obvious pleasure, stacking and sorting and swapping to complete their color sets. Richie was a bit of an outlier, preferring a "rainbow" approach to ownership and often trading for a color he didn't have or happened to fancy. Odd phrases of monetary assertion became commonplace, things like "Rent is owed, please, in the amount of fourteen dollars," or less formally, "That'll be twenty-eight buckaroos."[27] And, well-financed as they were after weeks of rent-free circumnavigation, they blanketed the board with housing, maximizing every buildable lot. "Looks like Vegas circa 1950 in there," said Dasher, referring to the squat hotels that lined the four sides of the board.[28] Money began to change hands by the armload, and the PA sounded

---

27 "Buckaroos" was a term of uncertain and dubious origin. Most of us suspected Dasher of the introduction.

28 Scott went into the second set for more hotels in addition to the cash, the conformity of which with the rules of Monopoly was a point of some contention around the Project.

with little cries of anguish, in particular squeaky bursts of "crikey," a term they'd picked up from some of the less dignified nature video. Shiftless little bankrupts began to drift in the darker corners of the nursery while the surviving tycoons battled smugly for dominion.

Management, as you might imagine, took a keen interest in these developments. Brio had been reasonably impressive in a rudimentary sort of way. Line dancing had been entertaining in a hoedown, lowbrow, middle-America kind of way. But before us now were the essentials of unfettered capitalism, distilled, crystallized, and fiercely contested in just the second month of life. The financial disasters were somehow more visceral than I recalled from my own childhood games. Money didn't simply pass across a table. Our little debtors had to gather their grossly oversized bills in both arms and trudge around the board in a loop of shame wide enough to clear their peers, who sat Indian style or lay like little pharaohs on their elbows among the stacks of their riches; and thereupon to present to the profiting landowners, who stood grinning like golf champions handed giant made-for-TV checks. Chuck Hansen himself was rumored to be considering a visit, but those who did come were the same suit-and-tie crowd that had patronized the line dancing, primarily a financial group. Their hoots and hollers from before gave way now to more deeply felt gestures, private little nods and chuckles, quiet fist-bumps and grunts of appreciation at the spectacle of smaller landowners, helplessly outpositioned, passing through their financial death throes. Our cameras zoomed obtrusively on the distressed little faces, flashing them Times Square style, full-screen on the great PrismViews. Dasher gave a sardonic smile and sidled over to join Falstaff and me.

Dasher: Look at Marcia Tompkins trying to make it with the muckety-mucks.

Me: Pathetic. She's got no more chance of breaking into that group than Richie has of surviving another trip around the board.

Falstaff: Agreed. His cash position is much diminished. Utilities and an assortment of purples, pale blues, and magentas can only take you so far. Too bad it's not a high jump competition – he would certainly fare better. By the way, Dasher, have you finished your overlays on the cagebreak video?

Dasher: As a matter of fact, I have.

Silence.

Falstaff: Well?

Dasher: Adjusting for reach, I've got his leap to the bar at 32 inches. If we project that to a six-foot male – an adjustment factor of 4.8 – the jump works to 154 inches.

Me: That's nearly thirteen feet.

Dasher: Fine mathematics, Dr. Edelman. The best standing vertical jump in the history of the NFL Combine is just over four feet. Inch for inch, Richie's three times better than anybody the league has ever trotted out there.

Falstaff: You could pretty much guess that just by watching the video – he jumped twice his height.

Dasher: I have the ratio at 2.1 to one.

Falstaff: The foot speed must be a little harder to gauge. Did you get anything there?

Dasher: With the overlays, I calculated his covering 54 feet in 1.9 seconds. Forget adjusting for size, in absolute terms that's forty yards in 4.2 seconds. The best forty in the history of the NFL Combine is exactly that, 4.2 seconds. Then we have to consider that our guy had no warmup, started from a standing position, and decelerated to zero, or what they call stopping on a dime, when he reached the birdcage. He may already be the most athletic person on earth.

Falstaff: Unless someone else inside that glass is even better.

Dasher: Entirely possible.

Me: I notice he's "our guy" and a real "person" now that we're dabbling in world records.

Dasher (ignoring me): The size-adjusted time is off the charts, by the way. It would have him covering 260 feet, or nearly ninety yards, in that 1.9 seconds. Think about that.

Falstaff: Some pretty astounding results, Dr. Dasher. Funny you should only mention them now, under direct questioning. Am I mistaken, or are you holding your cards a bit close to your chest? Considering a shift in your professional approach?

Me: From the *Little Lords of the Dance* to the *Mini-Masters of the Gridiron*?

Dasher: It may have occurred to me to run my own little combine.

Falstaff: What do you make of it, Dr. Edelman?

Me: I like the move from dance to sport. But I do see some problems specific to the combine. It's exclusively male and exclusively American, way too parochial for a global operation like BioSpore. And the events themselves just aren't that compelling. A dash, the bench press, a couple jumps, and a couple scuttles around some cones – is that about right?

Dasher: Very impressive Dr. Edelman. Six events total.

Me: I agree it's important that the results be quantifiable, numerically based, so you're on the right track that way. But again, I'd choose something with more global appeal.

Dasher: Like what?

Me: The decathlon, for example.

Falstaff: Ooh, I like it.

Dasher: Run those events by me?

Me: Um, three runs – 100, 400, 1500. Three throws – discus, shot, and javelin. That's six. High jump, broad jump. Hurdles and pole vault make ten.

Dasher: Sounds like you've thought this through.

Me: I haven't. But it seems like the more events the better. It makes for better entertainment, and extends the time before they top out. I've begun to think that sustainable progress on their part may be linked to job security on ours.

Dasher: No dead ends. Like with Brio.

Me: Or with line dancing.

Dasher: Touche! Still, decathlon seems pretty fussy. It would require a whole line of miniature equipment. At least for now – assuming they're going to start growing at some point. Customized shots – is that the word? – javelins, discuses, hurdles, landing pits.

Falstaff: Wouldn't they be "disci"?

Dasher: I don't think so.

Me: Me neither.

Dasher: And how would we manage the pole vault?

Me: You mean how would we teach it? I did it in high school. Not all that well, but I did it. Probably about as well as you danced.

Dasher: You are a source of constant amazement, Dr. Edelman. But no, I'm still on the subject of equipment.

Falstaff: The pole itself should be easy enough. Carbon fiber, right? That's right down Dmitri's alley. And I think he might actually have been a track and field guy himself. Back in Omsk. God, I loving saying that. The shots and disci would be metal alloys, pretty straightforward. We could sneak them into the budget, or the guys in engineering might just work them up in their off-hours. I'm not sure what they make javelins out of these days.

Me: The big question is whether we have room for a correctly scaled track in the nursery.

Dasher: So it's "we" now, is it?

We exchanged a look. Dasher extended a hand. I let it hang as long as I thought practical, then took it in my own. The deal was struck.

Falstaff: You understand you'll need to keep some semblance of independence.[29]

Dasher: How about I take track, she takes field?

Falstaff: That might do it.

Me: Works for me. As to fitting the track....

Dasher: We need hundred-meter equivalents on the straightaways. With the 4.8 adjustment factor I mentioned earlier, that's just over twenty meters. I think we have that.

Me: Pretty easily as it looks me. With enough margin to accommodate the end curves.

Falstaff: Agreed. We can project the whole thing on the floor with laser lighting – the track, the lanes, the field event markers.

Dasher: Speaking of that, I'm appalled that Jasper Scott's got little laser shows going with every roll of the die. Falstaff, you must be responsible for that.

Falstaff: I'm here to serve.

Dasher: Look at him hamming it up in there.

Me: Who?

Dasher: Scott. In a matter of days he's undergone a complete personality makeover. And it's much for the worse – from the quiet banker type to the smarmy gameshow host, the celebrity Monopoly MC. It makes you want to vomit.

Falstaff: I've often wondered about that expression.

Dasher: How so?

---

29 Joint projects between staff specialists were neither sanctioned nor encouraged.

Falstaff: Does anyone actually "want to vomit?" If you're feeling sick I suppose you may want to have vomited. But the act itself seems intrinsically unpleasant, enough so to preclude most people's undertaking it by choice.

Dasher: But the alternative, Doctor... "Makes you want to have vomited." Doesn't quite roll off the tongue, does it?

20. Richie

After some time that windowsill got a little uncomfortable. I couldn't sit on its bare wooden surface more than a few hours without my backside cramping up and my joints starting to ache. I'm just not built for that. So I hauled a few things up the lines to make my perch a little cozier. It was all lightweight stuff, very manageable – extra clothing, scraps of cloth and tissue paper, leaves, bits of soft bark, that sort of thing. Arranged just so, it was supple and reasonably supportive, though it shifted more than I liked. But it enabled longer sessions on the sill, and that paid quick dividends.

I noticed, for example, that magpies and butchers shared a certain voicing in situations that seemed to call for admiration or respect. A bird would swoop in with a fresh catch for the youngsters, and more often than not a nearby adult would vocalize what I took to be an expression of praise. I assumed that this phrasing was specific to a successful hunt. But one afternoon a pair of crows intruded on one of the home trees nearest my window, and the two birds most instrumental in driving them off got the same vocal acclaim in larger doses.

Because the call was relatively infrequent, it took me a few days to get it down. Again, if I had any decent recording equipment I'd have had it in an hour. When I had a passable rendition I began to praise any remotely positive behavior, hunting and defending of course, but also any particularly nice bits of flying, graceful landings, exceptional singing, even the more fastidious preenings. This liberal use drew a puzzled response at first, cocked heads and little inquisitive remarks. But one of my more consistent visitors, a particularly beautiful bird and a spirited preener, hopped toward me, spread her wings and did a little half pirouette. And shortly thereafter, when I sang the praises of a particularly intrepid flier, a true ace – she'd followed a breakneck entry through an impossible tangle of branches with a feather-light landing – she gave me a look, took back off, repeated the exact sequence, and looked at me again, as if gauging my continued interest. There was less vanity than you might imagine in either of these gestures. The intent was instructive. Watch what I do. Make yourself better.

At that point I was reluctant to leave that sill if I didn't have to. I hauled up the paring knife so I could cut my fruit without having to come down for lunch. That in turn required me to transfer my hashmark system to the boards that flank my sill. Those were a lot of marks to copy, but it was a softer wood up there, easier to carve, and I was happy with the result. Next, I turned my attention to my ever-shifting sill coverings. Despite some misgivings on the point, I made several tiny cuts in the screen and weaved fabric ends through each of them. This anchored the bedding and cut back on the time I spent fussing and rearranging to stay comfortable. And the process of cutting and weaving seemed to interest the birds more than anything I'd done to date. I wasn't quite sure how to interpret that – either they were genuinely encouraged at my progress, or they welcomed the damage to the screen, however slight, as a useful weakening of my defense.

That worry aside, the improved sill conditions were encouraging enough that I hauled up my blankets and started spending the nights up there too. I liked the big bed well enough, but right away the sleeps on the sill were the best I'd had in East Central. The sounds were soothing and the air was fresh, and there was something about that smaller more elevated area I just found cozier than the bed. And while there was no interaction with the birds after dark, sleeping on the perch seemed to give me a bit more credibility. I noticed a few of them looking in on me just after dawn, completely unsolicited, before heading off on their rounds. They didn't stop then to chat – mornings were far too busy for that – but it seemed I'd become a slightly larger part of their mindset.

At about this time I began to redirect my morning ambulations toward those trees, the idea being to expose myself primarily to birds more familiar to me. Rather than walking directly away from the house as I'd done to date, I hugged the wall from the cat door to the sill – the two sat at opposite ends of the house – and veered off from there. It made for a longer trip overall, but the house did protect me on one side for much of it. One hundred eighty degrees of exposure is just about manageable, even with my limited field of vision. By walking sideways I was able to cover myself until I reached the trees and headed out. The bad news is that attack frequency actually increased – I had some kind of incident virtually every trip. But these attacks were more of the swooping variety rather than the more familiar pummelings. Swooping was extremely unpleasant in its own right, with the same startling effect and the wings detonating all around my ears. But physical contact, the actual dispensing of blows, was infrequent. On a few occasions I even had the impression that my swoopers were being swooped themselves, and this, of course, was my best-case scenario. But I couldn't be sure. It's hard to be definitive while you scurry.

21. Jill

We began decathlon training within the week. As we'd hoped, Falstaff was able to project a track along the perimeter of the floor that scaled, on the 4.8 size adjustment factor, to an official 400-meter oval. We'd heard rumors of customized bathrooms coming in — Marcia Tompkins apparently loathed the kitty litter — and if it happened they'd almost certainly obstruct the track. "All the more reason to get on with it," Dasher said with his usual resolve. "They can't shut us down if we're breaking records by the bushel."

He began at once with certain running events. Weight dispersion flooring, with its superior grip and cushioning, eliminated the substantial complication of athletic shoes. Like the great Ethiopian, Abebe Bikila, the children ran barefoot.[30] Dasher spliced some Olympic footage into a video montage, and the pageantry of the events seemed to catch their fancy. Once they'd grasped the concept they were raring to go, and he had them circling the nursery like whippets. They were nearly incomprehensible in real time, the footwork too quick to track with the untrained eye. It took several runs before I could actually differentiate

---

30   Bikila won two Olympic marathons, in 1960 and 1964, running barefoot. Personally, I cringe watching anyone run barefoot for any distance. Unless I'm on grass or carpet, I won't run five meters without shoes. Maybe on the beach to catch a frisbee, but even then only on the soft part, away from the water. This was something I shared with Richie, who was the only one to complain about his feet.

strides. In the 400, with the extreme leaning on the bends – Dasher worked one out later at forty-four degrees – we began to appreciate the true grace of these little athletes. They were a remarkable sight, and all the more impressive for the black bodysuits, back in play for the first time since the wardrobes had arrived. Cast far larger than life on the PrismViews, the athletes were sleek and sexy, especially just after their runs, when they'd stand with hands on hips and shake out their legs with their little chests heaving.

To me they were all incredible, but Dasher, competitive bastard that he is, singled out certain performances – Uhura's in the 100 and Kirk's in the 400 – and claimed a pair of Size-Adjusted World Records, or SAWRs as he called them, before I'd even begun my field events. He'd bought himself an outrageous blue and gold polyester coaching suit and a whistle and stopwatch on lanyards. In the heat of the nursery, that suit forced him to shower after every session. But he seemed to relish it, assuming the air of having weathered an elite workout himself, of having run right along with the athletes. After the shower he'd drape the whistle and stopwatch back over his pressed workshirt for the rest of the day.[31] He insisted that we call him "Coach," and while most of us were reluctant to give him that satisfaction publicly, or without sarcasm, I did address certain respectful electronic messages to a "Coach D."

Field sports were largely delayed by the equipment issues we'd identified from the start. Dmitri had agreed to oversee fabrication of the miniature javelins, discuses, puts and poles, but it'd be several days before they began to filter in. He'd also agreed to advise us on the finer points of their use – Falstaff was right about his track and field background. I was able to get underway with the long jump only by crafting

---

31 That stopwatch was the key to our discovery that Dr. Morben's "five-minute buzzer" was more discretionary than we might have imagined. Over the course of several Little Gatherings, Dasher recorded times varying by thirty seconds or more in either direction, depending on the vitality of the given exchange.

a landing pit from a shallow box and some kitty litter. To familiarize the children with the proper landing techniques, I began them with the standing long jump. I wasn't tracking the distances they actually jumped, since the standing long jump was neither a decathlon event nor a standalone Olympic event. But Dasher, watching through the glass and running through some quick calculations, assured me through my headset that we'd just blown through the benchmarks set over the many years of the NFL combine.[32] I put more stock in the results of the next day's jumping, when I introduced the full running approach. All seven children shattered the long jump size-adjusted world record, or SAWR as we called it, by nearly triple. After half an hour, Falstaff and I had to shift the laser-light runway nearer the west edge of the nursery to prevent their jumping smack into the east glass wall. The only negative was the children's complaining of certain abrasions, the kitty litter, over the hour, proving too coarse for the purpose. I ordered in a bag of extra-fine playground sand for my next session, which, as it turned out, also solved the problem of Kirk's urinating in the landing pit.[33]

In private conversations I convinced Dasher to hold off on the 1500, that being more of an endurance event and therefore subject to the charge of impeding weight gain. The children's growth was still the Project's top priority, by a wide margin. They were still at their birth weights and heights, and that was the topic of virtually every call we overheard now between Dr. Morben and his faceless superiors. Morben had bowed to the will of the pediatricians, who'd finally scheduled the testing for human growth hormone. Bitsen was holding steady in her support of regular exercise for the children, subscribing to the theory that strenuous exercise should logically promote

---

32 In point of fact, the standing long jump was an Olympic event until 1912. We apparently blew through those benchmarks by an even greater margin.

33 Kirk could hardly be blamed, according to Dr. Bitsen, who was a frequent apologist for the boy children. "You put out a box of litter, what do you expect?"

HGH. The pediatricians were split on that point, Manly's predictable objections more or less cancelled by Hayes' position to the contrary. And the Senior Science Officers weren't intervening – at least that's how we read it, since, to our relief, we received no order to cease the workouts. To the contrary, we'd pulled virtually all the executive spectators from Jasper Scott's Monopoly Hour, a hand he'd badly overplayed.

Not hesitating to kick a man when he was down, Dasher circulated an unflattering video clip of Scott presenting at a Little Gathering. It zoomed heavily on a strand of partially desiccated mucus extending half an inch from one nostril, unfurling with each exhalation, and refurling in a delicate curling motion with each inhalation, like a tiny pulsating sea creature. The spectacle ran unabated for a full forty-five seconds, the footage extraordinary in its simplicity, the camera unmoving and unforgiving, before Scott finally cleared the matter with an absent-minded swipe of the hand. I'm not generally one for childish video, or for personally derisive video, but as a matter of biological curiosity, it did have some merit. And team-building benefits ensued among the small group of our supporters included in the distribution.

Dasher followed with a far bolder gambit. On the morning of P38, a day when his session was scheduled immediately after the Little Gathering, he had the gall to *present* in his polyester track suit. He guided his esteemed and presumably startled audience through both of the SAWRs established under his watch, and not at all in the manner of someone seeking to impress. On the contrary, he affected the dispassionate tone of the grizzled, cliche-ridden coach who neither enjoys the press nor seeks its favor. The Oklahoma drawl may have been slightly accentuated. A straight-faced brusqueness, laid over something resembling contempt, had supplanted the fawning manner we'd all adopted in addressing the Senior Science Officers. Dasher's briefings were soon the highlight of every Little Gathering, and Dr. Morben, who was not without some theatrical instinct of his own, took to scheduling him in the final slot.

For better or worse, my own briefings as field coach were less impertinent. My initial emphasis was not the long jump SAWR, though I did mention it.[34] For the most part, I focused on the apparent athletic parity between the genders. The girls had been up to snuff, if not slightly superior, in all three events we'd introduced to date. I've mentioned that Uhura had the fastest 100 meters of the entire seven. Samantha had the second-fastest 400. And in my long jump work, Laura was second behind Richie, who, having surrendered his brief and unofficial reign as World's Fastest Human, had countered with unmatched long-jumping prowess. With no experience to the contrary, none of the girls seemed surprised by their success. Similarly, none of the boys seemed put off. By private agreement, Dasher and I downplayed gender-based SAWRs altogether. The timer screens we had Falstaff flashing on the PrismView did not group by gender. In our unofficial conversations in and out of the nursery, and in each of our official briefings, we spoke only of human achievement and of human SAWRs. The children were even more broad-minded.

Uhura: What's the best cheetah time in the 100?

Me: I don't think we know that.

Samantha: Why not? That's the time we're after, isn't it?

Richie: Yeah, aren't they the world's fastest runners?

Me: Yes, I believe they are. But I don't think anyone's actually timed them in the 100.

Richie: What about the 400?

Me: Nope.

Kirk: Why not?

---

34 A review of the tape shows that I spent my entire P44 time allocation on the topic, but I didn't dwell on it unduly thereafter.

Me: I think it's hard to get them to wait for the gun to go off. Or to run in a straight line, or around a particular oval. Or to run at all if they don't feel like it.

Richie: We do it.

Me: Yes, but you're people. You understand instructions.

Uhura: I'd rather be a cheetah.

Richie: Not me. I wouldn't want to have to go out hunting every time I wanted to eat.

Laura: Yeah, well how would you like to be one of those little deer they trip from behind – the cheaters – and bite on the neck?

Me: You mean a Thomson's gazelle?

Laura: I guess so.

Kirk: Those ones look pretty fast too. What's their time in the 100?

Me: I don't think we know that either.

Kirk: Jeez, do we know anything? What's the point of all this running if we don't even know what times we're after?

Me: You should bring that up with Dr. Dasher. Maybe he could do some calculations.

My comment about cheetahs not running when they didn't feel like it may have had consequences I hadn't intended. Coincidence or not, over the next few days the children began, in Dasher's words, to "dog it." They still relished their solitary sprints, roaring out of the blocks at the sound of the gun,[35] firing down their lanes, and immediately turning to check their times. But placed together on the track in any configuration – twos, threes, fours – they'd often just meander along their ways,

---

35 Security would not allow handguns of any sort, even starter pistols, into the facility. We piped that noise through the sound system. And we had no blocks, something Dasher would cite with impressive detachment to enhance the children's performances even further. Though, truth be told, the children would sometimes act as human blocks, standing just behind the crouching racer whose feet would straddle their own.

each deferring to the other like the *Goofy Gophers*, Mac and Tosh, videos of whom Jerry immediately pumped to the PrismViews:

"After you."

"No, I insist."

"You're too kind."

Sometimes they'd skip, or hop on one foot. And sometimes they'd just stop and chat. It drove Dasher up the wall. He berated them, goaded them, chided them, bribed them. But nothing he did could get them to focus in their competitive heats. He talked to us about integrating blinders and crops – I believe he was actually serious about the blinders. And he formally requested that Falstaff rig up what you'd see at a dog track, a rabbit lure on a rail, racing along ahead of them. Falstaff refused on both ethical and logistical grounds, and on reasonable doubts that the children would actually chase such a thing.

To my mind, the behavior was all quite charming. The children would strive for their own personal bests, and stand and cheer for each other's, but they wouldn't overtly compete. I was told that my approval of this approach, however subtle, came across. And this on top of my cheetah comment was the start of Dasher's protracted irritation with me. But the more interesting matter to me was reconciling the children's non-competitive behavior on the track with what we'd seen in the later cutthroat Monopoly sessions. I brought that up before one of our long jump sessions.

Me: What's the problem in there with Dr. Dasher? You don't seem to run your best unless you're running alone.

Samantha: I'd rather have everybody cheering for me than crowding up the track.

Richie: Yeah, me too. Why go all at the same time?

Me: I can't say I disagree with you. Though in the videos you've been seeing on the big board, they always run together.

Laura: I don't know why they want to do that.

Me: They're competing with each other. It's called a race. Everybody wants to win. Just like when you all want to win in Monopoly. The theory is you go a little faster if someone's racing along right next to you. The competition is supposed to bring out everyone's best performances.

Kirk: I just like when everybody watches. That's when I go my fastest.

Richie: Or jump the farthest.

This didn't provide much clarification about the Monopoly money lust. Ironically, it was Dasher who offered what I thought was the best explanation, though it was more parable than science: "When we were kids in Oklahoma we used to catch grasshoppers in the school play-ground. Bigger than any grasshoppers you've ever seen. We'd hold one between the thumb and forefinger of each hand and put them face-to-face. At first they'd just sit there, but if you held them long enough they couldn't help but get a little agitated. Eventually they'd start grappling, until one of them pulled the other one's head clean off. Same with the Monopoly, more or less. You make 'em play that long, even the social-ists are going to get a little agitated."

22. Richie

Jill couldn't help but notice that I'd relocated to the sill, though I down-played it as best I could. I knew she was proud of the house she'd arranged for me and might reasonably object to my using "literally, one square foot of it."

"For the record," I said, with my feet dangling off the sill, "it's one and a half square feet. The window is three feet wide, and the sill is six inches deep."

"Funny."

"But seriously, I use more of the house than the sill."

"I don't see that you spend much time anywhere else. You're sleeping up there. You're eating up there. Speaking of which, you need to clean up all these fruit peels. You can't leave that kind of stuff all over the floor."

"Yeah, you're right. I'll pick it up later."

"It's not like you're pressed for time, right?"

"No."

"You'll get mice, and you won't want to see what comes in after them."

"Like what?"

"Snakes. Big ones."

"Maybe confining myself to the sill isn't such a bad idea after all."

"If you didn't have to go to the fridge I don't think you'd ever come down."

"I still use the fireplace in the mornings when it's cold. And I have to walk all the way to the cat door to get out."

"Do you ever change your clothes?"

"Yes, occasionally."

"Do you have anything for me to wash?"

"No, thank you."

She took a deep breath to dramatize her exasperation. I couldn't really blame her on that one. My dressing habits had gotten a bit sloppy – I'd come to enjoy a bit of my own scent up there on the sill. But those deep breaths could also mean she was making a conscious effort to shift her tone. This had become common for Jill when she arrived from the city – she was always full of agitation and needed to bark herself out before settling in.

"How's your birdsong coming along?" she asked in a friendlier tone.

I called out a few bars.

"Wow, that's very impressive. Does it mean anything?"

"Yes, that one's a call of distress used primarily by the fledglings. Here's an adult responding now." One of the butcherbirds, the pretty preener, settled just outside the screen.

"Jesus, Richie. You actually get them to come over."

The preener and I exchanged a few phrases and settled into an easy silence, as we often did, perching quietly in each other's presence and taking in the subtle sounds and movements of the day. I was getting better at picking up the quiet bits of communications – shifts in posture, for example, or erections of certain parts of the plumage. Jill was not at ease with silence.

"Can you sing some other things?"

"Well, I'm a better listener than talker, at least for now. But I can hold my own."

I started chirping once again. The preener and I fell into a passable little chat. It was actually one of our better exchanges, to the point that I forgot Jill was even there, at least for the moment.

23. Jill

Watching the old tapes has made me wonder at my reserve about Richie's shattering the long jump SAWR. My briefing from P44 seems overly clinical, analytical, and reserved. It's almost dismissive, as if from someone hesitant to harp on the exploits of her own child. And I suppose it was beginning to feel a little like that with Richie. I'd started to call him Richard about then — I couldn't help myself, though it was pretty clear from the start that he didn't like it. After a couple days he'd had enough and made me stop.

His approach to me wasn't what I'd consider filial. He took to flirting with me during other people's sessions, wandering over near my workstation and pressing his face into the glass, which was the best way to see through the shading, and also to make silly pig faces, with his nose turned up, his mouth open, and his cheeks blown into fleshy little bellows, his breath steaming on the PrismView. I couldn't help but laugh every time he did that, though I had complaints from two or three of the SCPs, Jasper Scott foremost among them. A conversation with Richie on the subject was notable for his early sense of cause and effect, and for his early tactical reasoning.

Me: Richie, I love your sense of humor, but it's disrespectful to Mr. Scott when you leave Monopoly to make pig faces in the glass.

Richie: What do you mean?

Me: You don't know what disrespectful means?

Richie: No.

Me: It means you don't think highly enough of the person not to disrupt what he's trying to do. In this case, that would be Mr. Scott and the Monopoly game.

Richie: But I'm not disrupting anything. Why should I have to just sit there when it's not my turn?

Me: Well, for one thing, somebody might land on your property.

Richie: I can always run back. I'm pretty fast, you know.

Me: More to the point, you should be asking Mr. Scott for permission to get up.

Richie: But he'd probably say no. Then it'd be worse than if I hadn't asked in the first place.

Me: Hmm. Well, I can't say I disagree with you. But hasn't he already asked you to stop?

Richie: I just pretend I don't understand what he's saying. That way it doesn't hurt his feelings when I do it.

Me: Your speech comprehension is getting very good, Richie. I don't think you'll get away with that approach much longer.

Dasher was anxious to get on to his next event. He spent one late evening with precision cutting tools and wooden tongue depressors, and the next morning was underway with the high hurdles. This is a more technical event than simple sprinting, requiring proper form for clearing hurdles and measured strides between them. It was the perfect opportunity for Dmitri's consulting debut. By now the children were highly conversant, if somewhat selective in their hearing and comprehension, and privately Dasher would remark that Dmitri's chore was a lot easier than ours had been when we'd taught Brio and dance without language. Nonetheless, Dmitri's progress with the children was impressive. They mastered an excellent hurdler's position in a single session, heads forward, lead legs rod-straight, trail legs tucked nimbly to the side. Prodigious leapers that they were, they did tend to overjump and lose time in the air, but Dmitri attacked that the next day. He demonstrated a tighter, more efficient clearance with several leaps of his own, skimming repeatedly over a folding office chair, perspiring through his workshirt and drawing raucous applause from the whole staff. "I think he may have split his slacks," said Dr. Sloboth, hopefully. But further observation, and later video review, showed no evidence of that. In short order, Dasher had his third SAWR, the honors going this time to Samantha.

I benefited from Dmitri's experience just later, when I took delivery of a set of javelins packed in a customized dart case. Despite the exposure to National Geographic and the BBC, the children had no direct experience with injury or death, and they seemed inclined to turn the new javelins on each other in fun. But Dmitri's stern words, uttered in Russian, unintelligible but menacing, had more effect than my own well-reasoned but feeble pleas in English. Without him I could never have installed the strict safety protocol for which I'm thankful to this day.

While the javelins could certainly have penetrated little bodies, they couldn't penetrate weight dispersion flooring, clattering and skidding with a displeasing effect. This made for difficult measurements, and it undermined the dramatic impact of running out an old fashioned measuring tape, as I liked to do rather than simply triangulating with the lasers. We solved the problem, somewhat ingeniously I thought, by rolling out a large section of corkboard, which accepted its piercings with understated but thoroughly pleasing little thumps.

The more persistent problem was that the children were less gifted throwing than they were running and jumping. Just as gender equality had shown itself in the running and jumping, so it did here – they all, to coin a phrase I've always loathed, threw like girls.[36] It took most of them a while just to decide which arm to use. And they lacked flexibility in the elbow and shoulder. Only the incredible speed of their approaches made them even respectable in the event. Their best size-adjusted tosses might have won them a high school meet, but another SAWR seemed a long way off, at least with the javelin.

Dasher was waiting at the airlocks.

"Well, that sucked."

"It was perfectly fine. They're just not natural throwers, that's all."

"You gotta coach 'em up, Jill."

"Coach 'em up? That was our first session, for god's sake."

"One session was all it took for a couple SAWRs on my watch."

"Yeah, I had one of those too. And that SAWR was no more my doing than what we saw today. It's just possible they're not going to set records every time they try something."

"You need to rethink your approach for tomorrow."

"Don't take yourself too seriously, Coach."

Dr. Morben lurched past us as the chime struck noon. I shifted my focus to Morben's Gait, but before it could have its usual calming effect the big man ducked into the airlock. He hardly ever went inside. Even Dasher went quiet to watch.

---

36 Plenty of boys wished they threw as well as I did when I fired a complete-game, eight-strikeout, one-hit shutout my final start in Oswego Little League. And, for the record, any decent right fielder would have made the play on that so-called hit.

Morben had arrived that morning with a battered old plastic case shaped something like a lunchbox. Gray duct tape covered every surface, but in gaps along the edges you could just make out the original pink. It sat with him through the Little Gathering, and accompanied him to his normal post in OB1 and on his ambulations to the restroom, never leaving his person the entire morning. He'd brushed off all of our inquiries, and only now, as we all watched through the glass, did he open the box. It held a toy dining room set – a small wooden table with chairs and place settings for eight.

While Bitsen still drove the lunch menu, Morben, by agreement, was now driving the lunch. Rather than sitting Indian style on the floor and eating with their hands from a communal plate, the children sat upright at the table, with individual little plates and glasses and full sets of cutlery and cloth napkins. They sat three to each side and one on one end. Morben sat Indian style at the other end, his plate in his lap, demonstrating the proper use of cutlery and the napkin, and conducting genial conversation across a range of topics.

That first formal lunch, the first of many, was one of the most touching moments of my time at Genesis. Here was gigantic old Dr. Moribund, who lurched around and betrayed hardly a feeling for anyone, now showing a gentle side none of us even knew existed. We took our own lunches in quasi-reverential silence, each at our own workstations, exchanging occasional looks but mainly just watching inside, where the children took knives and forks in hand, cut their food into manageable little bites, and fed themselves like little lords and ladies.

24. Richie

The light is down, the sky orange in the west. The birds are into their final chases, in the last throes of their day when the social order for sleeping is both contested and confirmed. This dusk-lit drama used to have me on the edge of my sill, straining against the screen to see as much as my position would allow. But I've learned that the outcomes are pretty inevitable, the same groupings settled in place by the end. For the most part, these late-day chases are just a series of feints. The outsiders, young adults mostly, may probe and test, but they've little hope of breaking through. They're chased off, with varying degrees of enthusiasm, as if they're all going through the motions.

On the floor below me several insects, some of them as big as my foot, sound their death rattles. This is the distasteful residue of an initiative I put forward not long ago, when, eating lunch on the sill, I had another idea to increase my peaceful avian interactions. Taking up my paring knife once again, I cut a small section of the screen away altogether. Believe me, I had no plans to crawl through. For all the apparent niceties, I expect I'd still be mobbed and beaten to the ground. And that's a longer drop than I care to contemplate. Nor did I wish to draw any of the birds inside. A houseful of raptors is about my worst nightmare. I cut the hole only as big as my hand, and only to slide out a small portion of my lunch. I tried it all that day, and over the course of several more. Bread, dried meats, seeds -- nothing seemed to appeal.

But one afternoon when I'd pretty much given up, I had a hit with, of all things, the pomegranate. One of the noisy miners settled in when I was hardly even paying attention. She pecked almost randomly at first, as if getting her bearings with this new fruit, then shifted to a more systematic approach, piercing individual seeds and taking the nectar like the honeyeater she is. Others joined her shortly. There was even a bit of squabbling over rights to my sill.

The magpies and butchers showed no interest in pomegranate, but the commotion drew their attention more generally to my sill. And soon I had hits with them as well, dried meat for the magpies, dried fruit for the butchers. I learned how to allocate certain times for certain foods, and cultivated a steady hour for each of them. I was careful to stay ahead of it, placing the portions in advance and all at once, rather than risking my hand when they were already perched. I'd suffered enough gouges on the ground, through and around my umbrella, to needlessly risk more.

Several days into this, and maybe fifteen minutes after the dried fruit distribution, a butcherbird flew in and settled on the sill. She carried what I can only say, even now, was a bug of some type. I'm afraid I've never been able to distinguish, by name, between the countless insects they so enjoy. I can't bring myself to do the research as I've no interest in any of them. This particular specimen was alive and squirming, but crushed so badly in one section that the butcher could drop it near the hole in my screen at no risk of its running off. Shocked as I was at her intent, I did manage to sound her praise. But there was no question I was going to decline as politely as I could manage. I couldn't eat that thing, no matter how much it might benefit me socially. And I couldn't expose my hand reaching out for it, even in this case of apparent generosity. She nudged the bug a time or two closer, and looked at me first with curiosity and then with exasperation. At last she picked it up, stuck it through the hole, and dropped it just next to me. In my horror I flicked it to the floor, but I regained my wits quickly enough to scramble down after it, hoping she'd interpret that as a suitably avid intent to devour.

I know I should have been gratified, even flattered, to have received such an offering. And I was, at some level. But there was something so revolting about that wriggling morsel, and something so off-putting about that deadly beak jabbing through my screen – it pierced the veil of my safe little sill and strengthened the feeling I'd been battling all along, that I was fundamentally unfit for such a world.

Even so, it's in my best interests to go along. I accept a half-dozen daily deposits from two butcherbird females, the preener and the ace, insects of many sizes and shapes in various states of mutilation and disfigurement. I continue my practice of flicking them to the floor and chasing down after them. To my winged benefactors it looks like appreciation. But down on that floor, where I'm safely out of sight, I kick them to the corner and leave them to die in a pile of their peers.

25. Jill

I'd hoped Dasher and I would return to our collegial state, but we continued instead on a downward spiral. With three size-adjusted world records under his belt, Dasher had reached a tipping point in his workplace persona. What had started as light comedy – the sweatsuit, the lanyards, the coaching impersonations – became a different kind of farce, an affectation of what he'd actually become. Beneath the tongue-in-cheek façade he was deadly serious, completely obsessed with his, or our, quirky run at decathlon history.

We'd initially agreed to focus on individual events and to avoid mentioning the decathlon at all. I'd considered adding field events that weren't in the decathlon, the triple jump and hammer throw, as red herrings, just to boost our independence quotient. But that all became moot when he not only dashed the agreement, but leapt to the far other end of the spectrum. Suddenly he was preaching to anyone who would listen, and to many who wouldn't.

"The decathlon is the greatest athletic concept of all time. Dating into ancient history. Spanning all the world's major cultures. No judges, no subjectivity. Pure numbers, quantifiable and indisputable. Ten diverse pursuits requiring speed, strength, coordination, and endurance. The best decathlete is, by informed consensus, the world's greatest athlete. And we've got that very athlete within these walls."

While no one actually called us out on our collusion, I was uncomfortable flouting the guidelines, and more so with Dasher becoming such an embarrassment. Our interactions were increasingly combative. Some version of that had been our shtick from the beginning, but affectation had once again become reality. He began to ride me like his minion. I was lagging in my duties, an impediment to the greater glory. While I'd "delivered" on the long jump, my javelin results were "bringing us down." And if one or two of my other results were as poor, it would "sink the project." Given that two of my remaining events were throws of some kind – the shot put and the discus – this seemed more likely than not.

He'd wander over and sit on my desk, clacking his baby food jar down like a gavel. "How's it going? Any revelations on javelin technique? I've been reading about the importance of hip turn." Or, "When is Dmitri getting you those discuses? Have you talked to him?" Then he'd call Dmitri directly. An hour later he might repeat the whole process. This was particularly aggravating to Dmitri, since he was helping us on his own time and neglecting his own work in the process.

The discuses did arrive, on P50, like polished little coins in a pull-string bag. Dmitri was there to introduce the children to the proper techniques, but this event didn't start well either. Most significantly, the children had a tough time with the spinning that preceded the throws. Maybe it was a function of their youth, but they seemed overly susceptible to dizziness. It was not uncommon to see one of them, after a throw, staggering like a drunk and toppling right over. This was a source of great humor among them, and among all the staff specialists with the exception, of course, of Dasher. Dmitri's gentle reproaches couldn't squelch it, and I'm sure my passive complicity didn't help much either. I couldn't help myself – it all reminded me of birthday parties long past, when a kid would put his forehead on one end of a baseball bat, set the other on the ground, and spin until the fluid sloshed in his ears like lakewater at the bottom of a rowboat. I suppose I'd reached a point where I didn't mind letting Dasher or anyone else squirm at "the unforgivable waste of precious session time" while the kids had a little fun.

Given their pervasive vertigo, the children, as you might imagine, struggled to release the discus into the proper vector. I set the dining table on edge, and the six spectating children took to huddling behind it, like Romans under a hail of arrows, while the seventh set up to throw. And while "Huddle up for safety!" became our singsong catchphrase, the ping of the errant discus striking off the PrismView was the real soundtrack to our buffoonery. For the first time, I was enjoying myself thoroughly, as I believed were the children. I couldn't help but feel a little naughty – even Dmitri cast me a disparaging look or two. At the Little Gatherings, I managed to speak with the appropriate gravity, declaiming on the biomechanics of balance and the comparative rates of its acquisition. But the vertigo videos were simply hilarious, to the point where Dr. Sloboth's hyenine laughter, in particular, infused my briefings with unprofessionalism. And the fact is, it didn't bother me.

Dmitri was more hopeful about the shot put. For one thing, it didn't require excessive spinning. While most competitive shot putters did spin, others used a gliding technique that involved a mere 180-degree twist. Moreover, we'd seen the children toss the full-sized Monopoly dice, and they seemed to have both a knack and an enthusiasm for that simpler kind of heaving. The shots arrived on P53, packed like little musket balls in a jewelry case. Dmitri was not available for coaching on that day, and I indulged the children with a reversion to the Scottish log toss technique they'd used with the dice, rocking once, twice, three times, and heaving the shots with two hands from between their legs. This, I suppose, was as much to get Dasher's goat as to please the children. Predictably, he was in my headset within minutes, the Scottish technique being highly illegal, and when I'd switched off the volume he was up and pounding on the glass.

Only when he'd thrown up his hands and sat back down did I begin the proper instruction, with a grapefruit I'd pilfered from the kitchen. I held it in the legal starting position at my neck, executed a passable glide step, and gave it my best heave.[37] But old habits were hard to break. The children complained bitterly about the new technique, particularly the starting position. "It's like scrunching your neck onto a super uncomfortable pillow," said Samantha, who then, as if on cue, dropped the cast iron shot square onto her foot. She collapsed to the floor with an awful howling, and the others joined in, weeping in immediate solidarity. It was our first real injury, and the first time we'd had all seven of them in tears – on my watch, of course. I was very nearly in tears myself as Dr. Hayes carried Samantha out for her x-rays. I berated myself for allowing some levity into the training, though the video would show we were serious enough at the time of the accident. Needless to say, field events were done for the day.

Our best put – Kirk's second try – had sent the shot barely two body lengths. That was a size-adjusted effort of about twelve feet, not a sixth of what we'd need for a world record. Once again, Dasher was waiting at the airlocks. The results, apparently, were disastrous enough to derail any hope of a decathlon SAWR, even if we hit SAWR-level performances in all nine of the other events. "Do the math," he snarled. "And now we're down our best hurdler and maybe our best overall athlete. I liked her chances in the 1500. That's what happens when you let them screw around in there. What are we going to do if the foot's broken?"

---

37 That grapefruit, incidentally, made a very satisfying and authentic-sounding thud on the corkboard, very similar to what I remembered of heavy shots pounding onto the infield grass.

"I guess the only merciful thing would be to put her down, Coach. We'll just have to shoot her. Probably should've done it right there on the track."

As it turned out, the x-rays were negative, though she'd be out for a while with a bone bruise. For Dasher's session on P55 she sat with her foot propped up on one of Morben's little dinner chairs. I could see right away what Dasher was doing with the other six. They were taking multiple laps around the track and at a slower pace than anything we'd done to date. Without consulting me, Dr. Bitsen, or any of the others, he'd begun training them for the 1500. Falstaff, who'd been required to project the start and finish lines on the track, was in the know, and assumed I was as well. He was at my desk before they'd finished their second lap.

Falstaff: I think you two are making a big mistake here. There's no reason to push into endurance events.

Me: I've got nothing to do with this, Alton. Dasher and I are barely on speaking terms. We'd agreed to hold off on the 1500. He's doing this on his own.

Falstaff: Moribund will not be pleased.

I checked my watch. They were flashing by us about every thirty seconds.

Me: That's strange. They're running in a group, and running well -- probably on pace for another record.

Falstaff: You're probably on pace to getting your programs cancelled.

Dr. Bitsen wandered over, followed shortly by several others.

Bitsen: Am I missing something, or does this look very much like distance training?

Me: It looks like he's got them going on the 1500.

Bitsen: I thought we'd agreed...

Me: It's as much a surprise to me as it is to you.

Falstaff: Isn't the 1500 supposed to be just under four times around?

Me: Yes.

Falstaff: I'm counting eight going on nine.

Manly: I knew this whole track and field thing was a bad idea.

Sloboth: Somebody needs to get in there and shut them down.

Morben: I think we can let them proceed at this point.

We all gave a bit of a start. For a seven-footer, he could really sneak up on you.

Bitsen: What do you mean?

Morben: The Senior Science Officers tell me they're conceding the notion of growth.

Me: The HGH testing came out negative?

Morben: Dramatically suppressed levels of both HGH and IGF-1.[38]

Dasher: But they must have been sufficient at some point. The fetuses developed.

Morben: Evidence points to rapid dissipation toward the end of gestation.

Sloboth: So wouldn't the next step be a re-introduction?

Morben: I believe supplements were considered.

Sloboth: And rejected?

Morben: Yes.

Sloboth: Why? What's to lose?

Morben: We have no idea how they'd respond. There are any number of negative outcomes. Experimentation on that basis would be considered inhumane.

Bitsen: Agreed. They're not laboratory animals.

Me: Since when?

---

38 Insulin-like growth factor 1, another highly relevant hormone.

Bitsen: Even on the off chance that it worked, people wouldn't like the idea of HGH infusions.

Me: How is that any worse than the idea of genetic manipulation?

Bisten: Think about vegetables. Practically every vegetable you eat has been genetically manipulated. But if they don't use chemical fertilizer it's considered organic, and everybody's happy. Synthetic HGH would be our equivalent of chemical fertilizer.

There was a certain lightness in Bitsen's voice, something irritating, something she was trying to suppress in a cloud of inanity. I realized it was joy. Sheer, unadulterated joy. She was off the hook. Nutrition was no longer, and had never been, the problem. And at least for the moment, the most ostensibly unselfish person on the staff didn't care about anything else.

Henderson: Dr. Morben, you say they're *conceding growth*. They've written off any prospect of its happening naturally, and they're not going to pursue it through supplements.

Morben: That's right.

Henderson: Where does that leave us?

Silence.

Falstaff: With seven footlings in permanent stasis. And employed in a project that's headed for shutdown.

More silence.

Falstaff: Look, we can all agree that they're gifted children. Clever children. Likable children. And it's been exciting science. But for any of this to have any commercial application it had to be clean. If it doesn't make childbearing and early stage childraising easier without being completely freakish, then it doesn't work. For all the enthusiasm we've seen, I'm sure there's also been a lot of concern. And now it's confirmed that they've engineered the growth right out of them. Not exactly what the marketplace is clamoring for.

Still more silence.

Falstaff: Maybe there are applications here for different projects down the road. But for now we're more of a problem than an asset.

Sloboth: Yikes.

Falstaff: BioSpore's got dozens of projects in development. From all those, they get just a handful of wins. That's how it works. They're big wins, giant wins, enough to carry the whole company. But we're no longer in that category, if we ever really were.

Bitsen: So now you think they cut their losses, clean it up, and move on.

Falstaff: Or we all just go away. Whichever narrative you prefer.

PART TWO

26. Jill

We understand spoken language to be a dynamic construct, but its mutations are often speedier than we think. The right term, in the right group at the right moment, can run from its first tentative repetition to full communal usage in a matter of hours, or even minutes.

Footling was just such a term. Falstaff had broken it out on the morning of P55, and by noon it was project-standard vernacular. As abruptly as the Greek alpha-names had yielded to 60s TV, *children* had given way to *footlings*. It wasn't a particularly accurate designation – our footlings were nearly fifteen inches, or a foot and a quarter, tall. And it wasn't particularly empathetic – I, for one, found it condescending and derogatory. But empathy reduction was, in all probability, at the heart of its appeal. You could make half a case that the term was endearing, and I heard that justification more than once around the building. But its primary effect was to separate our subjects from ourselves, to adjust our notion of *the proper distance*. Implied was the tenet that permanent miniaturization made them clinically inhuman, and that sooner or later we'd all have to start letting go. Even the kindest, most generous people in the group, Drs. Bitsen and Sloboth, adopted the term so casually you'd have thought they'd never used any other. Coming from them, it sounded so gentle and non-disparaging that I found myself tempted to join in, though it'd be a while before I got there.

However we may have tempered our in-house approaches, the greater entity of BioSpore wasn't nearly so subtle. Falstaff had predicted that the negative HGH tests would end corporate interest in Project Genesis. What he hadn't conveyed, or, like the rest of us, hadn't initially understood, was how quickly that would happen.

The caterers cut our breakfast rounds the very next morning. It was no one-time scheduling lapse – they'd suspended our entire service. This came as a great shock not only to staff members who'd come to rely on our culinary entitlements, but to the children as well. Dr. Bitsen and the techs scrambled to keep them fed from woefully inadequate kitchen facilities. Apollo-era provisions – instant oatmeal, dried soups, Tang – would soon become the new normal. The rest of us trudged out for takeaway lunches and sat back to our screens, chewing absently and slurping through plastic straws. And with dinner promising more of the same, the facility emptied promptly at 17:00.

Dr. Hayes, Jasper Scott, and two of the four techs disappeared overnight, complete with personal effects, sucked into that mysterious vortex known as reallocation. Hayes had been an awful bore, but useful as a counter-balance to Manly – we'd realize her true value only in her absence. Scott, who'd floundered badly once his Monopoly sessions had lost their luster, was not mourned, to say the least. Nor were the techs. But it all meant more work for the rest of us, much of it menial.

And most telling, from the day of the test results forward, not a single executive passed through our airlock doors. Not as spectators for sprints or hurdles, or for any other tricks we could muster. And not as responsible administrators with announcements, or explanations, or the slightest word of condolence. They all just stopped coming. Dasher was the last to grasp this. He interpreted the first day or two of the executive absence as "an understandable period of strategic regrouping." But as the days ran on and spoke to a more permanent detachment, he changed his tune. "The bastards," he said in his ludicrous Oklahoma coach-speak. "They've scampered off like calves from the gelding pen."

For all his irreverent façade, Dasher took it harder than anyone. He would never have admitted, even to himself, that he'd been giddy with the attention, real and imagined, he'd received on his short run to athletic history. And now, in our sudden isolation, his alternating voices – learned elocution and simpleton drawl – seemed more the product of bipolar disorder than of humor or defiance. As for me, I'd always thought myself immune to the more juvenile forms of workplace reinforcement. But I too was mistaken. While there was consolation in seeing my last of Marcia Tompkins, the lesson was as inescapable as it was humbling – you don't realize your dependence on even the shallowest forms of recognition until they're gone.

As you might imagine, these developments prompted a good bit of fretting about our futures. Job security became a frequent point of discussion, though not within earshot of Morben, who insisted on our maintaining a certain level of professional decorum. "We've survived the first cut," as Bitsen put it, "but by the end, we'll be lucky to have done as well as Hayes and Scott, reassigned and not released." Any speculation about the children was so unpleasant and so uncomfortable that it generally disintegrated into a series of off-color jokes, none of them particularly funny. Worst case, they'd be spinning hamster wheels and pushing levers for food pellets in subterranean kennels. Best case, they'd be scooped up by military special operations, running cyber espionage centers from clandestine crawl spaces. We hadn't the slightest idea what the future might hold for them. And after a few days of fretting we weren't inclined to dwell on it. We had to maintain the core operation, and not only were we suddenly short-staffed, we were just as suddenly burdened with the many annoyances of corporate contraction – equipment recalls, mandatory time allocation sheets, Machiavellian supply cuts. Working capital had dried up, as Dasher put it, "like spit on a hot summer sidewalk." I had to buy a bag of seed on my own dime just to keep The Chief on his perch.

The timing was something of a shame, the project contracting all around us just as the children were taking their most impressive academic strides. Drs. Sloboth and Henderson had been hammering at the mechanics of written language, and it all kicked in around the time of the HGH tests. The children began to read, and in the most extraordinary manner. The transition from single words to phrases and simple sentences was nearly immediate. Once they had cat, they had "The Cat in the Hat" and "The Cat in the Hat Comes Back." Longer words — catastrophic, catatonic, cataclysmic — and complex sentences weren't far behind.

This budding literacy brought a profound transition for the footlings. Child's play was abruptly passé, and any session that excluded reading became a drudgery for all parties. My field events were at the top of that list. The children didn't engage with anywhere near the exuberance they'd shown before, and they'd given up all pretense of seeking improvement. Dmitri was still making his daily visits from Engineering. He, like Dasher, had a hard time believing the Project would be terminated. But the apathy from our little athletes quickly exhausted his well of demonstrations and exhortations. He soaked through one too many business shirts, sank into streams of despondent-sounding Russian, and on P58, with a speech that extolled the life lessons of effort, commitment, and persistence, he resigned from coaching. The children liked Dmitri and were respectful enough during his sendoff. And he did promise to return "when their hearts come back to it." But the fact is, they didn't care if he coached or not, or if they ever took part in another field sport, associated life lessons notwithstanding.

I can't say I blamed them. I'd become nearly as disengaged as they had. The fun had gone out of it, and their performances were not only down, but now almost certainly irrelevant. Given the general state of flux, I felt no particular mandate to continue. As so it was that the day after Dmitri's departure, without reservation or regret, I suspended the field events entirely. In their place I chose the path of least resistance, or, less cynically, the path of the children's greatest enthusiasm. I launched a reading module of my own.

Dasher was surprisingly supportive. He'd seen the same falloff in his track sessions. I knew how invested he was in the decathlon venture, and watching through the glass I'd found myself genuinely disappointed on his behalf. But he believed the footlings' interest would return at some point, and I suspect he meant to pick up my field events when it did, consolidating all the athletic training under his own authority. Suffice it to say I didn't feel threatened.

Henderson and Sloboth had leaned heavily on automated reading, lines of text scrolling up the PrismViews while one of them, or one of the footlings, read aloud. I'd always preferred printed books, and wanted that more traditional exposure for the children. From the beginning, Genesis had stocked a great starter library, the complete works of Eric Carle, Julia Donaldson, Dr. Seuss, and others of the early readers' ilk. The problem was that turning the full-sized pages – many of them in stiff and bulky cardboard – was tougher for our diminutive students than actually reading them. I bought half a dozen bookstands, again on my own dime, and set them in a circle on the floor. The children began to work in pairs, one flipping the pages, which involved grabbing an edge and hauling it in a semi-circle of several paces, while the other stood back to do the reading. Three of the pairs fell in as might have been expected – Kirk and Uhura, Samantha and Darrin, Rob and Laura. Richie could have inserted himself into any of those groups – none of them would have purposely excluded him – but he seemed more comfortable paired with me. The resulting four-pair system kept four children reading aloud, an obvious improvement on the participation rates in Sloboth's and Henderson's hours. When they finished one book they'd shift one stand to the right, working counter-clockwise until they'd gone through all six titles I'd set. At the end of the hour they'd fall in for impromptu discussion groups, assessing the binge eating of the Hungry Caterpillar, the Gruffalo's hygiene, or the inherently evil nature of the Grinch.

Within just a few days my nursery hour had regained its former prominence as the children's clear favorite. I was happy enough to be back on top, even if no one on the outside was paying any attention. Richie took to reciting from Seuss each night before bed, and the others would often join in. One particular stanza from *One Fish, Two Fish* became something of a happy mantra for them: *Today is gone, today was fun, tomorrow is another one.* And that was true enough, at least from their point of view. While the project was quietly unwinding around them, I believe this period was their most contented. We as a staff had become less imperious, and while the children had become less inclined to physical play, there was a cer-tain equanimity about them, as if they'd settled on a track of their own choosing.

They blew through the early reader stuff we had on hand, and while I'd placed an order for more advanced titles – A.A. Milnes, Roald Dahls, and the like – they were destined never to arrive, pre-dictable casualties of our derailed budget. Henderson and Sloboth could load cost-free material on the PrismView, but my session had been built on printed books, a preference the children all shared, and a commodity now in short supply. I lugged in my own childhood volumes of *Pooh*. Worn as they were, decades earlier by my sisters and me, and more recently by my own nieces and nephews, they proved to be great favorites. I sat in the middle of the nursery, the children arrayed on the floor all around me, and read in my most kindly narrative voice:

> *The Old Grey Donkey, Eeyore, stood by himself in a thistly corner of the Forest, his front feet well apart, his head on one side, and thought about things. Sometimes he thought sadly to himself, 'Why?' and sometimes he thought, 'Wherefore?' and sometimes he thought, 'Inasmuch as which?' — and sometimes he didn't know what he was thinking about.*

"Can you read that part again?" asked Richie.

"And what caught your interest there?" I asked when I'd gone through it a second time.

"My own brain works a little like that sometimes," he said.

"Mine too," said Laura. "Mostly at the end of the day."

"Yeah, I suppose we all have periods like that," I said.

"What's thistly?"

"Do forests really have corners?"

I began daily runs to the local library to keep us in books. Many of my fellow specialists, nearly all of whom were parents with their own children's libraries, chipped in with offerings of their own — an encouraging sign that we'd begun to move beyond our internal competitions. But by the late P60s, those books had run their course. The children's reading abilities were moving too fast, and their interests were beginning to diverge. Henderson had squeezed in a tablet allocation just before the capital shutdown, and she made the distribution at this critical point, one to each child. She'd installed the three approved applications — Word, Dictionary, and Wikipedia — and within days the children were reading exclusively from these devices, propped, ironically enough, on the stands I'd introduced in defense of traditional printed books.

Reading articles at the Wikipedia level was impressive enough at first. Henderson would introduce some basic topic like trees, birds, or cars. Falstaff would pop relevant visual images on the screen. The children would do some introductory reading and ask a few questions. Henderson would set them onto related searches. And off they'd go. They were soon making that kind of leap on their own, stringing series of articles together in impressively logical progressions. They moved to more esoteric topics, geographical and biological items of interest, political developments, astronomy, the nuance of cultures. The study of historical events in particular spurred waves of additional research. What events led to that? What followed? They discussed these matters with us and among themselves.

By the mid-P70s, personal areas of interest were taking shape. Darrin had a budding specialty in world affairs, Kirk in trade and economics, Samantha in Asian history. Richie took to classical architecture, Laura to botany. Henderson encouraged this by having the children begin daily presentations to each other, complete with five-minute buzzers, just as we'd done in our Little Gatherings. The first occurred on P79, the children sitting around their dinner table, the speaking party standing at its head. It was beyond impressive. Richie's presentation on the flying buttresses of certain European cathedrals was so compelling that it drew a series of questions not only from the other children but from those of us outside the glass, a significant break in the general protocol. We dubbed these presentations, quite cleverly, the Tiny Gatherings.

Daily deadlines made writing a staple of the footling life. They made ample use of the dictionary and thesaurus functions, expanded their vocabularies, began to develop their own unique elements of style. Uhura was particularly academic, with the prose of a budding professor. Samantha tended more to the preacher or politician, fiery, self-assured, full of bluster. Richie dabbled in the poetic. Intrigued by

170

the couplets and rhyme schemes in many of the early readers' books, he was deeply gratified by the anapestic tetrameter[39] of Seuss. Accordingly, he steered his prose to the flowery side of the spectrum. In time he began to fancy he had some flair for it. And who was I to discourage the notion? "Listen to this," he'd say, and start babbling out original poetry or random literary impressions from his tablet. Those sessions could get tiresome, but it was obvious he liked me to listen. It was the least I could do. And I suppose he did have his moments.

To whatever end, self-paced, presentation-based education was firmly underway, eclipsing anything Henderson said she'd seen from the most gifted children at the most well-endowed institutions with the most liberalized approaches. While the Wikipedia curriculum was academically sub-optimal, the process was self-sustaining and almost geometric in its progression. I made a log on P81 that these children, who'd never actually been out of the nursery, had a broader world-view than any grade-schooler I'd ever encountered, or could even imagine.

By all rights, those Tiny Gatherings, with children expounding to one another on quasi-academic topics at eighty days, should have drawn bigger corporate crowds than the track events, the line dancing, the Brio, or the Monopoly ever had. But as I've mentioned, the crowds were gone for good. Exciting as the recent developments had been, a couple of specialists listening in was about as much as we could summon. The Tiny Gatherings were recorded, but only as a matter of procedural inertia. To my knowledge, no one ever reviewed them.

Our own Little Gatherings had undergone what most observers would have considered a radical decline. Morben never officially acknowledged that the Senior Science Officers had stopped watching,

---

39 Henderson, who turned out to have majored in English and American literature, claimed that anapestic tetrameter was verse in four measures with a beat on every third syllable. I thought that level of recall preposterous and looked it up, but she was correct.

but he'd dropped the five-minute presentation limits, which we took as confirmation. We grew steadily bolder, egging each other on until we'd transitioned from disciplined daily presentations, with each of us building a tight body of work in carefully phrased, well-documented five-minute increments, to rambling, wide-ranging discourses from anyone with the slightest hunch about anything. And while most of us, by the nature of our training, were uneasy with that degree of informality, something in the approach was scientifically liberating. On occasion, it actually produced some decent thinking.

Falstaff, for example, made an unscheduled presentation on P84. He'd cleaned himself up a bit – trimmed his beard, donned a newer shirt, and somehow found himself a decent lab coat, despite the shameful state of Project laundry. He spoke without notes, and with the air of someone who'd done quite a bit of it before. Not two minutes in, it was clear he had more biological training than we'd thought. He was a better speaker, and probably a better overall scientist, than the lot of us.

"A mammal weighing less than a kilo and carrying a standing pulse rate of two hundred should, by all logic, be more closely related to smaller mammals than to human beings. While we've documented physiological and cognitive characteristics in the footlings that are strikingly similar to those in humans, it would be imprudent to project human characteristics, simply on that basis, to all facets of the footling biology. The far broader range of empirical data tells us that certain physiological eventualities are almost certain to fall within ranges predicated on mass and on pulse rate.

"Mindful of that, we can begin to rationalize certain of our expectations. The first and possibly foremost of these concerns longevity. Take a moment to consider other mammals in a comparable weight class. The lifespan of the southern brown bandicoot is four years. The black-tailed prairie dog, five to seven. A resourceful and extremely fortunate meerkat may last ten. Removing predatory and other stress factors is a help, but there's no reason our footlings would project to something dramatically outside this four-to-ten-year range. Most likely they'd be at the lower end of it."

I was thinking something along the lines of, "Of course! He's right! How did I not think of that?" when Dr. Bitsen burst into tears. It was a shocking break in amphitheater protocol, a display I would never have allowed myself in any professional setting, or, to be honest, in any private setting beyond absolute solitude. But some part of me admired it all the same.

"Look," Falstaff continued, in as comforting a tone as he could summon, "it's only theory. But there's no precedent in the animal kingdom for animals this size and with these pulse rates living more than a tiny fraction of the eighty or ninety years we've come to expect of humans."

"But there's no precedent for most of what we've seen here." I mentioned this only for the benefit of Bitsen, who'd removed her jar-bottom glasses to rub at her eyes.

"That's true," said Falstaff. "Until very recently we'd not encountered fifteen-inch mammals with this kind of cognition, or speech. Or with such human mannerisms, or such a similar anatomical makeup. But projecting into areas where we have no specific indications to the contrary, we must still default to the laws of the biological world. It's only natural."

27. Richie

Dawn on the sill. Today's hash marks another milestone, my eight hundredth day in East Central. I'm well into my third breeding season, once again in proximity to several active nests. While this is advantageous to my learning, and at least theoretically to my social advancement, it does have the drawback of shrieking chicks, all day, every day.

The adults, for their part, have submitted to their servitude. Already, many are hard at it, hunting for chicks' breakfasts in the half-light. I'm reminded how I exploited this my first couple times around, co-opting the chicks' needy calls to attract several already beleaguered females for visits to my sill. It's not something I'm proud of. And looking back on it now, it's hard to believe they paid me any mind. The more I watch, the more obvious it becomes that they've no time for my kind of sideshow. It's hard enough securing your borders against a steady stream of intruders and keeping yourself fed while giving all your best bites to a horde of insatiable little tyrants, let alone tending to some freakish interloper.

That said, they seem to accept their lot with a certain equanimity. Living so entirely in the present seems to minimize fretting, though it rules out what I would imagine to be their most comforting notion, that this all will pass in time. On the other hand, maybe it's best that they don't think too far ahead – they might mislead themselves into considering this indenture an exercise in delayed gratification, a downpayment on future contentment. With just two seasons under my belt, even I can tell them that a good number of these chicks will be dead within the next few weeks – I've already seen the first little body parts in the grass. And that the chicks who do manage to fledge and fly, rather than maturing into sources of ongoing joy and support, will carry on with their badgering and their freeloading, well past the reasonable due of youth. Granted, they've got hunting skills to acquire, but it does get a little pathetic watching a perfectly adept flyer, as big as or even bigger than his mother, shrieking for service. He'll accept her hard-earned fare in the beak-to-beak manner afforded to infants, without a hint of shame or the slightest peep of gratitude. When she flies off for a moment's peace or a bite to herself, he'll follow right after, demanding her next bit too. It's a wonder she doesn't snap before she does. Only after several months of this will she even begin to chase him off. If she does it often enough and with a convincing enough vigor, he'll fly to parts unknown, and she'll not likely see him again. And if she doesn't, he's likely to turn the tables and chase *her* off instead. His own mother, deemed no longer of use and coolly discarded. I've seen it with my own eyes.

Speaking of badgering, Jill's given up trying to talk me off the sill. She's come to respect my time there as part of my "linguistic immersion." When she's cheery enough she'll rave about how much of the birdsong I've picked up. She asks for new vocalizations every time she visits. I'm perfectly willing to entertain her that way, though I doubt she'd notice if I repeated the exact phrasings from the prior week. She doesn't have much of an ear for it. Nor, in my view, does she have the temperament. But while her compliments are grossly uninformed, I do appreciate her notice, and, I suppose, her enthusiasm. "Jesus!" she says. "What I could have done at Genesis with this! We'd still be in business over there."

Her interest seems grounded in process. From what she tells me, countless birds have picked up snippets of human language. Humans, for all their acuity, have done no better – they've picked up certain calls, but nothing approaching mastery of an avian language. So she's curious as to how I've done so well across multiple species. A few ideas seem to make it more understandable for her:

The songs of the magpie and the butcherbird are nearly identical; the song of the miner is quite different from those; and the song of the cockatiel, at least as much as I picked up from The Chief, is even more remote. But they're all built on many of the same principles. It's not that birdsong is fundamentally less complex than the language of humans. Magpie sounds and rhythms, for example, span a far greater range than the sounds and characters in English. And I'll grant that the higher range of my voice gives me certain advantages. But the conceptual scope of birds is so much more focused compared to that of humans that if you do have any kind of an ear, and you take the time, you can keep right up before too long.

English, I should mention, is the only human language I know. I wasn't aware that other human languages even existed until just before my transfer over here, though I do remember some strange bits of what I'd assumed was jibberish from Dmitri. Looking back on it, I'm surprised the Genesis people didn't expose us to a little more that way. Maybe if we'd had more time, Jill says. She also says that, given their reliance on tone, the birdsongs resemble some of the Asiatic tongues more than they do English. Though, as she readily admits, she's no expert in human linguistics either.

But imagine, for example, the English lexicon stripped of all the exclusively human constructs; the verbs calling out the huge range of uniquely human activity; the nouns denominating the tens of thousands of man-made objects and abstract human concepts, and the endless convolutions of history, culture, science and art. Shrink the geography and the ambition, and, in particular, shrink time. That keeps the few remaining verbs to one simple tense, the present, though I've found a surprising emphasis on the imperative in all birdsong. Eliminate past and future, conjecture and review. Eliminate articles and adverbs, redundancies, synonyms. Eliminate the flowery stuff, the whiny stuff, and everything else that's just not worth talking about. Pare it all down. And then find the nuance in tone.

There are, of course, a few areas of increased complexity – subtleties of flight, fine distinctions of air currents and feather conditions, an impressive list of edible crawly things. But none of that pertains to me, and I've been able to tune it out to concentrate on the things that really matter – like which individual birds are most inclined to knock me senseless, and how I can have them persuaded otherwise. Given their predilection for the blind side, direct observation of my attackers has been difficult. But it's clear by now that magpie males are the main culprits, and occasionally miners of both genders as it turns out, though the miner women will admit to nothing of the sort. The miners are too quick for gender determination in the air – I've gleaned that information only from the others, and only after quite some time and effort.

Getting information from any of them just isn't that easy. You'd be surprised at how an unshakable fixation on the present limits questions. It's not that they're incurious creatures. Quite to the contrary. They're curious about almost everything they can see, and, of course, their eyesight is astounding. They can spot the tiniest grub, all but concealed in the grass, at forty meters. It's just that most questions you or I might ask can't even be expressed. Concepts like "when" and "why" and "what if" don't exist in birdsong. Questions themselves hardly exist beyond their one seemingly eternal statement-query. "I'm here, where are you?" This single message, in calls from all three species, is the most prominent thing I hear in these trees. When I mentioned that to Jill, she found it "cute" and "very touching." They do seem extraordinarily concerned with each other's whereabouts.

One other question I hear popping up from time to time is something to the effect of "What needs doing (at present)?" It comes from only the meeker birds, and is generally dismissed with the slightly condescending "Nothing at present. Be still and see (more) around you." Which, I suppose, is instructive enough in its own right. But given how naturally these birds take to bossing each other around, you have to wonder why the question exists at all. The most overbearing of them seem to consider it forever implied, answering well more often than asked.

You can imagine my quandary trying to deal with them in hypotheticals, with, for example, attack mitigation models that marry past experience with future probability. I can't stress enough that the past, in particular, does not exist for them as it does for us. They learn from their experiences, which implies memory, but only in that it informs the eternal and overriding present. Memory seems non-existent in that they move on from disappointment, and from tragedy, with such remarkable dexterity. I've observed this in particular around the deaths of their chicks, for whom, as I've mentioned, they labor devotedly, but who with shocking frequency succumb to some natural cause; or are torn in the teeth or talons of nocturnal predators; or are driven from the nest by cruel siblings. It's the worst sound I've heard in nature, the fallen chick, thumping from one branch to another and then to the earth. But there's a certain stoicism that limits the emotional range in these birds, and for the better. Anger, for example, is checked to tactical aggression. Fear is reduced to more clear-thinking caution. And, as Jill pointed out, they dispense entirely with the completely unhelpful emotions. Disappointment, regret, and self-pity, to name a few – these are just not in their makeup.

28. Jill

Long after I'd taken home my Poohs and suspended my trips to the library and everyone else had stopped bringing in their own children's books, Dr. Morben, who had no children of his own, made his only literary contribution. On the afternoon of P85, after chairing an otherwise unremarkable lunch from his customary spot at the head of the children's table, he produced a worn, leather-bound, pocket-sized volume, and proceeded to read like a thespian:

> Now, fair Hippolyta, our nuptial hour
> Draws on apace. Four happy days bring in
> Another moon — but O methinks how slow
> This old moon wanes! She lingers my desires
> Like to a stepdame or a dowager
> Long withering out a young man's revenue.

I didn't know one Shakespeare play from another, and no camera angle could pluck the title from the obstruction of Morben's massive hand. But suddenly, three seats from my own, Henderson was reciting right along.

> Four days will quickly steep themselves in night,
> Four nights will quickly dream away the time;
> And then the moon, like to a silver bow

New bent in heaven, shall behold the night
Of our solemnities.

At that point I wouldn't have been more surprised if Morben and Henderson had flown around the room like The Chief. "*A Midsummer Night's Dream*," Henderson gasped, with a blush and a quick look to the rest of us. "I played Hippolyta in college."

The footlings had heard nothing like it. And from the look of them, they'd have been happy to hear nothing else, for the rest of their days. With the last bits of cutlery set reverently onto plates, Morben's gentle baritone was the only sound in the nursery PA. None of us had been able to hold their attention reading aloud in many days, but Morben was leaving them speechless. Months later, Richie would tell me that even he, the true bard of the group, couldn't describe the effect of that moment. "I'd say the only introduction even remotely as impactful for me was the song of the butcherbird,[40] and probably not even that."

We were similarly dumbstruck on our side of the glass. Falstaff scrambled to set the text scrolling on the PrismView, and some of us read along, while others kept our eyes on Morben and the footlings. When he'd concluded the first act, Morben returned the book to his pocket and opened the little table for questions. "It's theater," he explained. "I'm reading all the parts here, but the way it really works is that different people play the different parts. Only they don't read them. They memorize them and act them out. It's typically done on a stage, in a theater with seats where other people can sit and watch."

"Can we do that? Can we play the parts?" asked Richie.

---

40 Richie would become obsessed with having me hear the butcherbird song, and always seemed disappointed with what they'd summon when I was on the premises. "For some reason they're just not at their best with you," he'd say. What I did hear was certainly pleasant, but well short of sublime.

"Oh, I think it's a little early for that. Why don't we read some more of the play, and we'll see what you think then."

Morben resumed that evening, and the impromptu dinner theatre continued for several days running. We were as devoted an audience as the footlings, rotating through the local takeaway options to enjoy our Shakespeare with pizza, curry, or gyros. When apprised of Henderson's theatrical background, Morben insisted she join him to read the female parts. On occasion she'd stand to her lines, striding to an imagined center stage, her hands clutched to her heart, clenched to her brow, or pointed to the heavens. In heated exchanges between female characters she'd pivot nimbly to distinguish between the two, adding slight changes in intonation to seal the effect. Even Morben, from time to time, unwound himself from his seat in the thrall of his more impassioned deliveries.

The response, if possible, was more rapt than before. Falstaff had cameras trained on the footlings, and he'd sprinkle certain closeups on the big screen beside the scrolling text – Samantha laughing, Laura gasping, Richie squirming with silent emotion. Morben and Henderson would pause between scenes to walk the footlings through any confusing bits of plot. But they all seemed to follow the action better than we did. At least that was my impression, given their relative calm compared to the feverish consultations on our side of the glass. We'd barely be back up to speed when the reading would begin again and Falstaff would hush us up. If Morben's goal had been to overcome the discontinued catering and keep his staff engaged into the early evening, he could not have done better. We were perched in our seats five nights running, through the play's conclusion on P89.

Perhaps the timing of this dreamy, entangled, and romantic tale was purely coincidental, but the theme of the P91 Little Gathering was love among the footlings. Or, more rigorously phrased, subject sexuality. I noted with some irony that such speculation had been unconscionable when they'd been children, but footling fetish seemed fair game.

Sloboth: Even a cursory examination would lead one to believe that the footlings, in their present condition, have the physical attributes required for intercourse and breeding. The females are full-breasted and just enough developed in the hips. The males are notably pendent – observational consensus indicates a gonadosomatic index far greater than we typically see in adult human males.

Dasher: Objection.

Sloboth: Overruled. And yet, we have several counter-indicators – the lack of hair in the pubic regions or, in fact, anywhere below the shoulders, the failure of the females to menstruate in any discernible manner, and, perhaps most telling, the lack of even the most rudimentary sexual activity to date.

Bitsen: That last point, do we know that for a fact? The night watches have never been particularly vigilant. I'm the first to admit that mine have not. And to my knowledge there's been little or no review of night video.

Sloboth: We see them off to sleep. And we know that those sleeps are almost impregnable.

Dasher: A play on words, Dr. Sloboth?

Sloboth: We know that those sleeps are practically undisturbable.

Dasher: A commonly observed post-coital phenomenon, at least among *homo sapiens*.

Sloboth: Yes, Dr. Dasher, particularly among males. We all appreciate your expertise in the field. The point is, given what we know about the remarkable depths of their sleep, it seems unlikely that they would rouse themselves for any activity, sexual or other.

Dasher: Think back to your own formative years, Dr. Sloboth, and to your own resourcefulness on the matter.

Sloboth: I beg your pardon?

Dasher: Never underestimate the power and perseverance of the reproductive instinct. Untoward activities could well be occurring behind that glass, even *during* sleep. Somnolent shenanigans, as it were.

Sloboth: I'm sure Dr. Falstaff would file this under "areas where we have no specific indications to the contrary," and should therefore default to accepted rules of nature. Even you will concede that mammals are generally awake during intercourse.

Bitsen: I would hope so.

Sloboth: Even if Dr. Dasher is correct, it only reinforces our need to discuss birth control strategies. Waiting to the point of sexual activity, if it isn't upon us already, would be grossly irresponsible.

Me: We don't even know if the footlings are fertile. They don't grow, so what are they going to do, give birth to creatures their own size?

Dasher: In that case we'll have to insist on C-sections.

Sloboth: There's plenty we don't know about their reproductive capacities – estrous cycles, gestation period, litter size...

Me: Litter size?

Sloboth: Yes. For planning purposes we need to assume a natural conception model. When you compare the footlings to other mammals in their weight class, it's natural to suppose that the offspring would come in litters.

Dasher: Ah, many little footlings. All of whom would presumably share the HGH deficiency.

Me: And would then give birth to even smaller pups.

Henderson: As depicted in Seuss.[41] Little Cats A, B, and C, steadily decreasing. Little Cat Z being microscopic.

Me: In which case our problem is self-resolving.

Dasher: Maybe we should have Dmitri work up some tiny condoms.

---

41 *The Cat in the Hat Comes Back* (1958).

Falstaff: Dmitri's a fine engineer —

Dasher: And a helluva track and field guy —

Fasltaff: But he's not a contraceptionist.

Dasher: Is that even a word?

Me: If it isn't it should be.

Bitsen: Do you say he's not a contraceptionist because he's got a bunch of kids running around at home?

Falstaff: No, in fact, he doesn't have any kids, running or stationary. I say it because he works exclusively with metals.

Dasher: Wholly unsuitable for condoms.

Bitsen: Perhaps we could instill a firm commitment to abstention.

Dasher: Yes, very good. We'll introduce the notion of sin. Venial and mortal. Old school stuff. Eternal damnation, flames of hell.

Me: I think they passed the period of gross naïveté sometime in the P20s.

Sloboth: Maybe we should start with some simple procedural changes. Underwear. Separate sleeping quarters.

Dasher: We'd have some habits to break on that one. Every day here starts with the Roman orgy morning after, the seven of them draped all over each other.

Me: Many animals sleep in clusters with no sexual overtones whatsoever. Crocodiles, sea lions, rattlesnakes...

Dasher: Believe me, we've got overtones in there.

Sloboth: It might be just the blue lighting.

29. Richie

No sooner had I mentioned the emotional resilience of the birds than I noticed a somber and lingering undertone in the trees, a general melancholy that ran against my eight hundred days of prior observation. Granted, I'd seen plenty to justify it, this season and in breeding seasons before, to the point where I'd wondered how they hadn't developed a better sense of night security over the generations. Their system just seems so vulnerable with the nests open and effectively unguarded while the whole flock sleeps. And while incidents in the dark are generally lost to me, I see the mornings' remnants of terror, the baby body parts in the grass and the agitation in the parents, which I'd place somewhere between disorientation and distress. But that agitation has always been limited to certain factions of certain flocks, and to a short period of time, an hour or so at most. The mornings are such a glorious time here with the first shock of color and the warming sun that even the most aggrieved among them seem to spring back to life like it's the first day they've lived.

But this time the whole morning song was reduced to lament, and for several days running. It ran across all three resident species, as if any loss suffered by one was shared by the others. The early drop-ins at my sill were even more fleeting than before, alighting for no more than a second or two, just long enough to confirm me in my place before flying off without greeting or comment. It wasn't until the heat of midday that they'd return to their normal activities and resilient demeanors. You can imagine my curiosity, but they weren't going to revisit the horrors for my benefit, and my sleeping patterns wouldn't accommodate a personal night watch. I doubted I'd ever really get to the bottom of it.

But one morning I awoke to an utter cacophony, a racket so violent that I covered my ears and wondered how I'd slept as long as I had. Every bird on the compound seemed to have gathered in the branches near my window, and every one of them was shrilling at the top of its lungs. The effect was one I'll never forget, an overwhelming wall of sound in the middle of the range and dozens of individual shrills above that, high-pitched and piercing. They were as thick as leaves in those trees, likely the entire population of magpies, butchers, and miners over several acres. They'd positioned themselves in concentric spheres around a shapeless lump that I soon identified as a brushtail possum, holding motionless to an upper limb. All the birds were shrieking, but the attacks were left to a select few magpie males. I could see that group in its own ring closest to the possum, working in rotation to deliver blows on or around its head.

I'd never seen a possum except in pictures. It was a hulking thing, much bigger than I'd imagined, big enough to look badly out of place that high in the tree. It was frozen in a protective hunch, its rear aspect oriented toward me. What I could see of it was hideous, a coarse brown coat, grotesque hairless testicles, and a long tail with a hairless tip that gave the impression of an intestinal worm working free. Though my view to the front was obscured, I made out what I took to be a bloody chick in its mouth. If so, this seemed the very absence of judgment. The beast was too stubborn to let go, but too beleaguered to chew and swallow, and the ongoing spectacle of the dangling chick had to be inciting the flock to an ever-greater frenzy.

I couldn't understand how the nocturnal possum had come to be there in the first place. Had it simply missed its curfew in a careless extension of the late-night feeding? That was the only explanation I could muster. No evolved creature would willingly put itself in this situation. And given the error, if that's what it was, the response strategy seemed equally imprudent. Sitting still to absorb blow after blow, one every couple of seconds for minutes at a time, was tantamount to suicide. Perhaps it expected that the birds would lose interest in the face of its dogged stillness. But that was proving very much in error. The horrors of the last many nights were playing out with a vengeance unlikely to abate.

The possum had an unnatural ability to take punishment – I'll give it that. Blows rained down on its head and neck to a point that became difficult to watch. To this day I don't know how it managed to protect its eyes. But eventually, and to my astonishment, the birds *did* lose interest, or at least conviction. It wasn't simply fatigue – even if the original attackers were spent, countless others were in position to replace them. It was a flaw in their hierarchy. If the alpha males couldn't get it done, others weren't at liberty to step in. And on that basis, the possum had its opening. The wormish tail, in its particularly awful way, reached for an adjoining branch, and with that for leverage the possum reversed itself, surprisingly composed. It set to its retreat, if you can really describe a creature so apparently unhurt, unbowed and unrepentant to be in retreat. I noticed with some distress that its course ran along a branch leading directly to my sill. That was definitely a bloody chick in its mouth, dead but still pliable, and bouncing repulsively at both ends with every step.

I had an overwhelming urge to reach out and confirm the integrity of my aged and slightly corroded screen. I didn't, for fear that any movement would invite the beast's attention. But it noticed me anyway, with an interest far greater than its circumstances would sensibly allow. It pressed its head to the mesh, distending it horribly, its eyes leering grotesquely into mine. It sniffed wetly, its foul breath engulfing me and mixing with another pungency I realized, after a moment of puzzlement, was my own glandular output, the distinctive and repulsive scent of my most primal fears. I should have been scampering down the lines, but I stood there stupefied, staking everything, by default, on that screen. Against all odds, it held. The beast pivoted and settled on the sill. It could try me again later, redouble its efforts at a more opportune moment. But for now it had turned back to the several dozen birds, with an attitude, remarkably enough, of simple annoyance. I could see the head of the chick undulating with its killer's steady breathing. The overall effect was one of deliberate provocation, the closest thing to contempt I'd seen in nature. The birds held their positions, still gathered but no longer pressing. And while the shrilling persisted, the volume was dropping, a steady concession to shame and defeat.

Freed of the possum's face in my own, I began to feel like myself again -- or rather, like a slightly altered version of myself. I was indignant at the bristles of the massive hindquarters sticking through my screen, and even as I retched at its loathsome stench, I felt a rage building within me – rage at the carnage, rage at the insolence, rage at my own perpetual meekness. I was suddenly steeled to a purpose, gauging the several openings in the screen with the coolness of a killer. I rose to my feet and reached for my paring knife. The beauty of that implement, I reflected, wasn't its blade or its maneuverability, though both were excellent in their own right. It was the grip. I could get my hands a good way around, and its finely ribbed texture provided a no-slip quality I admired.

We'd never gotten to the pole vault back at Genesis, but we'd seen the videos. I took the starting position I remembered, backing to the very edge of my sill, bending at the knees and waist, weight slightly forward, the implement held level before me. Two hard steps, a cry, a thrust, and the blade was through the gap and deep into flesh. The beast sprang from the sill, and in the same instant I yanked back at the handle. My grip held firm, and I was fortunate not to tumble off the sill in the recoil. If not for the counterweight of the weapon I would surely have fallen. I leapt back to the screen, pressing my face for the best look down. And there, far below me, the possum shuffled off in a pronounced limp. The stab, the fall, or both – one way or another I'd inflicted an injury that was somewhere beyond superficial.

What followed I'll never forget. The birds went deathly silent, a silence all the more stunning for the racket that had sounded since I'd first awakened. Every bird faced me directly. A butcher began a chirp I recognized as the song of tribute. All of them took it up, the volume rising as it had before, an overwhelming drone at the mid-range with a few select voices sounding higher, each of them curiously in focus. I stood square to face them and lifted the paring knife overhead, my best attempt at a salute.

30. Jill

Our sex talk at the Little Gathering may have set a few things in motion. On P94, a thick package arrived for Manly. I happened to sign for it, and noticed the return address of a prominent law firm known to do a lot of work with BioSpore. Manly sat at the far other end, but I had him on Camera 16 when he opened the document. He flipped through some pages, took a quick look around, and stuffed it in his bag, presumably for a longer look later.

Early the next morning, he and Morben slipped into the amphitheater as if by prior arrangement. This attempt at discretion was so unusual in our open culture that it had the exactly opposite effect, grabbing everyone's attention at once. They emerged after twenty minutes, both of them agitated.

Morben was subdued, even by his standards, for the next several hours. Word began to circulate -- even in our small group I had no idea where it originated -- but by all accounts Manly had a new and independent agenda, one that might not sit well with the rest of us. Just after noon, Dr. Henderson got into a heated conversation at Manly's desk. I was considering how to work myself discreetly into earshot when Dasher, Sloboth and Bitsen walked over with no regard whatsoever. I followed them directly.

Me (to Bitsen): What's happening?

Henderson (to me): Manly has instructions to neuter the four males.

Manly (to all of us): And I'm not looking for any discussion on the point. This is straight from the top.

Me: Whoa, I guess they've been watching the Little Gatherings after all.

Sloboth (to Manly): You're doing this personally? What qualifies a pediatrician to perform vasectomies?

Manly: I'm not doing vasectomies. In this case that would be something approaching microsurgery. Not my area of expertise.

Bitsen: So what's the plan?

Manly: Standard male neutering. Bilateral orchiectomies.

The room erupted as never before. I caught a glimpse of Morben running over – he looked like a daddy longlegs at full gallop. It took him the better part of a minute to bring us to order.

Sloboth: What are you, some kind of savage? You can't just go around castrating people!

Manly: As a reminder, these aren't, strictly speaking, people.

Me: Oh, come on.

Manly: It's not a particularly difficult procedure. Don't tell me none of you have pets. And there's no question that it needs doing. Dr. Sloboth, you were the one championing birth control just the other day.

Sloboth: Castration, in this case, is not an acceptable form of birth control.

Manly: For virtually every domesticated species it's the *only* form of birth control. I've ordered the equipment. When it arrives you'll all be dismissed from the premises until further notice. Security's been instructed accordingly.

Sloboth: By whose authority?

Manly: Mine as presiding medical officer.

Dasher: Per the charter, that kind of authority is triggered only in cases of medical necessity. There's no such provision for elective procedures.[42]

Bitsen: Not that any of this is the slightest bit elective from their point of view.

Manly: The procedures have been deemed both mandatory and urgent.

Dasher: By whom?

Manly: By the only medical officer with authority on the project.

Me: I thought you said this was coming from the top. Which is it?

Manly: It's my decision, Ms. Edelman.

Falstaff: With a certain corporate remuneration involved in its formation.

Heavy pause.

Bitsen: What about hormonal contraceptives for the females?

Manly: We have no idea about safe doses or effective doses, and frankly we're in no position to be experimenting here.

Me: Hasn't there been some recent progress on the chemical sterilization of males?

Manly: Not that I'm aware of. Do you have any particular information on the point?

Me: No.[43]

Pause.

Me: You need to bring in a microprocedure specialist.

Manly: Unfortunately, Ms. Edelman, no one has the experience to justify that kind of security breach. Micro-vasectomies aren't generally performed in the medical community. Nor are tiny tubal ligations,

---

42 I looked it up later, and Dasher was absolutely correct. I could not have been more impressed.

43 I'm afraid I reddened slightly at this point. More on this later.

miniscule IUD implants, or anything else of the sort. That shouldn't come as a great surprise, even to you.

Dasher: No one has experience with footling anesthetics, either. You'll be completely winging it.

Sloboth: Yes, what is the anesthetic plan?

Manly: Strictly local.

Dasher: Even dogs and cats get general anesthesia during spaying.

Manly: Too dangerous in this case. We just don't have any history for determining dosage.

Dasher: You don't have history with local anesthetics either.

Manly: That's correct, though it entails much less risk. I've consulted the veterinary literature to determine the drugs and dosage most likely to succeed.

Dasher: What about sedation?

Manly: Far too dangerous in this case. The local anesthetic should do the job.

Dasher: You mean it'll have to.

Me: Jesus, are you planning to use restraints?

Manly: Let's not be overly dramatic here. I'm under no obligation to present you people with the entire surgical plan. I'm comfortable with it, and that should suffice. I'm the only medical doctor on this staff. I have the only authority and the only relevant expertise.

Me: As it pertains to numbness in the groin, I'm sure that's true.

Sloboth (to Morben): Any chance we could bring back Dr. Hayes?

Henderson: I assume we'll be explaining this all to the children beforehand?

Manly: Absolutely not. It's a simple, time-honored procedure. There's no call for pre-surgical consultation.

Henderson: There'll be permanent physiological and psychological effects.

Manly: That may be, but it's still a mandatory procedure. And it doesn't require consent. The likely outcome of unnecessary consultation is pre-surgical stress, resistance, and increased risk.

Henderson: The almost certain outcome of no consultation is exacerbated psychological trauma.

Manly: They're not going to be happy in either case.

Henderson: But there are ongoing issues here of trust, violation, and betrayal.

Manly: My charge here is to optimize the chances of surgical success. Once the medical procedures are completed you educators and counselors can do as you wish. Until then, you're all forbidden to discuss the matter with the footlings.

We all looked to Dr. Morben. He nodded in unhappy agreement.

31. Richie

The next morning's birdsong – at least what I heard from the adults – was the cheeriest in many days. I enjoyed what I could of it, but the chicks were as insufferable as ever, too ignorant to appreciate that they'd not been reduced to possum fodder. I rolled on my side to admire the light in the leaves, but my glance fell instead to the mass of insects on my sill. In the hours after I'd routed the possum, the birds had set me a quantity large enough to obscure much of the wooden surface. At its peak it'd been a teeming swarm, but most of the offerings had expired mercifully in the night. Give or take a few little twitches, the mass now lay inert. I felt a little guilty about the waste, though the sheer volume had made that inevitable, even if I were inclined to eat bugs. Because the birds had left them on the sill and not poked them through the screen – another sign of my newly won respect? – I hadn't bothered with my normal charade of knocking them to the floor and chasing down after. And I might not have in any case. In the wake of my conquest I felt decidedly less interested in currying their favor.

Rolling back from the screen, I lifted my paring knife for consideration. I'd intentionally not wiped it clean of the possum blood, which had now congealed. This left an unappealing tool for cutting breakfast, but it didn't much bother me. I scrabbled awkwardly down the sill lines with the dirk in one hand, resolving to ask Jill for needle and thread to make myself a scabbard. I bypassed the slippers and skipped the fire. I trotted directly to the cat door instead, pleased to feel some warmth flow into me from just that simple exertion. The skeletal umbrella beckoned from its normal spot, but I left it where it stood. Wielding the knife in its place, I pushed through to the outdoors.

With the house protecting me on one side and my blade flashing on the other, I felt, if not invincible, then passably secure. I didn't even trouble to walk in my usual defensive manner, scuttling sideways with my backside pressed to the wall. But when it came time to veer away and out into open territory, I began to think it hadn't been such a good idea to leave the umbrella. I envisioned not only the familiar attack from the air, but now a ground attack as well, the possum charging like a spittle-spewing rhinoceros, its eyes asquint with the bloodlust of revenge. When neither materialized, I felt relief, gratification, and, to my surprise, a tinge of disappointment. The birds weren't much for reflection, but was one more chorus, even the most cursory morning-after song of tribute, really too much to ask? Instead, from the branches above, came two glops of anonymous excrement, one hitting to my immediate left and one to my slightly less immediate right. "Keep it in your cloacas," I snarled, pointing my blade to the trees. I immediately regretted both the comment and the gesture. While the birds couldn't understand in any specific sense, I'd been around long enough to know that there was always meaning in tone, and in the odd threatening gesture with a blade.

But my luck was holding. While I myself am not blessed with a cloaca, I was able to empty my own anatomical equivalent without incident. I felt a sense of empowerment in doing this more or less as I pleased, before breakfast, without the bother of a fire, and without weathering a series of assaults. What better time, at last, to expand my range? I pulled up my pants, kicked a few blades of grass behind me – this a ridiculously ineffective nod to hygiene, recidivist behavior from the ancient days of Genesis litter — and set off to the west. A grassy incline topped off some fifty meters distant. I'd never seen over it.

My stride was confident, even brash, but I was quickly into a military mind trick. Twelve steps to a meter made six hundred, and I counted every one of them, a distraction from the spittle-spewing possum with its telltale limp and the twin specters of disfigurement and death. As I neared the crest I had the laughable notion I might drop to my belly and crawl, but I'd no idea I'd actually do it until I did. There was nothing humorous, or soothing, about scrabbling along with my face in the earth. I released another pungent cloud, my second glandular voiding in as many days, both of them involuntary, this one even more repulsive than the first. How counter-selective it seemed, skunks notwithstanding, to raise an olfactory flag at the critical moment, pinpointing one's position for one's large and toothy stalker. As it happened, no such stalker was anywhere near. I reached the crest, and at last I had my view.

The land sloped away, and there before me were hundreds of trees, not scattered and clumped in the randomized way of nature, but ordered and spaced as if by some greater design. I'd seen this sort of thing at Genesis, in our many images of agriculture. An orchard, they called it, trees planted all at a time and cultivated for their fruits. As I drew closer I could see that this one was not nearly as neat as those I'd seen in pictures. Several trees had toppled at their roots, their underparts bared, dessicated, and clumped with dirt. Countless limbs lay shorn and scattered about the grounds. Others hung broken and despondent, clinging in futility, the visual definition of the lost cause. I wasn't more than a few rows into the trees when I myself was knocked to the ground. I leapt to my feet, shouted, and waved my blade in rage. But my stage anger didn't translate to intimidation, or to deterrence. I went down twice more, struck from behind each time, never laying eyes, let alone a blow, on an attacker. My narrow field of vision was having its normal detrimental effect, but it was vanity, leaving the umbrella for the sword, that had put me in this position. I rose for the third time, wielding the blade in two hands and taking two steps toward home. Certain of another attack from the rear and acting completely on impulse, I spun one full rotation on my left foot, scanning my full perimeter, albeit with blurry, imperfect results. Three more steps and I spun again, slowly enough this time to maintain my vision, just quickly enough to maintain my balance. Four more steps and another spin, this time with a corresponding loop of the blade overhead – this improved my balance while conferring, I thought, a certain panache to the maneuver. I hadn't done this much spinning since we'd thrown the discus, and was pleasantly surprised to feel less dizzy than I had then. I'd hit upon the ideal frequency, one spin every four steps. Any more frequent and I risked my equilibrium. Any less frequent and I compromised my coverage.

I carried up the incline, perfecting my pirouettes as I went. Twenty meters out I recorded my first interception, a magpie swooping in from what had been my rear. He seemed startled to be seen, pulled up, and settled back on a branch, suitably chagrined. Eight hundred days in, and it was the first time I'd managed anything of the sort.

32. Jill

Others followed Hayes and Scott into reallocation, leaving more empty workstations and just seven of us in regular attendance – Dasher, Bitsen, Sloboth, Henderson, Falstaff, Morben, and me. Manly had been ostracized to the point where he'd begun to absent himself for the better part of each day. None of us knew when his dreaded equipment might arrive, but we understood that when it did we'd be escorted promptly from the premises. The prospect cast a pall over all of us. And yet, for all the gloom, something beautiful was taking root.

Morben and Henderson, on continuous prodding from the children, had begun to organize a stage production, an act or two from *A Midsummer Night's Dream*. In their first halting hour, as the footlings struggled through their opening lines and stepped stiffly through their paces, the last sad vestiges of our individual ventures began to slip away. When Henderson's scheduled hour expired, I waved her on, ceding my own. Bitsen and Sloboth followed in turn, and suddenly the whole concept of assigned hours, the backbone of our operational structure to date, had collapsed, swept away in the wave of this single, suddenly unified production. The day belonged fully to the stage, as did the next, and the next. The arrangement, spontaneous as it was, suited both footlings and specialists alike.

While the footlings assumed all the theatrical roles, each of us dove into some facet of the production. Morben and Henderson were co-directing. They seemed perfectly paired in the endeavor, never stepping on each other's toes, seizing on the best of each other's ideas, plying their personal quirks to prod the best from the cast. Bitsen and Sloboth morphed into dialogue coaches, drilling the young actors on their lines, both individually and in small dramatic groups, and doing so with a steady, indispensable cheer. It was largely their doing that the footlings responded so brilliantly to the dialogue and the memorization, and that we expanded our production to the whole play.

Falstaff managed lighting and sound to astounding effect. His command of spots and darkness obviated the need for curtains and offstage areas — the actors simply stepped into the light and then back into the void. Dasher, who'd suspended his pursuit of athletic immortality with unexpected grace, leapt back into choreography, chasing a spritely brand of dance with more energy, if that were possible, than he'd brought to the line.

I directed logistics. This, I found, was as close to my natural calling as anything I'd experienced. As one day wound down, I'd consult with the various parties to pull together a rough schedule for the next. I'd finalize it that evening, and present it at the Little Gathering in the morning.[44] That might generate a few suggestions, a few clarifications, and a few tweaks. But the adjustments were minor and the meetings uneventful. I'd post the final schedule on the PrismView and fix a hard copy to an old-school clipboard, which I'd brandish through the day, browbeating the participants in an unending crusade for compliance. Overbearing as I may have been, everyone seemed to take it in the spirit intended.

---

44 While we suspended the Tiny Gatherings during these theatrical pursuits, the Little Gatherings survived in the form of daily production meetings. My chairing them was a great relief to Morben, who was too immersed with the muses to concern himself with administrative detail.

We broke the day into fifteen-minute segments, with breaks at mid-morning, lunch,[45] and mid-afternoon. Morben and Henderson often filled roles so certain actors might break away, singly or in pairs, to be tutored on their lines or walked though their choreography.

The dedication of the footlings was every bit the match of ours. From the moment they awoke until bedtime thirteen hours later, they were constantly in role, or rather, in roles, given that they were each playing several parts. Richie couldn't walk by any of us without the greeting that was his first line of the play, "Happy be Theseus, our renowned Duke!" At any spare moment, two or three of them would pull together to rehearse dialogue. Snappy exchanges came easily to them. It was the longer speeches where they'd tend to bog down and lose the thread. "When you've got a section you're struggling with, you have to attack it," Henderson urged. "Take your biggest weakness and work it into a strength. That's when you're really making progress."

Looking back on it now, it's hard to explain the urgency we all seemed to feel in pushing this production. Maybe theater just does that to people – outside of Genesis I've no experience in the matter. From the specialists' standpoint, and I had this conversation with two or three of them, the footlings' astounding rate of progress was inspiration enough. In a matter of days they were bellowing and cackling, strutting and enunciating like accomplished Shakespeareans. And with the Project in its death rattle, I suppose we all needed this final act for closure, and for some form of validation. As for the footlings, they knew nothing of BioSpore politics, but even they could sense the change in the air, and maybe, to some extent, the end of their adolescence, however brief it had been.

---

45 I'd pressed the other specialists for personal contributions, and pitched in myself, to reinstate the noon catering.

P96 was our fourth day of rehearsal. Six of us sat waiting in the amphitheater for Morben to appear for the Little Gathering. He was a man of extreme punctuality, so his running even three minutes late was a cause of some concern. I was heading out to check on him when he opened the door and stepped to one side. I didn't see them at first – my glance, naturally, was aimed too high. But there in single file, and oddly on stride, were Kirk and Uhura, Rob and Laura, Samantha and Darrin. They looked straight ahead, without expression, elite infantry on parade before the gentry. Richie brought up the rear, slightly out of step, his head swiveling by degrees.

It was the first time any of them had been out of the nursery. Strangely enough, we'd never really discussed the possibility. But for slight drops in temperature (they'd prove more robust in that regard than we'd thought) and the risk of their actually escaping outdoors (a virtual impossibility given the setup of the doors) there was no compelling reason to keep them behind the glass. Morben swung the door shut and followed them into the room. "Seven little ducklings and papa giraffe," said Dasher. No one laughed, not because it wasn't funny, but because it was so perfectly accurate. Morben was truly enormous trailing his little troop.

"Rather than rehashing everything, I thought it made more sense if the cast heard the schedule first-hand," Morben said coolly, as if it were perfectly normal to have seven footlings drop into our production meeting. They passed in front of the podium and, without a word, hopped several steps up the aisle. Their aptitude as leapers was more striking in this kind of everyday setting than in staged athletics. I remember a feeling of admiration at first, but then a tinge of nausea, or vertigo, as I watched these tiny human forms springing so unnaturally, like a swarm of oversized locusts. They sat all in a row, legs dangling, maybe eight steps up, high enough to give them a good vantage point. Their faces gave no indication that anything remarkable was going on – even Richie had fallen in with the rest.

"Go ahead, Ms. Edelman," said Morben. "Proceed as usual."

I ran the meeting as I always had, or at least I tried to. The footlings didn't miss a beat, and weren't afraid to chime right in. "I think it's about time we had all seven of us in choreography. Can't we do that?" And, "I don't think we can go straight from choreography into Scene Two rehearsal. We're going to need a break." And, "Wouldn't this be a good opportunity for me to do my dialogue drills with Samantha, since she's really not a big part of Scene Three?"

All the suggestions made sense, and perhaps I was a little irritated I hadn't thought of them myself. But they entailed more changes to my schedule than I was used to. "The little prima donnas are full of ideas this morning," I said. It came off more grumpily than I would have liked.

"What's a prima donna?"

"Never mind," I said. "I'm only joking. I'm really happy to have you in the meeting, and your ideas are all good ones."

My apologetic tone had fallen a little flat. An awkward silence followed while I took a moment to revise the schedule. Dr. Morben rose to request a moment at the podium, and I was more than happy to oblige. "Thank you, Ms. Edelman," he said. "We appreciate everything you do to keep us on schedule. I'm sure we can all agree it's no easy chore." I thought for a moment he was being ironic, but that was not like Morben.

"Bravo!" said Dasher. A few others called out in support. I stole a look at the footlings – they were quietly applauding with the others. I blushed what I knew to be a deep crimson.

Morben let me squirm for a period of inhumane duration, ten seconds at least. "Now I have an important announcement," he said, pausing again just long enough for my ears to cool. "We've secured a very special venue for our performance. High-ranking people have made extraordinary concessions, and the arrangements are in place. We have use of the Icosagon, any day this week. It's only after business hours – not before 18:00. And we need to give security a couple hours' notice. Beyond that, we're good to go."

We all exchanged astonished looks. How could a project in its death throes score such a corporate coup? And given the confidentiality imperative, how could we expose the footlings like that? I'd find later that everyone was as dumbfounded as I was, with the exception of Dasher. Prior experience with Morben had given him unique insight. "Moribund has some surprising clout in BioSpore's higher echelons," he'd tell me. "More than you'd ever expect."

"For those of us who don't know the Icosagon," – Morben turned to the footlings – "it's believed to be the most authentic replica of a Shakespearean theater in the entire country, and by some estimates, in all the world. And it's our great fortune to have that theater just a few minutes' drive from here." We all nodded. "In a car," he added, clarifying for the footlings.

Morben popped the virtual Icosagon tour on the screen. We were outside at first, panning the whitewashed plaster walls, the laths and staves, the weather-blackened thatch roof, the gables with their flapping pennants. We approached, paused, and panned up for one last exterior look, this from a tight angle, making the walls even more formidable, the most pertinent view, I reflected, for the footlings. We passed through the wooden gates, up the aisle, and onto the straw-strewn floor of the open-air pit. There we stood for a full 360-degree pan – three tiers of seating, impressively steep, and catwalks and trusses and dozens of theater lights.

"Just like the lights we have here," said Kirk.

"Yes," said Morben. "Everything will be just as we've practiced, except that when your part is done, instead of stepping out of the light you have to step all the way off the stage, out of the audience's view. We'll go over all that."

Morben made a slight shift with the controller, to the effect that we'd suddenly leapt onto the stage, with its rough wooden floorboards and its exits left and right. From that vantage point we panned the seating area once again, then exited to a holding area and a well-appointed dressing room with plush stools and a well-lit mirror.

"Where's the litter?" asked Rob. No one answered for a moment. "Did you ever notice," he went on, "that when you get a little nervous, sometimes you have to pee?" We all had a good laugh.

33. Richie

On her next visit, Jill seemed impressed with my having wandered as far as the orchard.

"I just wanted to see over the crest," I said. "I was surprised to find all those trees standing in their rows. I'm planning to go out there again now that I can defend myself a little better." I grabbed my blade and demonstrated, once again, my new pirouetting technique.

"I didn't know you'd studied the samurai," she said, amused in a way I didn't much appreciate. She could be a little demeaning. And she wasn't much for apologies. But she'd generally sense when she'd gone over the line and move quickly to change her tone. "And yes, it must have been a nice little orchard in its day. Mostly avocado and mango trees, I was told, along with a few macadamias and oranges. They're all pretty much ruined from age and neglect, as I'm sure you could see. We can walk down there together if you want."

I took her up on that, and we proceeded under the cover of her full-sized umbrella. It protected us, in her view, from the blistering sun, and in my view, from winged marauders. I imagined the orchard to be teeming with them, though while I'd been attacked my first time through, I'd not actually been mobbed. But I'd never been attacked at all around Jill, and I felt good enough in short stints to venture out of her cover.

"Would you mind if I tried a little climb?"

She stood by while I eyed a particularly inviting avocado tree. I felt it with my hands, pawed it with my feet. The holds seemed good, so I started right up. It wasn't much tougher than climbing my lines. I walked out at the first branch and jumped into the relative softness of the grass at Jill's feet.

"Pretty good," she said. "I guess we should have had a couple trees in the nursery."

We walked a little further and I noticed a branch hanging low and bare, an invitation. I took three running steps and leapt up onto it. Both feet stuck, but my weight was too far back. I recovered in the only way I could, by dropping and catching the branch in a clamp between my arms and ribs. That hurt, but I tried to ignore it and pulled myself up. I walked back and forth along the branch and dropped again to the grass.

"Impressive," she said. "Now you're going to have to work on those landings."

I leapt again at the next opportunity, sticking the landing this time. A series of similar maneuvers took me further up the tree. Working the perimeter that way made a better show for Jill than if I'd just scrabbled up the trunk. Sometimes I could just reach up for the next branch, but usually I'd have to jump for it, or work laterally for better angles. The lateral leaps were pretty basic. But vertical jumping from one branch to another proved a bruising endeavor. I landed cleanly only about half the time, and on the misses I'd slip painfully to my shins, or catch the branch in that brutal clamp between arms and ribs. I didn't dare stray too far up – Jill's umbrella, after all, wasn't going to protect me at ten meters. And with Jill as an audience I probably did more that first day than I should have. But there was more to it than just impressing her. I liked the physical exertion and the excitement of going up, of changing one's grounded perspective. And I liked the tactical focus, the reduction of all life to a series of simple choices.

We wandered to the far edge of the orchard and found a few trees that were still bearing. The mangos were too green, Jill said, and we didn't pick any of those, though I dropped one at her feet for a laugh. But she grabbed a few avocados and we filled a little cloth bag she had with macadamias we'd gathered in the grass. It had a strap that fit nicely over my shoulder. "That's a nice little rucksack for you," she said. "You should keep it." Nice as it was, the nuts were heavy enough that I had to switch shoulders after a few dozen steps back toward the house. I'd already walked to the orchard and all through it, and happily accepted when she offered me a ride the rest of the way. I was feeling the effects of all that climbing, and I hadn't been up on her shoulder in ages. I settled in like I'd done so many times before. It was just as I remembered, her familiar scent, the touch of her hair, the lobes of her ear. I enjoyed the perspective from that height and the gentle sway of her gait.

For the longest time we couldn't crack those macadamias. Jill sat on the edge of her Adirondack chair with a glass of wine on one of its arms, gripping a pair of pliers with both hands between her legs. Her face went red, but the nuts were unfazed. She tried cracking them "caveman style," setting them on a boulder shelf and bringing another stone down with both hands. This crushed them completely, producing bite-sized bits for me but nothing useful for her. Finally she went to whacking away with a hammer, but they wouldn't sit still for her, shooting to the side at impact. One of them hit me on the hip, and I contorted, teetered over, and played dead. That was one of the best laughs we ever had in East Central. She refined her hammer work soon after, tempering the blows to produce a fault line, then a crack, and at last an opening. It was a cool enough day, and we settled our chairs around the boulder in the late-day sun, cracking and nibbling at our leisure. All throughout, a kookaburra sat on a branch just overhead, not in hunting mode, but as Jill said, "well into his feathery siesta." We shared her bottle of sparkling water. It burned a bit on the way down, but by the end I was well used to it.

34. Jill

The tip-off came on P100. We were into our eighth day of rehearsals, just after lunch, when Falstaff missed a lighting cue and left the cast hanging for a good thirty seconds in half darkness. I was looking toward his station, trying to make him out in the dark, when I saw him strolling across the nursery floor.

"Dr. Falstaff," I said through the PA. "This is not a scheduled break."

He waved me politely off and went into consultation with Morben. Within minutes the seven of us we were all in the amphitheater.

Falstaff: Dmitri has a friend looking out for us in Logistics. Manly's surgical gear is scheduled for delivery this evening. My guess is he'll do the procedures in the morning.

My heart sank – I guess some part of me had been counting on a last-minute stay. Morben and Henderson remained commendably on task.

Morben: I was hoping we'd sneak in an extra day or two, but we'll have to give it a go as we are.

Henderson: Meaning you want to do the performance tonight?

Morben: I think it's our best shot.

Henderson: We're not ready. Why not wait until after the procedures?

Morben: It's going to be a long way back for them, in more ways than one. They're not likely to take well to it, not likely to return in the same frame of mind. And by the time they get there, if they do, I doubt we'll have another shot at the Icosagon. They're all looking forward to it, and in my view their hard work should be rewarded.

Me: If that's what you want to do, I suggest we tell the children now and give them the rest of the afternoon off. They can review their lines if they'd like, walk some things through, or just relax, whatever they think is best.

Everyone seemed to agree.

Me (to Morben): I assume you'll personally want to notify security. Falstaff and I will handle the rest of the logistics. How do you propose we transport them?

Morben: I've modified a cat box – it's out in my car. If we have Manly's timing right, by the time the play's over we won't be allowed back in here. So we should all take our cars and plan to head straight home afterwards.

I spent an hour alone with Richie that afternoon. We both knew he needed work on his first speech, the first long speech of the play, two hundred words that set the stage for all the action that followed. We'd worked on it privately before, and he struggled now, just as he always had. But this time I made a conscious effort to limit my corrections, thinking confidence more important than precision in these final hours.

At 17:40, the whole troupe had assembled for departure. Morben had the footlings buckled in their box. They sat grim-faced in two rows, backs to both sidewalls. I couldn't help the impression of infantry in an armored personnel carrier, headed onto a path of peril. But just before they were packed away, Richie met my eye with an encouraging nod. "Happy be Theseus," he said, and then, in a muffled tone from under the lid, "our renowned Duke!"

We pulled out in a string of cars, and held the line as we went, moving in convoy, ramping onto the highway and off two exits later. Morben cleared us all at the security station, and we rumbled onto campus. We may have driven boring practical cars,[46] but we did so with admirable precision, wheeling into seven consecutive spots near the theatre gates.

Henderson, Sloboth and Bitsen would be the staffers backstage. Henderson would suffice as backstage director – Morben couldn't bear to miss the view from out front. Sloboth and Bitsen would handle the madness of the wardrobe changes driven by the actors' all playing multiple characters. At the back of the pit, Falstaff would work the soundboard, a giant panel of switches, slide levers, and lights rising strangely from the straw-strewn floor. Dasher, Morben, and I were left to make up the audience. The three of us took the center section in the first tier, leaving seats between us to look as expansive as possible. Morben rested his feet on the chairback two rows in front of him – Henderson would later tell me he looked like a small crowd all by himself. Dmitri strolled in just after we did. I hadn't seen him in some time, and was pleasantly surprised to see him now. He smiled a wordless greeting and took a seat next to Falstaff. In addition to handling lights and sound, they'd be filming the production. With no prior access to the facility we hadn't managed any technical rehearsals, or Q-2-Q sessions as Falstaff called them, so they were reviewing Falstaff's annotated script and familiarizing themselves with the equipment as best they could.

There was only one other person in attendance. I'd seen him walk in just after Dmitri, just before we'd heard the gates rattle closed. With his silk print shirt, sunglasses, and impressive Afro he might have been Lincoln Hayes from *The Mod Squad* – but you had to get past the fact that he was short, white, and duck-footed. He climbed all the way to the third tier, stage left, and began moving to the center. I said, "That wouldn't be Chuck

---

46 Dasher was the exception, with a luxury vehicle that would keep his kids out of private school for years.

Hansen, would it?" But with the steepness of the tiers he'd gone from our view.

It being the heart of the California winter, the sun was in full retreat. The sky was a quilt of reds and oranges, and the diminutive cast members, in a slight professional lapse, wandered on-stage for a long look.

"We should have gotten them out a little more," I said. "Especially at this time of night."

"You're right," said Morben and Dasher in unison.

The biggest threat, after all, wasn't forgotten lines, technical error, or bungled choreography. It was the cast going to sleep on the set. They hadn't been up past dark in their lives, and this show wouldn't even have begun by day's end.

Ill met by moonlight, proud Titania!

We fairly jumped out of our seats. It was sound check, Kirk bellowing as proud King Oberon. The footlings all wore tiny microphones, but I'd venture to say Kirk could've reached the third tier without his. Falstaff jolted into his adjustments, huge fingers darting over the soundboard.

What, jealous Oberon! Fairies, skip hence; I have forsworn his bed and company.

Uhura's voice was set at a more tenable volume. She and Kirk had worn nothing but Star Trek outfits in what seemed like forever, but the boots and velour were still a bit startling in this setting, though perhaps not inappropriate, in an off-Broadway sort of way, for their roles as fairy royals. We hadn't the means for customized Elizabethan garb, but would make do by digging deep into the original clothing collection – Sloboth and Bitsen had all four of the silver valises loaded up backstage.

Beyond that we'd had time for only two customized additions. Morben, who apparently had some ability with needle and thread, had stitched up some handkerchiefs to serve as robes and capes. And Dasher had pilfered a thumb puppet donkey from a toy box at home, which Bitsen had altered to function as a mask. For footling purposes, it made a fine head of an ass.

All went silent. The sky had gone dark, the house lights dim. Center stage held a single blue cylinder of light. Falstaff had a way with these things. Evoking both a Star Trek transporter beam and the drone lighting that had tracked the footlings their entire lives, the cylinder made a fine dramatic effect, silent and unmoving, illuminating only the occasional flitting moth. It was unsettling that no one slept or danced in its glow. We'd never managed a full rehearsal, never actually strung together more than a couple of scenes. And while we'd simulated as best we could, the children had never been on a real stage. They'd never even been out of the building. Or, as I've mentioned, up past dark. It was way too much to ask, and grossly unfair that this was the only crack they'd get.

Then the cylinder was gone, and three players were lit before us, Kirk booming out the opening lines as Theseus, Duke of Athens; Uhura answering full as Hippolyta, Queen of the Amazons; and Richie marching in as Egeus, the father aggrieved. As Athenian elders, they wore the Jedi robes in which I'd first met them, in what seemed such an earlier time. Richie had only one warmup line – *Happy be Theseus* – before his big opening speech, and when it squeaked out, rushed and unsettled, I feared the worst. But he bowed slightly at the waist, straightened back up, and lit into those two hundred words on cue. And he nailed them, every one of them, as if he'd been doing it for years, as if he'd been born to it, as if a stutter or a stumble were not even in the realm of possibility. In the context of the play, it was one long complaint by a sour, unlikable character. But in the context of this production, that delivery, the shocking joy of Richie's near-perfect execution, resonated through the entire building. It energized the cast and audience as one. I blanked for a moment, resurfacing only several exchanges later when Kirk sauntered through another flawless passage:

> *Therefore, fair Hermia, question your desires,*
> *Know of your youth, examine well your blood,*
> *Whether, if you yield not to your father's choice,*
> *You can endure the livery of a nun;*
> *For aye to be shady cloister mew'd,*
> *To live a barren sister all your life,*
> *Chanting faint hymns to the cold, fruitless moon.*

And with that I went from theater mom, stressing over every line and every cue, to theatergoer, transfixed by poetry and drama and dance. I'm a scientist by training, and by no means a theater critic. All I can tell you is that I laughed and I cried, and I hung on every word. And the way Morben rocked and guffawed in front of me, and Dasher hooted and hollered to my right, I was not alone.

Objectively, this production had a few elements no other could possibly have matched. The children had a unique ability for voicings – they could broaden their tones to sound fully human when playing Athenians, or revert to their fainter footling speak with, somehow, no sacrifice in projection, in the roles of the fairies. This had an otherworldly effect of its own, but when paired with the spectacle of the fairy dance, it became positively surreal. Dasher had given them concepts of movement, spritely bits rooted in ballet, but the choreography was nowhere near fully scripted.[47] And now, on the Icosagon

---

47 Dasher initially complained about insufficient rehearsal time, but afterwards would hint at his own aesthetic discretion.

stage, the children, left to their own devices, rose up as we'd never seen them do before. They were natural leapers, of course, but now they seemed simply to fly – if we hadn't known better we'd have thought them attached to guide wires. Inventing as they went, they flitted and gamboled and channeled the spirits they were meant to be, in boots and velour and handkerchief capes.

As Athenian maidens, Laura and Samantha brought us to tears in the pangs of their cruelly unrequited loves, and were catfight electric in their moments of hostility. Rob and Darrin, playing Athenian gentry, were as pliable and deluded and uncentered as all humanity, swearing angelic devotion to one maiden and hurling insults at the other, until, smitten with fairy dust, they reversed themselves to swear love with equal ardor to the maiden they'd just maligned. Richie was hilarious in the ass's head – he had a knack for physical comedy, careening and stumbling around the stage, braying and bumbling while the others played off him in turn.

But through all this, I couldn't shake the notion that it all might end with any number of them dropping off into deep, unwakable sleeps. We were now into the dark of night, and this play was littered with particular peril – Shakespeare had them sleeping at every turn in the forest. At one point, five of the seven were curled up and perfectly still, and I doubted that any of them would rise again. But they did, on cue, and with the same energy as before, through to the closing scene and *Exeunt*.

We sat stunned just long enough for the man upstairs to beat us to the punch – an immediate "Bravo" and one-man applause from the upper deck. Dasher and I snapped to with standing ovations of our own, and beneath us, Falstaff and Dmitri stood from the soundboard to join in. Morben, who seemed to suffer extreme paresthesia while unwinding from his seat, joined us shortly thereafter. We were an admirably raucous crowd of six, but our combined output in that building was, by definition, a bit feeble. Falstaff solved that with the flip of two switches, activating a feedback loop that pumped our crowd noise through the sound system and back onto itself. We swelled to rip-roaring effect, a full house by any audible measure.

Our little cast had no idea about curtain calls — we hadn't run through that at all. Dr. Henderson led them back out holding hands in single file, arranged them in a line, and demonstrated the bow and the curtsy, which they hastily and happily adopted. Both gestures appeared to be gender neutral. Henderson waved them off, and they returned a moment later to repeat it all without her.

This is where things got a little blurry. After the second curtain call Falstaff killed all the lights but for the blue cylinder, which returned to center stage. We sat waiting for the house lights, but they never came on. Eventually Dasher and I started picking our way through the darkness, headed backstage. We found Sloboth and Bitsen at the dressing room door, which they said would be opening in a few minutes. After an awkward moment or two it became clear that they were actually serious in blocking our access. It was weird and offputting, and I wasn't going to wait there for clearance from people who could well be considered my subordinates in this production. I wandered back to the stage, where I caught sight of Morben, sloping at the shoulders and in deep conversation with someone who'd positioned himself, for some reason, directly within the blue cylinder. It was the impressively Afroed Lincoln Hayes from the third balcony. As I came into earshot they caught sight of me and turned away.

By now the dressing room was open and fully lit, but whatever after-party may have occurred was already over. The footlings, apparently, were asleep and packed away for the return trip. Morben followed me in. "Security wants us out of here as soon as possible," he said. "If we each take one of these we can get to the cars in one trip." He handed silver valises to Henderson, Sloboth, Bitsen, and me, and kept the cat box for himself. I remember this only because Dasher looked a little disappointed to be left out. "Make sure you air them out when you get home, or they'll go a bit musty – the little people sweat as much as we do. Oh, and by the way, we're officially out of the Genesis facility until further notice. Enjoy the time off, and I'll be in touch."

At the rear of the line, Henderson snapped off the light, and we headed out. We moved in single file – it seemed like the safest formation in the darkness. I followed like a school child, one foot after the other, more aware now of the old plank floor and wooden posts, the scent of uncoated timber and straw, an old barn back upstate.

Two security officers waited at the gate. Morben handed the cat box to one of them. We all filed out, and the gate banged shut behind us. We dispersed to our various cars. No one said a word. In contrast to the earlier precision of our arrival, the exit was a disorderly, dispirited affair. Cars started indiscriminately, backed out in a jumble, and returned us to our private lives.

35. Richie

We've had a pack of sulphur-crested cockatoos in the area for the last day or two, a couple dozen of them. Jill, who was only here for about an hour this week, said it was like they'd flown in for a convention. They're big birds of the parrot family, pure white through the body with bright yellow crests on their heads, like something a child might draw. But they have a cry completely out of keeping with that picture, the ugliest and loudest of all the bird calls I've encountered. If I were a daytime sleeper I'm sure it'd jolt me awake again and again until I was a bleary-eyed mess, which would make me about as miserable as they seem to be. It's an outraged cry, a shriek, as if they were being gripped and plucked alive. This is a great mystery to me as I see them flying, perching, feeding, stepping along in the grass, doing all the things that seem to occupy any number of other quite contented birds. They have the company of their peers, which, if you'll forgive the sentimentality, is a lot more than I can say. Nobody messes with them, not even the miners. They have all the physical attributes I'd want as a bird – intimidating size, glorious white feathering, powerful jet-black beaks, and, of course, those great yellow crests. The Chief spent a lot of time looking in the glass to admire his own fine headdress, but he'd have been mortified, or, to risk a pun, crestfallen, in the presence of these vastly more majestic creatures.

While they've made several appearances around the house, they seem to be concentrating their time in the orchard. I've followed them down there a time or two, and I've seen them coordinate feedings in a way that suggests I'd underestimated their intelligence. They seem mostly interested in the oranges this time of year, and it's probably no coincidence that they've come now when that fruit is near its peak. They swoop decisively into a single tree, as if everything's been discussed and resolved in advance. Half of them work in the foliage, snipping at stems and dropping the oranges to the ground. The others man the base of the tree to work the fallen fruit. After a time they'll shift roles. When there's more than enough for all they'll move to a roomier tree to take the rest of the meal at leisure, perching on one leg and holding fruit in the other.

You'd think that kind of operation would be something to be proud of. And that the sense of community would be soothing. And that the meal itself would be settling, though a little acidic for my liking. But it all conspires to make them even more ornery. Feeding strategies notwithstanding, it seems they'd be better off in solitude. They demonstrate an inordinate number of hierarchy problems. While they don't openly bicker and fight like some of the other birds, they steadily bring out the worst in each other. As Jill says, they stew in each other's bitter juices. The squawking is unbearable – I wonder how they can even stand themselves. When they've eaten their fill they fly into my eucalyptus trees and start snipping branches – perfectly healthy, leafy branches – leaving piles of them on the ground, denuding the trees and hastening their demise, for no reason beyond spite.

They've gone into the macadamias as well. I watch those jet-black beaks at work, and I consider myself fortunate. They crack dozens of nuts with astonishing ease, and leave plenty behind. I'm happy to eat one on the spot and lug a few more back home. But what is truly providential is their apparent disinterest in small mammals. What they do to those macadamias they could just as easily do to my head. To some degree, I'm surprised they don't. And I suppose there's no guarantee they won't, again if only from spite.

Their crests are said to droop and flare with the flights of their moods. But from what I've seen, and to hear them squawk, their moods don't really fluctuate. They're consistently sour. Or, more accurately, they fluctuate within a narrow range on the sour end of the spectrum. It's as if the whole group is consumed with a series of pivotal and pressing injustices. I have no idea what's really at the root of it. I can't tell what they're actually saying – I'd need a much longer exposure to work that out – but their acute agitation would be obvious even to someone not the least bit familiar with birdsong. I can't help but contrast these birds with The Chief. He had no friends of his own and spent his life alone in a cage until I finally worked up the nerve to "spring him," as Jill used to say. After that he could make short little flights around our grim little building, which seemed a slim consolation for his dull and solitary life. He'd have been thrilled to live like these cockatoos, flying as high and as far as he pleased, perching in the tallest trees, admiring the views, eating what he pleased, spending time with his peers.

Watching them over these couple of days has made me wonder if we're all not wired a notch or two below contentment, regardless of the circumstances or apparent outcomes of our lives. The cockatoo is an extreme example, but I see it even among the more even-keeled species. Take the birds I'm most familiar with here. The higher-achievers, the top birds in each flock, seem no happier than those of the lowest standing, maybe even less so. They're constantly on edge – overworked, tired and harried. They feel the weight of leadership, the threat of the next internal rival, and the torment of other worries completely foreign to us. The lesser birds, even the ones rejected and run out of the roost at night, seem serene enough by day. Given ample foodstuffs and reasonably good health, even the basest of lives appear to bring their satisfactions.

I hadn't noticed this so much with people. Our exposure to the Genesis specialists was such that I didn't get a chance to observe them in their domestic settings beyond a few days I spent at Jill's. But she's confirmed the phenomenon, citing countless observations from her own life, both personal and professional. While she hadn't thought of any of this before I'd mentioned it, she quickly accepted the idea of a "pre-set range of potential contentment," as she called it. In fact, she was willing to embrace the notion as a "fundamental tenet of the human condition."

"People are programmed to accomplish things," she said, "and their dependence on that construct is constant and relentless." Great deeds or tiny deeds – she thought it almost irrelevant – satisfaction derives primarily from the most *recent*. "I can have a big professional breakthrough on a Thursday, something people really notice, something potentially life-changing, and I'll still be miserable on the Saturday. But then I knock off a list of perfectly mundane little household chores – check, check, check – things that mean nothing to anyone, and will mean nothing even to me by that very evening – and I experience a comparably powerful and completely unjustified rush of contentment, albeit equally short-lived."

It's all perfectly understandable from a Darwinistic point of view – continual striving is how individuals thrive and species moves forward. The downside is that even a lifetime of achievement earns people like Jill hardly an hour's peace. I could only respond by saying that kind of programming might have been best for an earlier age, when the core yearning – for a safe home, a stream of decent meals, a brood of healthy offspring – was less routinely fulfilled.

36. Jill

In a moment of desperation I thought of heading back to the facility to stop Manly however I could. But I knew I wouldn't get by the first passkey door, and security would have me the minute I tried. I drove home chiding myself for cowardice, defending myself, and circling it through again. When I pulled into my driveway I had no memory of any part of that drive. We seem to have that kind of affinity with our cars, whizzing within a meter or two of each other at lethal speeds, neither driver paying a whit of attention. Somehow it all works, and we keep ourselves between the lines.

I swung the valise onto the counter, hung my keys on the hook, and poured myself a cold glass of water. I took a long drink, staring past the edge of the glass to the valise. Recalling the orientation of the clothes, I set it upright and popped it open. The clothing on one side swung on its hangers, the way it always did, and I headed for my much-needed shower. But the other side hadn't processed somehow, and I turned back for another look. Richie hung there, vertically, by Velcro straps. I jumped nearly out of my shoes.[48]

A panicked check told me he was breathing. A slightly less-pan- icked check told me his respiration was something near his normal

---

48 When I have no science on a topic, I'm a simple pessimist. I consider that kind of adrenaline jolt an accelerator of cardiac arrest – each such incident moves the inevitable attack up a week, a month, a year, while also increasing its severity.

sleeping rate. It occurred to me to close the case right back up, but I knew how horrible it'd be to wake up in there. I also figured it'd get too stuffy – though I did now notice that someone, presumably Morben, had drilled several holes the diameter of a pencil into the sides. I thought about setting it back flat, but for some reason I left it upright. I could see Morben had done some clever work with the Velcro straps. A tiny piece had kept Richie's head from flopping around in the moving valise, and kept it from drooping too much now. A larger piece ran under his arms and over his chest – that one seemed to take most of his weight. Another over that held his arms comfortably folded. And two more, one at the thighs and one at the shins, held his legs in place, one ankle crossed over the other. He had a vague resemblance to the wooden Jesus who'd been hanging in my mother's bedroom for as long as I could remember – just the right size, his head at just the same droop. But that was the extent of the similarity – after all, he was beardless and fully clothed, and his arms weren't even out. Looking back on it, the better comparison might have been a tiny teenage vampire sleeping the day away, upright in an open coffin.

By now, as you can imagine, I was starting to do a lot of wondering. Why would Morben send Richie home with me? And why would he do that without warning or instruction? He'd mentioned opening the valises to prevent must, but as warnings go, I considered that one very much on the cryptic side. It was a given that his intention was to spare Richie from Manly's ministrations. And the drilled holes and Velcro strapping indicated a plan rather than an improvisation. So who all was in on it? Sloboth and Bitsen had blocked the dressing room door, presumably under instruction, but did they really know what was happening inside? Neither Falstaff nor Dmitri had been in the room when I was, and I didn't think they'd been there before me either. Dasher had been with me. Morben himself had been on stage, chatting with Lincoln Hayes. That left Henderson as the only staffer inside just after the play. Had she tucked Richie in the valise? Had she tucked the other footling males in the other three valises as well, or was Richie the only one sprung? Could they really hope to get away with it? And what did they expect from me?

At first consideration, either Morben hadn't had the time or opportunity to alert me in private, or he didn't want to give me the chance to say no. But as I thought about it, a third option occurred to me – that he was protecting me as much as he was Richie. The way it had been structured, I could legitimately deny any role as a knowing participant, though that option would expire pretty shortly if I didn't pick up the phone and report what I'd found, or, rather, whom I'd found. I thought long and hard about making that call, and about making a few others – to Morben directly, for example, or to Falstaff, or to any of the other valise carriers. But in the end, I didn't call anyone. If Morben wanted a conversation with me, he'd have initiated it already. Same with Henderson. I guessed that a call was something they were trying to avoid. As for the others, I had no idea what they knew, or how they'd react. After a good long while – long enough to get a pretty stiff backside on that kitchen stool – I concluded that if someone was going to blow the scheme and put Richie and, most likely, the other males, back in harm's way, it wasn't going to be me.

I unstrapped him as gently as I could and carried him on two open palms to my bedroom. I couldn't put him in the bed for fear of crushing him in my sleep, or on the floor for fear of stepping on him. Instead, I made him a little nest in my underwear drawer. I put the drawer on the floor in case he fell out, though, in my experience, sleeping footlings didn't do a lot of moving. I cranked the heat well past where I like it but slept surprisingly well regardless.

That said, I was wide awake before dawn. I looked immediately to the drawer. Richie was just as I'd left him. I lay back and started circling through the same scenarios I'd considered the night before.

But the sky grew light, and Richie stirred, and from that moment forward I wouldn't have time for much strategic thinking. Let's just say that the footlings had grown accustomed to a lot of attention. I've had the occasional overnights with my nieces or nephews, but they were nothing like this one.

"Where am I?"

"Good morning, Richie. You're in my house."

"Why am I here?"

"I don't really know. Dr. Morben sent me home with one of the clothing valises after the play, and you were sleeping inside."

"Why was I sleeping in there?"

"You must have been really tired after the play. You've never stayed up that late before."

"But why would Dr. Morben send me home with you?"

"I don't really know."

"Shouldn't we ask him?"

"Yes, we will. Next time we see him."

"When will that be?"

"I don't know that either. I'm guessing it'll be a few days."

"So what are we going to do now?"

"How about some pancakes?"

And that was it. Like most young people, he was pretty quick to adapt to his new environment. He did spend a lot of that first morning on my shoulder, which he hadn't done in some time, all through the breakfast preparations and then again during cleanup. I talked him through the various procedures, the mixing, the stovetop flame, the melting butter, the bubbles in the batter, the dramatic flipping. As to the play, his only comment was, "When can we do it again?"

Since I couldn't match Morben's convenient little place settings, Richie sat on the counter with his back against the wall and his feet splayed in front of him. The saucer on his lap, the smallest I had, looked as big as a paella pan. I'd made coin-sized cakes for him and drizzled them with real maple syrup. They were a big hit, a dramatic improvement on Bitsen's poor fare. He ate two of them, his total consumption amounting to about a sixth of a full-sized pancake. Impressive for his size, but I'd out-eaten him by thirty to one.

The first awkward moment came just afterwards, at the time for my shower. At Genesis the footlings took only baths – girls one day and boys the next. So Richie had never seen a shower, and he was plenty curious. After some discussion we agreed that he would sit through it on the soap dish.[49] It was the first time he'd seen me naked, and I was surprisingly self-conscious. But after a few bouts of staring he seemed well enough accustomed to the various features of my anatomy. We resumed our normal conversations through the running water and carried them on through toweling and dressing.

It was not yet 09:00, and I realized I hadn't the slightest idea how we'd get through the day. I certainly couldn't take him out in public, and thinking about the food in the house, or the lack of it, I started to wonder if I could leave him alone while I went shopping. One thing I had going for me was my little back yard. While I was probably the only person on the block without a dog – and I'd spent many a night plotting the murder of each of the neighbors' more persistent barkers – my property had come with the finest dog fence money could buy. It was built of solid timber, with footings to frustrate even the most spirited diggers. It was also eight feet tall, and even Richie couldn't clear eight feet, not that he showed any signs of wanting to. The fence height had the ancillary effect of making the yard completely private. So I opened the door for him, and he scampered right out. It was the

---

49 A tougher endeavor, as it turned out, than you might imagine. Those things are slippery.

first time he'd ever stepped in grass. I did have a nice little lawn, just cut, and he rolled around and hopped about like a delighted little fawn. I also had a mint patch in one corner – he approached it without fear and disappeared like Shoeless Joe into the cornfield. I had the thought that he might be relieving himself in there, which reminded me I needed to buy some litter. He emerged a minute later and hopped around some more.

I blew up an old birthday balloon – this was a point of extreme fascination in itself – and showed Richie how to keep it afloat with a series of kicks and finger taps and headers. He thought the headers were hilarious and took to them in particular, leaping like a little terrier after a frisbee. The grass made for more labored movement than he was used to on the dynamic weight dispersion flooring, but he loved the softness and the smell of it, and he was soon diving around and making digs like a professional volleyballer. We played well beyond my needing another shower – at one point we must have kept that balloon aloft for fifteen minutes straight.

I gave Richie a bath in the kitchen sink. Afterwards he stood in front of the valise, stark naked, flipping through his various sartorial options. Theater seemed to have piqued his interest in fashion. I told him he'd become a dandy and a fop. He'd look those words up a little later, dressed in a Nehru jacket, bellbottoms, and a floral shirt open at the neck. I made some mint tea, cutting and boiling the mint, squeezing the lemons, measuring out the sugar. Richie loved all the kitchen activity and was an adventurous eater. I ordered in plenty of groceries, and over the course of his stay I did some of the best cooking I'd done in ages. Over several sessions – on the couch, on the lawnchairs, and in the bed – we re-read Winnie-the-Pooh, both volumes, which I was happy to find still agreed with him. At the end of those days I'd be so exhausted I was tempted to go to bed when he did, just after sunset. I stayed up only for a bit of private time, and I retired progressively earlier every night of his stay. I have no idea how single parents do it, and I'm more perplexed by this now than I was before Richie. But for those few days, I was more than happy to have him.

37. Richie

Those first climbs in the orchard had left their marks. Contusions from the rougher jump-landings colored my shins and the insides of my arms and circled my ribcage with hues I'd never seen on an unfeathered body. Even my worst run-ins with the magpies hadn't left such palettes of purples and greens, oranges and yellows. Overlying those contusions were abrasions that had gone dry and crusty in the night. The overall effect, in both color and texture, was that of an exotic tropical lizard.

I'd never been particularly stoic in the face of injury, and it was strange to find myself focusing on something beyond my wounds. Through the din of the chronically underfed chicks, at least to hear them tell it, I sat on my sill and contemplated, of all things, climbing more trees. The orchard session, brief and painful as it had been, seemed to have sparked some dormant genetic disposition that had kindled and fired in my sleep. I'd awakened with a fresh outlook on every tree I'd studied since I'd been in East Central. Their familiar forms were presented anew, as riddles, fresh and endlessly varied. I spent hours assessing them as I hadn't before, gauging the distance between branches, judging the bark for the depth of its toeholds, tracing the many possible paths up.

Eight hundred days, and I'd never been higher than my sill. I'd been sitting in place, surviving for survival's sake. I thought back to the things Dr. Dasher had said about our physiques, and now for the first time I saw that they could actually matter. I was flexible. I could jump. I had decent balance and an uncommon strength relative to my mass. I was light enough to reach the tops of any canopy, places no man or possum could go. And I had no doubt that I'd get there. Because, at least in this pursuit, I could call on the attributes Dmitri had so admired – effort, commitment, persistence. My muscles twitched as I sat. I shot off the sill and ran to the bed. I jumped up onto it, scrambled down its lines, and jumped again – ten repetitions. I dangled my legs as dead weights and pulled myself up the sill lines – five repetitions – my arms and shoulders straining nearly to failure. I ran a series of interior loops, leaping from the floor to the arms of every chair in the house, wobbling on my first landings, but sticking more of them as I went on.

I could already imagine the heights and the views. Beyond my trip in the travel carton, which didn't really count, it'd be the closest I'd come to flying. I wanted a go at every tree I'd seen, and at the thousands I assumed were just past them. Certain eucalypts would present challenges with their daunting heights and paper-smooth bark, but I'd get to them soon enough.

Making the venture oddly more appealing was the fact that it couldn't realistically occur. Taking to the trees without Jill alongside, in broad daylight, with the nests full of chicks, was just short of suicide. When I considered it objectively, my bird-friendly, possum-toppling pedigree was almost certainly more in my head than in the birds'. It offered me no guarantee of local immunity, and quite possibly none whatsoever. Every one of those birds, at least in the daytime, would protect those chicks from any perceived threat in the most vicious and violent way they knew. They probably couldn't stop themselves, even if my favorable behavior had made them so inclined. They were wired to defend those trees, just as I was wired to climb them. If I'd been a night creature, things would have been different. But with all parties diurnal, I couldn't imagine a tree-climbing scenario in which I wasn't mobbed to my death. I couldn't take punishment like the possum. I lacked its bulk, its coat, and its brainless resolve. And while my defensive pirouettes were becoming more proficient in the grass, I couldn't take them into the trees.

The obvious course was to wait until the nests had gone vacant. As I'd become a more experienced victim I'd begun to understand the seasonal nature of the attacks. Beaks and talons took the lead during the breeding period, pecking and bludgeoning with full intent to injure and maim. The offseason brought a greater emphasis on wing-work, swooping and clapping, something more in line with standard pecking order maintenance. If the possum incident had raised me at all in the avian esteem, or at least tempered my despicability, I could entertain the hope of climbing then. Success would depend on projecting a treetop manner disarming enough to earn, if not their friendship, then their indifference. Maybe with such a foundation I could some day extend my range and move beyond the birds familiar with me. In any event, the sill would no longer suffice.

38. Jill

On the evening of the third day, Morben sent an all-staff message. We were to report back to the facility in the morning. I waited for the follow-up, the private message, some hint or instruction about Richie, but after an hour or two I had to concede that it wasn't coming. After far too long, I called Morben directly. No answer.

It was all getting a little aggravating. If Morben was assuming I'd keep protecting Richie on my own, he was badly mistaken. I'd conceal him for a short time in league with a right-minded group -- I'd shown that already. But I wasn't exposing myself to termination and possible criminal charges in isolation.[50]

There were other possibilities, and they were all over the map. Maybe Morben would greet us in the morning with a coherent game-plan. Maybe he'd lost his nerve and simply folded. Maybe he'd been busted and coerced. Or maybe, best case, something had taken the orchiectomies out of play -- something as simple as Lincoln Hayes' appreciating Shakespeare.

I decided to get in before sunrise with Richie sleeping in the valise. It seemed like a sensible hedge. I'd learn what I could and either return him to the nursery or haul him back out without revealing him to any cameras. Henderson was scheduled for the night shift,

---

50 Kidnapping? Felony theft? Looking back on it, the legal questions were intriguing.

a favorable setup since she was the one most likely in league with Morben.

My new early-to-bed regimen made the obscenely early alarm less painful than it could have been. In the soft light of the bed table lamp I pulled Richie from the drawer. Marveling as always at his pliability and resilience in sleep, I strapped him into the valise and closed it up, just as he'd been delivered to me. He'd slept through what must have been some rough handling a few nights before, but this time I placed the case gently and steadied it with my free hand at every stop along the way.

It was the morning of P104, though the official record has the Genesis Project ceasing operations neatly on P100. I understood that protocol had been upended for the last three days, but it was still a surprise to find the parking lot empty. I'd expected Henderson to honor her night duty. Still more unnerving was finding the other six footlings completely unsupervised inside. For there they were, fully dressed but sleeping soundly, in their normal tangle under six blue cylinders.

I'd hoped the other males would be off somewhere in safe houses of their own, but it looked like Richie had been the only lucky one. The Chief seemed agitated, as if in confirmation that bad things had happened within those walls. Then again, he'd had no attention for several days. I put him on my shoulder, where he nibbled a bit too aggressively on my ear as I checked out the rest of the facility. There was no sign of any surgical equipment, and while they could always bring it back for Richie, Manly's personal effects had vanished as well. If history served as our guide, we'd seen the last of him. The systems were up, but when I checked for video from the last three days it either hadn't been recorded or had been deleted.

Overall, there wasn't a lot to go on. And on balance, I didn't see much argument for extending my risk. What was the end game for my increasingly solitary intervention? A life with Richie on the lam? The notion was absurd. Not that I regretted my actions of the last several days. I'd been handed Richie's custody by my Project Supervisor and would be returning him to the facility when first cleared to do so. Hard to fault me for that. And as a result, in all likelihood, they'd be settling for three castrations and barring Richie from the womenfolk. I went back inside, unpacked him, and set him with his peers. Like them, he was dressed for the day, having chosen a sleeping ensemble of silk slacks and a navy turtleneck. He sighed, rolled into the group, and went still. His drone floated over to add a seventh cylinder of blue. I cleaned the birdcage and waited for the others.

Sloboth and Bitsen trickled in over the next half hour, each toting their assigned valises. There was something particularly communal at that ungodly hour and in those uncertain conditions. It reminded me a little of the polar bear swim clubs in Oswego, where people would congregate at dawn, strip in the snow, and jump into the frigid lake.[51] There were awkward hugs all around, all of us talking at once, allies in the common cause. All the same, not one bit of meaningful information passed between us. Henderson's arrival made things even more awkward. At least two of us, and maybe all of us, were saying a lot less than we knew or were lying outright, reading each others' faces, trying to piece it all together. I checked the other valises with as much nonchalance as I could muster. They all had airholes matching mine.

Dasher and Falstaff arrived just later. I could see Falstaff immediately churning. He was a quick hand at assessing disorder. Dawn was upon us, the footlings would be waking shortly, and we had no semblance of a gameplan.

Falstaff: Well, I see that we're all in early.

---

51 Mostly those were people my parents knew. I would never do something that stupid just to fit in with a group.

Dasher: With the obvious exception of our fearless leader, the esteemed Dr. Moribund.

Me: And of the slightly less fearless Dr. Manly, who, by the vacant look of his work station, won't be in at all.

Sloboth gave a Bronx cheer, and, one by one, we all joined in. It was strange, six accomplished and more or less dignified adults all blowing raspberries with no humorous intent.

Falstaff: Has anyone checked the video record for the last three days?

Me: I did. Nothing there.

Falstaff: I haven't been able to reach Dr. Morben. Has anyone else spoken to him?

No one indicated that they had.

Falstaff: Can anyone confirm that the surgeries actually happened?

No one indicated that they could.

Falstaff: Then our first priority would seem to be a physical assessment of the males.

Henderson: Agreed. But in the unlikely event that they've been spared, it'd be best if they didn't know what was intended. They're going to wake up any minute now, so let's not risk the assessments just yet.

Dasher: We don't want to get caught with their pants down.

Me: Good one.

Henderson: We should hold off until their normal dressing sequence.

Bitsen: But they're already in their day clothes.

Sloboth: Yeah, what's with that?

Falstaff: I don't know, but it means the best opportunity for our extremely subtle physical observations (nodding here to Henderson) will be the individual morning litter visits.

Dasher: Litter-cams?

Falstaff: Nothing embedded in the litter, but we'll have cameras where we need them.

Dasher: I'm assuming they'll be limping around and complaining, and it won't be all that mysterious.

Henderson: If that's the case then we're directly into counseling mode.

Bitsen: They're going to hate us.

Sloboth: And with good reason.

Henderson: But if they seem normal, we proceed with business as usual.

Me: Whatever that means at this point. It's hard to imagine we'll be diving back into reading modules.

Henderson: Or rehearsing a play we just crushed!

High fives and awkward embraces all around.

As if on cue, the footlings began to stir. Kirk, as usual, was the first one awake, and while he didn't exactly crow, he greeted most mornings with yawns violent enough to wake the others.[52] This day was no exception.

The males arose without difficulty and walked without limping. Bitsen fed them their breakfasts, trying, and mostly failing, to act normal. The footlings volunteered nothing out of the ordinary. They weren't impressed with the instant oatmeal, but that was par for the course. I was dreading Richie's babbling about his stay at my place – I'd be the first to have to come clean. But he was as oddly tranquil as the rest.

Darrin was the first to the litter box. With all the cameras Falstaff had in place it felt like a high-tech corporate peep show. Nine different angles lit up the PrismView. I thought Darrin might kick up a fuss

---

52 While almost nothing could wake the footlings at night, they were light sleepers once the sun was up.

– the footlings, after all, were not completely oblivious to camera placement. But he settled in, and when he dropped his pants and the cameras zoomed we were barely breathing. We saw no bandaging, no sign of insult, and yes, there was the proof – Camera 5 had it clearly – he was fully intact. Falstaff shouted, and we all whooped like our horse had just won the Derby. Henderson had already shown herself to be a very good actress, Shakespearean and otherwise, but the others were either fair players themselves, or they really didn't know what had transpired over the past few days. Either way, it was a good moment for our sound-proofing – the uproar would almost certainly have disturbed Darrin at his labors. "For God's sake," yelled Dasher. "We've seen enough. Kill the video."

But it was back up soon, when Rob ventured in. He too was unscathed. We gave another roar of joy. By now we were starting to babble. "What do you think happened?" "What happened to Manly?" "Do you think they all got out of it?"

Richie was next, half an hour later, and here my historically poor acting was put to the test. But either all the theater exposure had rubbed off and I did a little better than usual, or no one paid me any attention. Kirk completed the assessment shortly after, he too in full flower.

We assigned Henderson to the debriefing. She entered the nursery and gave them all big hugs. "So tell me what you've been up to the past few days," she said. Six little voices chimed in at once. They'd been at Morben's place. We looked at each other in astonishment, real or feigned. Apparently Morben had cooked up a storm. They couldn't get over how well they'd eaten.[53] And for dessert all three nights he'd served some special apricot nectar, which, he'd said, "was a little like

---

53 I felt badly for Bitsen at this moment. She lacked suitable kitchen facilities, and any hint of culinary talent, but she did her best to keep the children fed.

the fairy dust" and made them act a little silly. They'd read another play, *The Merchant of Venice*, and had even begun acting out a few scenes.

"Moribund is quite the wit, isn't he?" came Henderson's voice through the PA. "You know, *The Merchant of Venice* -- Antonio, Shylock, the whole 'pound of flesh' thing," she added when our silence made it clear we hadn't understood. I, for one, still didn't. Falstaff explained it to me later.

In a moment of relative silence, Laura's little voice came through loud and clear:

"But where were you, Richie?"

"He wasn't with the rest of you at Dr. Morben's?" asked Henderson.

"Nope."

All eyes were on him. That was probably for the better since I felt myself going red, and more so the more I tried to look casual. He hesitated for a moment, took a stride forward, and puffed out his chest.

"I was on my way up!

I was seeing great sights!

I was joining high fliers

Who soar to high heights."

Seuss.[54] I never thought he'd get away with that. But the others responded with only a laugh. And just like that, they all moved on. Richie had kept his visit strangely secret. The others had just as strangely supported his evasion. And Henderson, for reasons of her own, declined to pry any further.

---

54 Richie had improvised from Seuss's last book, *Oh, the Places You'll Go! (1990)*.

39. Richie

I was still getting regular visitors to my sill, in bigger numbers than I'd ever had. For good or for bad, spearing that possum had raised my profile. I'd continued to promote the species-specific visiting times with regular hours and the judicious use of the favored foods. The birds were still edgy – it's in their nature, especially at that time of year – so they'd flit between bites to the nearby branches, where they'd sit for a moment to monitor the nests. On the flip side, they seemed to appreciate the food all the more. The butchers had begun delivering bits of my dried fruit to their nestlings. They hadn't done that at first, though they'd always been happy enough to swallow it for themselves. I hadn't taken it for selfishness, but rather that they considered the food inappropriate or unsafe for the chicks. Either the chicks had grown enough to diversify their diets, or the adults had developed more trust in my offerings. I clung to the latter, chalking it up as another small step in my journey to acceptance. And I waited for the miners and magpies to follow suit.

With the increasing number of adult visitors, and with the butcher-bird chicks now in the mix, I was running through more and more of my food stores. Jill seemed a little bewildered at my weekly consumption of dried meats and fruits, and at my constant call for pomegranate. I kept my responses as vague as I could, not daring to tell her that her hard-won deliveries were going largely to the birds. Toward the end of the week I'd be running short for my own consumption, and I'd trek off to the orchard to tide myself over. I was starting to like that food as much as what Jill was bringing me. And I'd gotten a little smarter at hauling it in the rucksack she'd left me, dragging it when the size of the load – an avocado and a store of nuts, for example – required it, and waving my blade overhead as menacingly as I could.

While the magpies still scared the hell out of me, my comfort level was growing with the others. I was doing my linguistic best with all of them to float the idea of my venturing into the trees. Theoreticals, of course, don't come naturally to them and aren't a part of their discourse. So my delivery was more along the lines of "me in the tree," repeated in as many intonations as I thought could make the slightest sense. Admittedly, none of it made much. As they could plainly see, and repeatedly insisted, I was not in a tree, but firmly ensconced in the "hideous dwelling" – I apologize for the awkward translations – perched as usual behind the screen. This earnest and perfectly logical refutal accompanied expressions of resigned pity, their stares between bites even more sidelong than usual. But in those few fleeting moments when I fancied we understood each other, none of them seemed to oppose the notion. I hoped I was only imagining the special glow in the eyes of the magpies.

When Jill finally brought me the sewing kit, I started work on my scabbard. By now I was considering it more in terms of climbing trees than climbing lines. It was hard to imagine leaving the house without the blade, though for purposes of defecation the skeletal umbrella still served best. But approaching a tree with a blade in hand wasn't going to set the appropriately passive tone, even if I left it leaning at the base. And while I could climb the sill lines with one hand, albeit awkwardly, trees were a different proposition. I cut a sleeve off a leather jacket that had been swinging in my clothes locker, unworn for eight hundred days. It was perfect in length but needed tapering toward the end. I unstitched it, formed it around the blade, tried to re-stitch it, botched it, tried again with the other sleeve, and did better the second time. The final product slid nicely onto my belt and held the blade firmly enough for stability and loosely enough to draw. It was well suited for climbing. I wore it shooting up and down the lines to my sill. But for now, I mostly just liked the look of it. On those hot afternoons, that belt and scabbard were all I wore.

I took to marching the length of my sill and back again. When the birds took less notice than I thought appropriate – I was still competing, after all, with the shrieks of a few dozen chicks – I began clacking a macadamia shell against the side jamb at every turn. This provided a cadence they found more difficult to resist, to the effect that I was able to draw some small audience most of the time I paced. At least a bird or two would flitter over for a bit – it seemed a respite of sorts from their labors.

I was still carrying on with my quasi-theoretical but mostly moronic monologue – me in the tree, me in the tree – but at that point the birds would hardly respond. Much as I tried to intersperse my chirp with other more sensible statements, a certain irritation had crept into them. Even birds can get their fill of nonsense. It occurred to me that, all my handouts notwithstanding, I couldn't risk irking them any further. I had to stop talking about it, and either do it or not. And so it was, despite all my perfectly logical reservations, that during one of the pomegranate sessions, with half a dozen miners on the sill, I took my blade, cut a large slice in the screen, and stepped through to the outside.

"Me in the tree," I said just once, as firmly as I could. The birds skittered off to nearby branches, calling out in alarm. I knew the gradations of their shrieks, and this was not a high level of panic, more an expression of surprise and a call for steady surveillance. I'd set out less food than usual, and now I stooped to place some more. Then I stepped to the far edge of the sill and waited. Either they'd mob me, or come back for the food, or fly somewhere else altogether. Or, just as easily, all of the above. With my blade in my scabbard I could draw as needed, though there was ample question as to whether I could do so before being driven off the sill, or if doing so would even prevent that. I kept my hands loose at my sides and acted as calmly as I could, though my heart was beating in my ears.

One of them returned to the far end of the sill, not going for the seeds just yet, but eyeing me steadily. I found myself staring into her eye flap with more interest than was necessary or advisable. I felt my diligence beginning to wane in the depth of that yellow hue. I barely noticed when another miner flew past me and settled on a branch just behind. Or when a third settled less than a meter over my head. This, of course, was the flanking maneuver I was so accustomed to from the magpies. Trying again to look casual, I tucked my back to the screen. It was the moment I'd long dreaded. Unprotected on a precarious perch, I was sure to be struck down and crippled like the possum before me.

But the first bird broke off her stare and dipped for a ruby seed, piercing the skin and taking the nectar like the honeyeater she is. One by one, the others fell in alongside her. I remember a surge of exaggerated happiness, giddiness even. I was up among them, and they were accepting me in their midst. I'd only intended an incremental step, a quick venture to the exterior sill and back inside. But I took a quick look at the nearest branch – I'd studied it so often from inside the screen that I hardly needed to – and I jumped. Stuck the landing. Walked several steps along the branch, away from my sill, toward the trunk. Made a series of short drop-jumps, wobbling on a few of them but never losing my footing. I wouldn't let myself look back – I knew it'd betray my fear and slow my progress – but I felt the presence of those birds above and behind me like a rucksack on my shoulders. I couldn't get out of that tree fast enough. With no accessible branches just below me I executed a quick traverse around the trunk, dropped to a branch on the far side, and from there to the ground.

I drew my blade and headed directly for the cat door, pirouetting at every fourth step. Several birds were tracking my progress, though none threatened me directly. I pushed through the flap, sheathed my blade, and leaned on the wall. My knees gave way, and I slid to a seat.

40. Jill

I was reading the footlings some Nietzsche just after noon when we heard the sound of the bell. They'd carried a recent demand that we stop shading the glass, so they and I could clearly see Dr. Sloboth scurrying to the entrance and returning with an armful of packages. She handed one each to Bitsen, Falstaff, Dasher, and Henderson, kept one for herself, and held another in my direction to indicate it was for me. They all sat to tear them open, looking like kids at Christmas expecting lousy presents and getting them. The contents, I knew, were legal documents. I started back to the reading, but we'd all lost our train of thought. I closed the book, and we sat there in the nursery, the footlings and I, observing the staffers as they leafed through their contracts. The footlings were in full observation mode.

"There seems to be a lot of stress within the group."

"Yes, we can see some nibbling of the fingers, and some wringing of the hair."

"Rapid tapping of the feet."

"Irregular breathing, general unrest."

After ten or fifteen minutes the staffers all came together, conferring and reviewing as a group. I caught Falstaff's eye, and he gestured for me to join them.

"I guess you'd better go out there," said Samantha.

Falstaff handed me my package as I pulled up a chair. "There are contracts for each of us," he said, "and from what we've seen so far, we've all been offered the same basic deal. We're to be engaged, more or less, as security contractors. Individually and collectively, we're securing the intellectual property of the entity formerly known as the Genesis Project."

I acted like this was all news to me, but the fact is, I'd been through it all before.

At this point I suppose I'll have to provide a little background. I've held out mostly by force of habit. You may have picked up a hint or two about my previous assignment in the city, mostly around City Hall and down into the Tenderloin. I mentioned that it had gotten pretty heavy and was even more hush-hush than most of the BioSpore stuff. I've also mentioned my moment of panic when Manly threw my question about chemical sterilization back in my face. I still don't know whether that was coincidence, or an indication that he knew more than I thought he could or should. But by now it doesn't much matter.

I'd been at Project StopValve, a male contraception initiative operating well off-campus – like four hundred miles off campus – in San Bernardino. We'd been chasing the science pretty hard for a couple years, and had come up with a potable liquid antagonist. Preliminary testing had shown it to be highly effective and free of major side effects. It was time for more extensive clinical trials. That much was business as usual. It was the nature of those trials that was surprising. I'm guessing that some BioSpore people were making a little run at social engineering, with critical support in important places. Or the regulatory process had drifted into some cryptic cross-agency collaboration. Either way, I can't say I really objected.

The basic premise was to restore some semblance of the natural order. At some point the human selection process had become unlinked from intelligence, or advantageous physical adaptation, or any of the survival characteristics we've traditionally valued. Instead, it began to correlate to backwardness and ignorance, and in many cases, to outright stupidity. In a Gathering just before I'd joined BioSpore, Chuck Hansen called this phenomenon *Reverse Darwinism*. I'd watched that video several times over – it actually made more sense to me than most Gatherings. Hansen made a convincing case that we'd been practicing this Reverse Darwinism for more than a century, and that it was proving, directly or indirectly, to be the root of nearly all of the world's problems. The species that's overrunning the planet has got it all wrong. The more functional, advanced groups – we'll call them the Alphas – are quite rationally limiting themselves to small families, generally three children or fewer. But the incompetent, the backward, and the irrational, the theoretically unsuccessful Betas, are multiplying at geometric rates. They benefit from the improved living conditions developed and implemented by the Alphas, and from direct material support from the Alphas. The Alpha population sees small declines in absolute terms, and massive declines as a percentage of the human pool, which becomes progressively less intelligent and less competent as it grows ever larger.

So when it fell out that at least one component of our StopValve trials would be more opaque than usual, I had no real problem with that, at least beyond any personal legal exposure – and that issue was resolved by agency immunity grants. I wasn't dispensing the treatments directly, but rather coordinating a group of volunteers. They were good people, high-minded, idealistic. They operated with the understanding that the doses held heavy concentrations of vitamins and minerals known to be depressed in the target population, which was completely true, and certain useful vaccines, also true. What hadn't been expressly mentioned was that three doses in seventy-two hours rendered male humans permanently sterile.

Working three-day stints, our volunteers combed through the heavier concentrations of the homeless population, dispensing single serves of our concoction. It was generally well received, as we expected, given its substantial alcohol component and a taste between apricot nectar and apricot brandy. The volunteers targeted men and women alike. There was no contraceptive effect on women, but no harm either, and the evenhanded approach eliminated a lot of potential questions. I handled distribution logistics, supervised the field, mapped the grids, tracked the data. After a few weeks, I was coordinating the two mobile semen collection units. And that's where things got a little dicey.

We'd known from the start that operating those units was going to be problematic. It was just a matter of how much and how soon. They were stock vans, each of which we'd outfitted with a reclining chair, a video player, and a locking refrigeration unit. We'd also had them hand-painted with hippie-looking exteriors, giving them, we hoped, a more or less harmless appearance. But the police were on to us from the very first afternoon, and quasi-authentic documentation could take us only so far. Two of my drivers were arrested, one of them twice, and I was very nearly arrested myself. By day five, for all practical purposes, we'd been shut down. But by then we had what we needed. The data, though more limited than we'd liked, indicated that we'd achieved sterilization rates as high as 85% in the targeted male population. These were spectacular results considering the difficulties of administering three doses in three days to an itinerant and intrinsically unreliable demographic.

That was basically the end of it, at least for me. Within a week, I was happy to have a transitional contract. As I've mentioned, I was ready to move on. And I could see right away that the terms were generous, guaranteeing my full salary while I sorted through relocation opportunities within BioSpore or with other companies. But near the end, it ventured into a completely different and unexpected realm. Suddenly, there were provisions for an escrowed six-figure bonus and for additional annuity payments. I realized that this was the meat of the contract. It shouldn't have surprised me.

Immediately following those heady financial provisions was a section titled PROHIBITIONS. It defined and described certain impermissible developments, primarily the release of any records, written accounts, or descriptions indicating the true nature of the StopValve street initiative. Any breach originating from me, directly or indirectly, or from any other source not even remotely related to me, would terminate my benefits, both the escrowed bonus and the annuity payments. Even certain forms of speculation by completely unrelated third parties would trigger termination. The language was very tough in this regard. But the way I saw it, this was found money, and potentially a lot of it. I signed and returned the document without much hesitation. If anything was going to leak out, it wasn't happening from my end.

Falstaff was still leading the Genesis crew through their terms and conditions: "Granted, the lion's share of the bonus is escrowed for fifteen years – that's a big part of the confidentiality lever and probably common to any deal they do like this. But I can't see that they have any legal access to what they've already given us. So even in our worst-case scenario we keep the unescrowed portion of the bonus and whatever annuity payments we've already received. And in the mean time, we've got the generous transitional provisions."

At this point, I pretty much checked out of the conversation. A quick look through my contract showed its similarities with my earlier deal, and as Falstaff described them, with all the deals around the room. But there were some critical differences. My contract made no mention of other opportunities within BioSpore, or with any other company. I was looking at a much larger bonus than the others were getting. And my annuity was particularly lavish – twice my existing salary, with cost of living escalations to the age of sixty-two. But for all that, it was another provision that had my attention. It explained the extravagance of the others.

In one spectacularly lawyerlike paragraph, filling an entire page and spilling well onto the next, this section, headed ADMINISTRATION OF TRUST, named me "sole Trustee of the facility known as A-19 and described in Appendix C," and, additionally, as sole Trustee of the account designated for its upkeep, "the A-19 Realty Holdings and Facilities Trust." I would administer these assets "in my sole discretion." And thus provisioned, I would assume "exclusive responsibility for the entity known as Delta Male." Yes, the Greek designation had made its triumphal return. Curiously enough, Delta Male was not described within the contract, but in a link to another document I couldn't immediately access. I assumed, and later confirmed, that it referred to the former Delta Boy, our own Richie Millipede.

Also lacking was any description of the nature of my "responsibility" for Delta Male. Beyond the stipulation that I would make my "primary residence within three hundred kilometers of A-19 so long as Delta Male shall live," my duties were sensationally vague. A comprehensive list of them – compiling data, filing reports, and so on – were specifically waived. Remarkably, Delta Male's wellbeing was not mentioned, contemplated, or even implied. It seemed a point of contractual irrelevance, of legal disinterest.

Falstaff was still holding forth. "Confidentiality has always been a big part of the deal here. At this point, it's second nature to all of us. Only now we're getting compensated for it. We're forbidden from communicating even with each other on the subject, though I'm not sure how they'd enforce that. But providing there's no breach, this is as close to corporate tenure as we could get. It appears to be fully guaranteed, immune to layoffs, internal reorganizations, changes of management…"

Appendix C provided geographic coordinates for the facility known as A-19. I went to the mapping data, which placed it in Australia. There were certainly more remote places in Australia, but it appeared to be three hours from the nearest population base. This would all make relocation a bit dramatic. But I figured it'd be warm there — I'd had enough ice and slush in Oswego, thank you. Australians speak English, which would certainly be helpful. And, as we know, it's an ever-shrinking planet.

41. *Richie*

By the following morning I'd recounted every step of my "climb" many times over. I've placed climb in ironic quotations – Jill does this in speech with her fingers – because I'd gone down the tree rather than up. And yet, from a technical standpoint there was a lot to be happy about. Under serious and largely unplanned duress, I'd pretty much stuck my branch landings. Granted, down-jumps are easier than up-jumps, but they'd been a useful trial for my feet, which had fared better than I expected. And when I'd run out of branches on one side I'd executed a smooth traversal around the trunk. There was no question I'd be going out again – the quicker I could acclimate the birds to my tree-based activities the better. The only question was how soon.

Common sense said I should stick to what had worked. That meant coupling the climb with a feeding, when the birds were most relaxed and most favorably disposed toward me, and preferably with the miners. But the miners were last in the daily feeding rotation – I always put out the pomegranates sometime after noon. If I were to go out again on their watch I'd lose half the day. Admittedly, a couple hours wait after eight hundred days idling shouldn't have been much of a problem. It's a reflection on the sudden change in my mindset that I knew I couldn't manage it.

If I were to try my luck on another species' watch, the butcherbirds were the obvious choice. They were the most stable of the bunch – I considered myself on nearly familiar terms with three or four of their females. They'd never, to my knowledge, taken part in any attacks on my person. They'd demonstrated a certain level of trust by relaying my bits of dried fruit directly to their chicks. And of course the only other option was the magpies, which was out of the question. This is not to say that the magpies couldn't attack me during a butcherbird feeding. But the birds of all three species had exhibited a certain deference at the feeding times of the others. The food choices I'd settled on didn't cross species lines, and once I'd established the schedule, the off-birds would generally cede the space.

And so it was that I found myself outside the screen once again, this time surrounded not by the miners, but by the much larger and longer-beaked butchers. I couldn't help but focus on the little jagged bit at their beak-ends, perfectly suited to turning small perforations into far uglier tears. But when I made my leap onto the first branch only two of the butchers registered much alarm, and those, I believe, were the preener and the ace, two of the friendlier females. To my great surprise, they seemed more concerned *for* me than *about* me. I made it a point this time not to rush down the tree, but to take some time, to acclimate us all to each other's presence. I walked along the branch to the trunk and took a seat. A slightly more dubious butcher settled just next to me, close enough that I reached for my sword, but she reached for a cluster of small crystalline globes affixed to the bark and flew off again. I scooted over for a closer look, reached for one of the globes, and on some impulse – maybe as simple as wanting to fit in – I gave it a try. In another pleasant surprise, it was sweet and delicious. For tactical reasons, I needed a few more minutes in that tree, and they were more happily spent snacking on those newfound crystals than fretting over possible attacks. I cut a chunk of several globes with my blade and ate them all. I dropped a few more in the grass, climbed down, and made a pouch of my shirtfront to carry them inside.

At the same time the next day I went back for more. I knew I shouldn't eat things I didn't know about, but these were too good to pass up. I soon developed a regular craving for them. First thing in the morning, a little more after every meal, and I felt better all around – more energy, better digestion, a brighter overall outlook. Jill guessed what it was as soon as she'd heard my descriptions.

"It's gotta be lerp, Richie."

She had an annoying way of pausing at moments like those, forcing me to ask the obvious question rather than simply continuing the explanation.

"What's lerp?"

"It's an exudate from certain insects. People took an interest some time ago, but no one could make it work for commercial purposes. So now it's largely unknown except to biologists. Birds are the primary consumers."

"What's an exudate?"

"Something secreted from plants or insects. In this case from insects. There's too much sugar in the tree sap as compared to the proteins they need. So they excrete the sugar component, and that's what you're eating."

"You say they excrete it."

"Yes."

"Through what body part?"

"The anus."

I considered that for a moment.

"Well, that's disappointing."

She didn't answer.

"That is to say," I continued, "it's a little gross for eating, isn't it?"

"I suppose. But a lot of food is pretty gross when you think about it. You'll get over it."

"You mean I'll get over eating it, or I'll get over its grossness?"

"I suspect the latter."

Time would prove her correct.

42. Jill

As far as I could tell, BioSpore had dozens of those kinds of properties, or at least access to them, all over the world. A-19 was by no means a perfect fit, but I could see that it met our basic criteria. It sat in a country friendly enough to allow the occasional irregularity at customs. It was remote enough to preclude anyone's stumbling onto our resident footling. And to all appearances it had come at moderate cost. For all that, it offered an attractive environment, indulgently spacious and nestled into a truly beautiful setting. Granted, it would have taken a hell of a lot of work before I'd have ever moved in there. And to be honest, I wouldn't have lived that far out if it were the Taj Mahal. Within a week I'd bought myself a place in the heart of Brisbane, which I'd quickly found to be a perfectly livable mid-sized city. I spent too much for what I got, and the ceilings were a bit low for my liking, but it did have a nice deck with a river view. The 300-kilometer contractual stipulation turned out to be anything but arbitrary – my drive to A-19 was almost exactly that.

I never did get much background on A-19. My guess now is the same as when I first looked it over, Richie in tow, my first day in Australia – that it housed some kind of biological research, presumably agricultural, from some time after the Second World War, and had lain more or less dormant for a period of some decades. It was a little more run down than I'd expected, but I talked it up to Richie as best

I could. Beyond the mangy-looking corrugated metal roof, the place had a real greenhouse feel, long and featureless with primarily glass walls. Even as a newcomer to that part of the world, I could tell that was a lot of glass for a place without air conditioning. But the trees threw a fair amount of shade. And the footlings, by their nature, liked it warm. The bigger problem, surprisingly enough, was the lack of heating. The nights would get cool certain times of year. In Oswego we'd call it sweater weather, but things are different when you carry less mass than a Chinese hamster and lack the benefit of its fur. Fortunately, footlings weren't much for nightlife, and Richie could bundle up when he slept. The house did have an open fireplace I taught him to use, and the grounds had an endless supply of eucalyptus debris small enough to gather on his own. I could have done the gathering for him, but I thought it important that he took some responsibility for his own upkeep. It was small stuff, kindling really, but it burned like nothing I'd ever seen, like someone had prepped it in a giant kiln. It got him going in the mornings anyway.

While A-19 resembled a camp more than a house, I wasn't in any position to renovate. I couldn't bring workers in without stashing Richie somewhere, and if that were an easy thing to do he wouldn't have been out there in the first place. And the Facilities Trust wasn't nearly as well funded as I'd hoped. When I did the math I figured it would cover basic expenses for a decade, maybe longer, and that was about it. The place was a step down for Richie, but when you're brought up in a big-budget care center with round-the-clock attention from dedicated specialists, I suppose that's pretty much inevitable. On the other hand, he now had mountain views and an open schedule, and a huge swath of outdoors to explore and enjoy, all things he'd been sorely lacking.

I did a lot of cleaning my first couple trips out there, a lot more than I'm used to. I swept. I mopped. I dusted. I squeegeed an absurd amount of glass, inside and out. And I tacked up some netting to help him get onto the various elevated surfaces. My plan was to paint the interior walls over time – I'd take a day every once in a while and we'd paint a room together, make a date of it.

Amazing as it seems in today's world, there was no phone or internet reception out there from any commercial provider. I'm a scientific person, and as much as I researched it, I couldn't come up with any solution short of building my own cell tower. I don't think Richie and I would have done a lot of telephone chatting in any case, but the ongoing communications blackout caused us a lot of logistical headaches. It put him out of reach in case of emergencies, which didn't make either of us happy. And I knew he'd be upset about losing Wikipedia. I did the next best thing, which was loading his tablet with all the Wiki bundles it could handle.

Having groceries delivered wasn't going to happen – services like that just weren't available out there.[55] He was completely dependent on me for food, and that was my biggest ongoing issue. The house had a mini-fridge like the ones we used to have in college. Or, rather, like the ones my parents had in college. We'd found it under a tarp, shoved into a corner. Like most everything left in there, I credited its presence to simple indifference – nobody'd ever bothered to take it out. It was a sickly looking thing, yellowed inside and out, but when I plugged it in it kicked right on. I wiped it out as best I could, and we gave it a try. It wouldn't make ice any more, but it did keep his food cool. The main thing was that Richie could open the door on his own. I did worry that it might swing shut while he was inside, but I packed some cardboard under the back legs to cant it forward, and that seemed to do the trick.

At the beginning I was schlepping out there every other day to stock that fridge, three-plus hours each way. It wasn't so bad at first,

---

55 Australia is a first-rate nation in every way. But with roughly the same area as the continental US and only 7% of the population, there's only so much it can cover.

refreshing in a way after years of battling the Bay Area congestion. Once I cleared the suburbs there was very little traffic, and beyond that there was no traffic at all, as in *no cars whatsoever*. I was just getting used to driving on the left, but sometimes I'd do stretches on the right just for the hell of it.

As you might imagine, the length of that trip began to weigh on me pretty quickly. I started packing a bottle of white wine in a cooler and pouring it into a plastic cup in the console. What began as a few little sips became half a bottle, and then most of a bottle. When I found myself listing a bit from the car to the A-19 front gate, and struggling more than I should with the padlock and chain, I knew I'd have to make a change.

The solution was pretty simple. I started picking foods with more shelf life, and that alone cut the trip frequency to every four or five days. I think that made things a little more lonely for Richie out there, but then I wasn't exactly living it up either, half a planet from anybody I knew. It didn't help that he wasn't as enthusiastic with the outdoors as I'd expected. From day one he obsessed over what he saw as the murderous intent of the native birds. He considered them a persistent and mortal threat. This was disappointing to me, and baffling, given how well he'd always gotten on with The Chief. I understand that his size gave him a more skittish outlook than you or I might have, but he was still bigger than most of the birds out there. He'd show me red marks from time to time and tell me they'd come from magpie attacks. But in all the many times I was out there, I never saw any sign of aggression toward him from magpies or any other bird. And nothing I read indicated that any of them would ever bother a mammal his size, unless it posed an imminent threat to their nests, which Richie clearly did not. I didn't challenge him directly, but he'd always liked his storytelling. Insect bites were the far likelier explanation, especially once he'd slit the screen and begun spending so much time on the windowsill, against my wishes and naked as a jaybird.

We looked at some maps together, and he started calling the area East Central. While this was accurate enough geographically, nobody in Australia called it that. The term evoked some crime-infested section of Los Angeles rather than a swath of bushland most notable for its marsupials and avifauna. I went along with it in a lighthearted way, as in, "It's a tough life out here in East Central," or, "It's a beautiful afternoon in East Central." But he was deadly serious, and his terminology reflected the irrational fear he'd worked up for the place.

While he did become noticeably more sullen over those first few months, I wouldn't pin that entirely on environment. A good portion of it may have been developmental. I don't have any science on the point, but it seems a fundamental truth that children become more sullen as adults. It's the normal course, the combination of difficult life experiences and the natural sobering that comes with the responsibility of adulthood. This was all accelerated in Richie's case. While he wasn't growing in the physical sense, he was running through his expected lifespan at a much quicker rate than you or I. Add the dramatic life changes and it begins to add up.

I had some serious reservations about selling my place in Silicon Valley, but only when I did could I begin to settle into my Australian life. I threw myself into it as best I could. I walked the river. I walked the city. I took exercise classes. I took meals out. I made day trips to the beach. I made longer trips to the bigger cities, Melbourne and Sydney, shopping and exploring but always returning after a few days to tend to Richie. By the time I started contemplating another job, almost a year in, it wasn't because I needed the money. Despite some uncharacteristically heavy spending – condo, car, clothes, furniture, art – I was better off financially than I'd ever been. And it wasn't because I was bored. Believe me, I'll take a free day over a workday any time. It was about isolation.

The headhunters loved my BioSpore experience, to the degree I could convey it. I was up front about having remunerative confidentiality agreements in place. The more privileged and confidential it all seemed to be, the more they seemed to like it. I was equally forthcoming about having retained some light duty. I called it *Ongoing Regional Oversight*, or *ORO*. Judging by my three quick offers, that didn't seem to bother anyone either. The job I eventually took, the meatiest of the three, was still pretty low-key compared to either of my BioSpore assignments. And the commute, believe it or not, was a ride on a fast catamaran they called the City Cat, buzzing a few bends up the Brisbane River, and returning in sunsets so pink or so orange you'd have thought we'd been transported to another planet. Work drinks out, a few friends, and I started to feel like I belonged again.

For the most part, the job limited my A-19 trips to the weekends. And the phone and internet problems put a lot of pressure on me to keep even those trips pretty short. For a while there I'd cut out of work at noon on Fridays, spend the rest of the day with Richie, and double back out on Sundays. But that burned both of us out pretty quickly, and I settled on single Saturday visits. Fond as we were of each other, we couldn't handle two trips in three days. He never showed much interest in my life, and his increasing obsession with the birds impeded my interaction with his. He spent most of his waking hours eavesdropping and mimicking their calls. And he spent his sleeping hours in much the same way, up on the windowsill, emulating their elevated nests and positioning himself as close to them as physically possible. With my zoology background I'm probably more receptive to those kinds of things than most people, and his assimilation of the various calls was impressive, even scientifically significant. But he had an amateur's tendency to anthropomorphism, and to over-deduction from small sample sets. Given the confidential nature of our situation, the science part of it wasn't going anywhere for me anyway. I couldn't match his linguistic proficiency, and frankly, I couldn't match his interest.

We managed to play a fair amount of chess. I'd picked up a nice wooden set for him in Melbourne, medieval characters on little pedestals, vaguely Shakespearean. I could tell right away that he liked it – he'd arrange the pieces in certain ways and admire them from different angles. As to the game itself, I knew just enough to move the pieces correctly. That was enough to get us going once we'd resolved the logistical issue of his seeing the board. He took to sitting on the windowsill to gain the vantage point he needed and dictating his moves from there. That dynamic got a little irritating, especially when he started winning the lion's share of the games. I did a little homework then, researching opening sequences and general strategic principles, but my winning percentage went up only marginally. And by then he was spending half of each game looking out the window.

At the end of our days together I'd always pull a couple rickety Adirondack chairs into the grass and make him join me for a sunset cocktail. He seemed to like that little ritual, though he never quite decided whether to sit on the seat or the arm and was always rotating his head in those exasperating little ticks, looking out for the killer birds. I never let him drink any alcohol, but in retrospect maybe I should have. The apricot potion hadn't seemed to bother the others at Morben's, not that I was going to give him that, or even had any access to it. But a tiny bit of alcohol, maybe some other sweet little mix, might have loosened him up. And he certainly could have used that. I was the one who shouldn't have been drinking, since I always had to rally for the late drive home. The place just wasn't set up for me to stay overnight. I'd see him to bed – he definitely liked that – then haul myself back to the city, exhausted as I always was.

Once I'd settled on Saturdays for my visits, I experimented with a few painting sessions, but they didn't work out the way I'd hoped. He'd do the borders along the floor with a little brush, making spectacularly straight lines – in different circumstances I could have hired him out. But most of the real work, naturally, fell to me. That part I expected, but it was always stiflingly hot in there, and it's hard to paint in a full-body sweat when someone's carrying on about the competing nihilism of Nietzsche and Wagner and expecting you to follow along and respond on cue. I suspected that the exaggerated intellectualism was a response to separation anxiety. He'd always been the odd man out among the footlings, but I'd never seen that as justification for separating him from the others. As much as I liked Morben, I couldn't help but resent him for it.

43. Richie

By now I've picked up countless strips of bark at the feet of the eucalypts. They're out there in the thousands, curling as they dry, like
great rolls of parchment blown in from an ancient and unknown culture. Many are scrawled inside with carven runes, the work of insect
legions long since gone to dust. When I find one that combines ornate
enough patterns with structural integrity, I spare it from the morning
fires and haul it up the sill lines instead. Beyond its aesthetic appeal,
it serves as an insulating mat, cool in the heat set flat, and warm in
the cold rolled snug. It presses its runes where it bears my weight,
marking me with declarations I can't decipher, untold wisdom from
the bottom of the food chain. Sometimes I'll lie still to set the prints –
onto one shoulder for example, or along the larger expanse of my
back – then jump up to admire the effect in the mirror.

I've mentioned the special light at the end of days in East Central.
While I understand it to be the refractory product of our extreme
southern exposure and our daily turn from the sun, it's no less remarkable for that. It's a reliably uplifting show. And once a fortnight or
so it jumps to a special gear, to something so glorious that it defies
passive observation. When I see that in the works, I'm back down the
lines, through the cat door, and out to the orchard edge, my biggest
vista to the west, unframed and unobstructed. As the sun dips behind
the mountains it kicks some colossal switch that washes the whole sky

in orange and violet. I carry my blade, but I've found the birds to be on their best behavior then, as if the whole living world has paused in admiration. At the peak moments the scene is beyond any imagining, exotic hues backlit on a prodigious scale. I imagine that by comparison, even the world's most revered stained glass collections are reduced to child's play – and I include that of Saint Chapelle, my personal favorite.

Most of our sunsets are just slightly less showy, and I'll take them in from the comfort of my sill, wrapped in my bark and watching through the leaves. Toward the end I'll roll onto my back to see the colors snuffed in the wooden ceiling, the last hints of orange dropping to brown and gray. At the convergence of my own fatigue and the fusion of darkness with light, the patterns in the wood begin to blur at the edges. And sometimes, just every so often, they'll move into murky animation, amoebic creatures pulling themselves upright and walking on the stumps of two legs. Their approach reveals them as the others of my kind, in robes that vanish in a low-lying mist. In this vision, I rise to complete the original seven, joining in the spectral stroll. Certain ground rules hold sway at those moments, a logic we've all come to accept. It's pointless to rehash events we've shared, and more so to babble about those we haven't. Speculation is specious, small talk mortifying. So we stride mostly in silence, nearly overwhelmed with each other's presence but effectively unable to speak.

44. Jill

At some point on most of my visits, Richie would ask about the others. I felt badly for him, but I could only tell him what I knew. And that was nothing. I had no idea where they were.

I still wonder what Morben was thinking, leaving Richie to me while keeping the other six. By now we know he bought a few acres somewhere near Crescent City and moved his footling brood up there within a month after the Genesis shutdown. His place abutted state parklands that ran to forty or fifty thousand acres. I hiked up there before I ever started at Genesis, and I can tell you that's real redwood country – old-growth stuff, never logged, trees like skyscrapers with diameters of twenty feet. I can picture them hiking through that brobdignagian[56] forest, even Morben looking miniscule at the base of all that wood mass, and the footlings reduced to almost nothing. He'd have had them on the remotest trails at the most desolate times. And he'd still have had them on perpetual alert for the sound of other hikers, each of them ready, like little sprites, to pop completely from view. It worked for nearly two years, apparently, everything to plan.

And then, from what Falstaff told me, Samantha got taken by what's commonly known as a *fisher cat*. To clarify, fisher cats aren't

---

56 A word I picked up from Dr. Henderson, the English and American Literature major.

cats at all – officially they're just called *fishers*, which doesn't make sense either since they hunt on the forest floor and don't, as a rule, eat fish. Rabbits are more to their taste, gamey things of that sort. Fishers are like smaller, faster wolverines, though at three feet long and eight to twelve pounds they wouldn't look small to a footling. Morben, apparently, never saw this one, but the little people did, and were unanimous in identifying the species afterwards. Samantha, according to their reports, drew it away from the rest of the group, probably thinking she could buy enough time in the trees for them all to get into Morben's satchel, then circle back herself. But the fisher proved the better climber, which reduced it all to a simple footrace. And in the end she couldn't outrun it on that forest floor, though I'm sure she would have on a level surface, certainly on weight dispersion flooring.

Even if I'd known all this, I wouldn't have had the heart to tell Richie. I feel horrible for Samantha, and for Darrin, and the four others, and, I suppose, for Morben. According to Falstaff, Morben took it hard, blamed himself. He took his crew back into seclusion, at a location unknown to Falstaff and, apparently, to anyone else either. Which means I won't get the chance to ask him, among other things, why he singled out Richie. While I wouldn't have wanted him in the clutches of a forest carnivore, he should have been there with the others.

One more footling wouldn't have made Morben's life much tougher. Did he really think Richie would be better off with me? Or was he thinking more along the lines of some theoretical favor he was doing *for* me? Financially, yes, the arrangement with BioSpore made me much better off for having Richie in my custody. But Morben wasn't about money, his or anyone else's. Anyone at Genesis would tell you that. And while it's no secret that Richie and I had a special connection within the scope of that project, how do you go from that to thinking we'd be inseparable in real life? Did Morben assume that because I was childless and single, and Richie was motherless and single, we'd make the perfect pair?

I'd always had my reasons for not having a pet. I never thought I could spend enough time with a dog or a cat to keep it content. And you know you're going to get attached to it, and then that it's going to die on you, probably sooner rather than later. We'd had a long line of pets in Oswego, and I remember every one of them as corpses. Oscar the guinea pig, unnaturally deflated on the floor of his cage, looking like somebody's lost mitten. Gemma the cat, dead under my mother's bed, and when we pulled her out, stiff as a board.[57] Sparky the Weimaraner, once all muscle and swagger, our pride and our protector, now an immovable corpse on the living room carpet, a thin greenish turd half-excreted. And Prudence, our unthinkably fat rabbit, ripped to chunks of fur and flesh in our own back yard by the neighbor dog who'd have never dared set foot there during Sparky's reign.[58] And just as I expected, when Richie went missing it was harder on me than any of those had been.

With plans for that Saturday, I was making a Friday afternoon food drop instead. I had the groceries packed and was ready to head out just after noon when things blew up so badly at work it took me another ten hours to clean it up. The logical play would have been to postpone the trip, but I had a hard rule about not letting more than a week go between deliveries. They were his lifeline. So I decided to go ahead with the drop that night, then go back on the Sunday for a proper visit.

---

57 Until that moment, I'd always considered "stiff as a board" a figure of speech.

58 No discussion of my pets would seem complete without some mention of The Chief, despite the fact that he wasn't really mine and that our relationship was brief. With no one left to take care of him, I released him into the California sky my last time out of the building. He seemed tentative, but possibly up for the new adventure. I worry about him to this day.

It was way too late to be making such a long and desolate drive, but I got a second wind once I cleared the city. The moon may have had something to do with that. It was right in my windshield the whole way out, so bright and full that on a whim I turned the car lights off for the last half hour. I fitted the key into the padlock, walked the gate open, latched it with the chain, drove down the driveway, and let myself in the house, all by its incredible glow. As always, I dropped my bundles on the bench, and, not bothering with any house lights, walked down to take a quick look at Richie sleeping on the sill. Only he wasn't there. At first I thought he'd picked another place to sleep. But he wasn't on the bed, and there weren't many other comfortable options in that house, even for a footling. Now I did turn on the lights, every single one of them. I checked the sill again, making sure I hadn't missed him in his nesting materials. I ran through the rest of the house, thinking maybe he'd built another little nest somewhere else. But there was no sign of him along the floor or on any of the furniture. There was a slight lip where the glass walls met the ceiling, and to rule that out I climbed a chair in ten-meter increments along the whole length of the house on both sides. Not there either.

I went back outside, circling the house and calling his name. If those calls lacked conviction, it was partly from shock and fatigue, and partly from knowing that no amount of calling would stir him from night sleep. And while the full moon was certainly a help, nighttime is hardly ideal for a small-object search over acres of untamed grass-land, not for one person with a mass-market flashlight. My work shoes couldn't have been more poorly suited for the job, and the prickly grass was doing a number on my bare legs, but I pressed on in expanding loops around the house, picturing the small leathery corpse, pushing it out of my mind, and picturing it again until the batteries faded and the beam went faint.

My feet throbbed, and an angry rash ran from my feet to my knees. Part of me wanted to punish myself, to spend the night without a shower or a change of clothes, lying awake in that miserable bed. But my rational side knew none of that would help in the slightest. Beyond sunlight, I had to have shoes and supplies. Now I felt terrible that I hadn't been out in a week – who knew how many nights he'd been gone? On the off chance that he picked the next morning to straggle back in, at least his supplies were there for him. I'd cancel my Saturday plans and come back for a better look.

45. Richie

To the degree I was marking time, I was doing so by the moon. At Genesis we hadn't done any work on the lunar cycle, so when I first arrived in East Central I didn't know how it all worked. But with more exposure to the outdoors I became pretty curious. What I read in the Wiki files I confirmed with observations of the daytime moon. Sometimes I saw it only briefly, as it dropped toward the western tree line at the beginning of my day, or as it popped up in the east when I was retiring at dusk. But the full-day matinees were the special treats, when it'd rise with me in the morning and I could track its long slow trip to the end. When that all-day moon went full I figured I'd seen the best of it. I might never have experienced the true night spectacle but by a single night's chance of its jockeying with the Earth.

On my sill, as I've mentioned, the tree cover is pretty thick. While that's excellent for mingling with birds, it's only passable for seeing colors in the sky. And it doesn't work at all for tracking the moon. But one particularly clear night pulled a harvest moon into perfect alignment with one of the more pronounced gaps in the trees, maybe the best spot in the entire sky for its light to reach me on that sill. At some level between dreams and waking I felt it come over me, like a warm and weightless cloak, and I began to stir. Very little can wake me once I've gone down for the night. At Genesis they tried a variety of noises and jabbing and shaking techniques before concluding that for all practical purposes we were unwakable. But somehow this moon did the job. Things had the quiet feel of dawn, but even in my foggy state I knew that daylight was still a long way off. This was light of a different sort, a strange glow in the deepest night. I hauled myself down the lines and tottered through the house to the first glass beyond the trees. From there I could see fallen limbs and textured grasses, everything in flawless focus but silvered over, like the colors had been drained from the Earth's palette. The great gums stood perfectly clear, both nearby and in the distance. Matching black patches stretched out before them. Moonshadows!

Without really thinking, I walked to the cat door and slipped into a world different than anything I'd seen before. Ten thousand stars were lit, but all of them together could not have rivaled that moon. I could feel its pull, and I teetered towards it, headed vaguely to the north. You can't look directly into the sun – I'd tried it on many occasions for no particular reason. But you couldn't *not* look into that moon. It locked my gaze to the point that I tripped in the grass every third or fourth step. I dropped to my knees once, and went flat on my face shortly thereafter. But none of it bothered me. I may actually have giggled. I watched some eastern greys, half a dozen of them grazing in silhouette, then fell into a kind of whimsical step with the nearest gum tree, tracing its shadow edge in the grass, up one side of its trunk, along the expanse of its foliage, and back down the other side. I skipped to the next, and the next, and the next, and as I finished my shadow loop of the fifth great gum, I sat for a rest at its base, catching my breath and scanning the craters of the moon. At some point I slid a little lower and nudged some bark into better distribution beneath me. I folded my hands behind my head and was gone.

The next light I knew was the sun's. I'd slept for hours, and I'd frozen stiff, but I sprang so hard to my feet I was half my body height in the air. Even before I landed it registered that I'd not been devoured in the night. I made a quick scan and a brisk walk back to the house, venturing only a few quick looks at the moon, nearly sunken in the west.

I passed through the cat door, and through the immediate exhilaration of the night's adventure I felt the dreariness of being back indoors. I noticed the bundles on the bench. It was just my luck to have missed Jill on the only night, or half-night, I'd ever spent outdoors. But I realized how little that food interested me any more, beyond my handouts to the birds. I clambered up the sill lines. It felt a little hard up there compared to the foot of that gum, and as a hopelessly diurnal creature I couldn't get back to sleep. As it turned out, I wouldn't sleep on that sill again.

46. Jill

I fretted away the rest of the night and awoke in a panic at noon. By the time I barreled down the gravel track to Richie's place, it was nearly 16:00. Normally, when I arrived in daylight hours he'd hear the tires and be waiting for me at the door.[59] As you've probably guessed, he wasn't, and that's when I figured I'd seen the last of him. It seemed a forgone conclusion that calling out would get me no answer. He wasn't a daytime napper, so I wasn't going to find him curled up and purring in his perch. The groceries sat exactly as I'd left them the night before.

I conducted another search of the house. The light fixtures in there were pretty dim, so I hoped that by daylight I'd pick up some sign of him I'd missed in the night. The blade and scabbard were missing, but that didn't tell me much. They'd become his constant personal effects – he wore them inside and out. Everything else was normal, his wardrobe against the wall, his umbrella in the corner, no sign of a breach or struggle. In more than two years he hadn't gone anywhere but to the orchard a time or two. I thought it just conceivable he'd be out there now, maybe working on his samurai spins. I headed out and walked it row by row. No sign of him.

---

59 After knocking him to the floor early in the going I took to opening the door with deliberation.

Most animals I've studied seek privacy in death. Somehow they just know it's coming. I could hardly process what had happened, but that had to be my working hypothesis with Richie, that he'd sensed the end and hidden himself as cleverly as he could. And if he was anything, he was clever. For all I knew, he'd gone up a tree to die – he'd done a little climbing with me a week or two earlier. My inclination was to have a good stiff drink, drive home, and never lay eyes on that place again. But I had to play it out, to honor the remote possibility that he'd stagger in like some horseless cowboy out of the badlands, with a torn ACL or a shattered femur, and what, by the way, was I going to do with that? Or worse, that he couldn't even manage that and was still somewhere out there, immobile and desperate. I began to walk the acres of grassland, doing my best to hold disciplined lanes while stepping over fallen branches in various stages of drying and decay, and hoping with everything I had not to step on Richie himself, or what was left of him.

I dreaded coming across the grim little body, but the more it eluded me, the more I wanted to find it. I didn't owe anyone a report, or even an explanation. But I wanted a decent burial – I'd made note of the rusty old shovel in the tool closet – and, I suppose, some closure, a cause of death. But even if I'd found the body I had no access to an autopsy, much less an informed autopsy.

Our projections at longevity were merely guesses. Without data from Morben's group, I had no idea if Richie's death was even a demographic anomaly. The elusiveness of the corpse suggested that a death of natural causes was unlikely to have been sudden, reducing the odds of a heart attack, an aneurysm, and things of that sort. But we knew nothing about proclivities to slower-acting systemic failures, or sensitivities to certain insect bites, allergies, or viruses. At some point I heard a dog in the distance – maybe one had worked its way through the fence. Maybe a snake. I didn't want to think about it. For all I knew, the little birds he'd spent so much time worrying about had finally had their way.

I knew all along there'd been substantial risks for him outdoors. Certainly he had an ample and even exaggerated aversion to those risks. I'll never know if something actually caught up to him out there, but cooping him up inside had never been an option. If I'd had the facility and staff we'd had at Genesis it would have been a different matter. But at A-19 the only option was a life that incorporated the outdoors. I never had a second thought about that, and never will.

After two hours the discipline in my one-person search party began to waver, and before much longer it broke down entirely. The afternoon was retaining its heat to the very end, and I realized I'd baked to the point where I was barely even paying attention. My tight little grid had given way to a broader, almost random wandering. As I grew more disoriented and delusional, I began to call out for him, but meekly, as if someone else might be lurking around, bearing witness to my derangement.

At dusk, I suspended the search. I pulled out both of the old Adirondack chairs – a maudlin gesture, as I well knew – plopped myself into one of them and poured myself a tall glass of wine. For the first time in quite a while, I wept. I missed his little voice. I missed his running along at my feet. I missed his perching on my shoulder, though he hadn't been up there much lately. And I missed reading together, though we hadn't done that in ages either.

At dark I settled in for something I'd long dreaded, a full night at A-19. I'd have paid a week's salary for a shower. After a halfhearted attempt at a sponge bath, my legs were still sticking together. I pulled up the sheet, kicked it off, and tried various half measures – sheet to the waist, one leg out, both legs out. The bed was even worse than I'd thought – pressing into it released a persistent scent of mold. I should have bought him a new mattress – how had I not done that? I regretted every omission I'd ever made with him, every withheld kindness, every moment of exasperation, every concession to myself. Then I shifted my incriminations to Morben, marshalling my many arguments against his isolating Richie as if I were prepping for a retrospective Little Gathering. Over the bitter hours, with that grievance bullet-pointed but far from settled, others slipped in to take their turns across the stage. Dozens of slights I'd suffered formed a steady parade, working backwards through time all the way to Oswego. I fidgeted and flipped myself crazy, then made myself lie still until whole muscle groups ached in rebellion. I'd never had much problem with insomnia – my father always said the key to beating it was eliminating the bedside clock – but now for the second straight night I understood something of its misery. I checked the time only twice – once at 23:45 and again at 03:10 – with never a hint of sleep. A single mosquito undertook an hour-long mission to orbit my head. A bird I couldn't identify – I imagined some kind of Australian loon – screeched out a doleful call every couple hours, as if in some scheduled mourning of the dead. It was suddenly clear to me that no effort on my part was going to bring him back. If I hadn't known the sun would be up so early I might have gotten up and driven home.

But there I was, back at it, just after dawn at the ungodly hour of 04:30. I retraced everything I'd done and then some, working through the orchard row by row, and through the grass in concentric circles from the house, this time for four predictably fruitless hours. After the single most miserable night of my life, and the single most miserable morning, I packed up and made my last long haul from A-19 back to the city.

47. Richie

There were still a few hours of daylight when I cleared the crest, dragging the rucksack behind me. The load was on the heavy side. The cockatoos had left a wealth of macadamias in the grass, and while I usually held myself to one piece of fruit, the avocados and mangos were too beautiful not to take one full-bodied specimen of each. As I considered the mango's sweet promise, it was all I could do not to stop and cut into it right there in the grass.

With a burden like that dragging behind I tend to use my blade as a counter-balance, a freehand walking stick, swinging and planting on the off-step. I understand logically that this must blunt the point, but I haven't seen evidence of undue wear, and I'm not sure I'd stop the practice even if I did. It brings a mechanical advantage I can't seem to resist. It enhances the physical rhythm, and it brings an auditory cadence I like – step, plant, step, plant, step, plant. On that afternoon I may have been caught up in the cadence more than I should have. It took me a moment to decipher the counter beat of pounding paws. This was no possum, no cumbersome hulk lumbering through the grass. At last, and when I least expected it, this was death.

It was a Staffie, of all things, a Staffordshire bull terrier in its physical prime, a furious blur of muscle and teeth rocketing over the terrain, its muscular haunches firing like automatic weapons, its forepaws swatting away great lengths of earth. This blend of power and stability was something I'd never imagined, low-set, nearly flattened in its aero-dynamic perfection, a killing machine at full throttle. I saw it at eighty meters – in less than a second I'd dropped everything I carried and was into a dead sprint of my own, and already it'd closed to sixty. Instinct pointed me directly away, a course driving me from the southwest and slightly but irrevocably from the sanctuary of my cat door. I processed this without regret – simple physics assured me I'd never reach it in any case.

The imminence of death, coupled with a desperate spew of adren-alin, seems to have a diversifying effect on one's thought process. Through the overwhelming wave of terror, I noticed, with some sat-isfaction, that I'd never run quite so well, at least without the benefits of weight-dispersion flooring The awkward steps of my earliest days in East Central were long behind me. I'd become a proud product of the bush, a natural phenomenon in my own right. Arms, legs, and breath in perfect cadence, cutting through the grass at a speed so pure I could barely feel my feet touch ground, though I felt nothing else. In spite of the terrain, the surface clumped and the grass to my shoulders, I was maintaining personal-best speed through a series of twenty-degree veers and feints ordered from some previously unknown command center within me. A surge of quiet dignity swam in the current of my terror. There was a certain gallantry in such a flight, in the race I could never win. I looked on as if through an overhead lens, the dog at fifteen meters, ten, and closing, but the focus on my own form at the height of its powers, a final moment of gratitude and the last fond parting.

I never actually saw what passed over me just then. But I felt the ripple, the parting in the air, and the disturbance just behind me. I had an impression for a millisecond that a tiny winged spirit had passed over, at deathly speed and in deathly silence, holding the tiniest clear-ance over the grass line. My first reaction was to deny it completely. And failing that, to ignore it, whatever it was. And with that I caught my feet and went into a tumble. It entailed exactly three rotations – my eyes were open, and three times I saw the flash of sky. Then I was back on my feet to meet the crush of jaws.

Instead, the earth itself seemed to heave. A mass of gray-brown matter thundered by me, and then the dog was out of its own tumble and back on its feet, not two meters away, with half a dozen miners and butchers swarming its face and others rallying to join. This was not the possum affair with only certain birds carrying the attack and the others keeping their distance. Every bird was a part of the swarm. The dog growled and yelped and rolled and jumped and fled to the north, clipped and bludgeoned every step of the way for as far as I could see.

I put my hands on my knees, dropped to one knee, and then to both. My chest heaved and my heart pounded in my ears. I vomited until my stomach was empty, then vomited some more. I rolled onto my back and tried to make sense, but couldn't hold the slightest coherent thought. After a while my mind just went blank. I flirted with sleep, or some highly stressed form of it, jolted myself awake, and succumbed.

When I came to, it was nearly dark. I could barely stand upright. It was too far to the cat door, but I didn't dare spend a second night on the open ground, not for any number of reasons, and certainly not with a Staffie on the prowl. Miraculous as my deliverance had been, it wasn't going to happen again. Not at night. Not ever.

I dragged myself twenty meters to the nearest tree, found a toe-hold and two fingerholds, and pulled with everything I had. My limbs were barely functioning, but the dead-leg training on the sill lines, or at least the thought of it, kicked in, and I started to climb. Two meters up, the tree forked into three main stems. I wasn't going any further in any event, but the crotch was filled with soft leafy material. It wasn't the worst place to end up. I made myself reasonably comfortable, but as wrecked as I was, I had no illusions that there'd be sleep. It's a lot different falling asleep in a strange place accidentally, as I'd done the prior night, and doing it intentionally, as I needed to now. Not to mention that I was still sick to my stomach, ached all over, and couldn't stop reliving the chase. I'd say I dreaded the night ahead of me, but dread implies a future misery, and mine was very much in the present.

I heard a soft landing above me, and a familiar call. I'm here, where are you? I had a thought it was the preener, but to this day I don't know if that was the unlikely truth or simple delirium. For the first time in my life that call seemed meant for me, and now when I tried to answer I could barely muster a peep. She drifted into a soft trill, and while I labored to take her meaning, nothing seemed to register. Either I was more compromised than I realized, or it was not a particularly directed message, but rather a song for its own sake, for the pure beauty of it. I gave up the struggle and let it settle over me. My heart rate slowed, my breathing softened. And there in that tree I slept like I"d never slept before, well past diurnal norms. When I finally awoke the morning was nearly gone.

48. Jill

Hardly a day goes by when I don't think about Richie one way or the other. Sometimes it's just some little notion, a memory behind a curtain that, if I let it, comes bounding out to center stage. There he'll be, lying on the floor to roll his Brio back and forth, or playing the balloon game on my lawn, or climbing trees in the abandoned orchard. Other times I'll go over it on a more rational level, wondering what we all might have done differently.

Once the Russians hacked the BioSpore systems it all came pouring out. Everything. StopValve, Genesis, and a dozen other projects just as juicy, all laid suddenly bare. It was way too much for one news cycle. And as far as I can tell, Genesis got more or less lost in the shuffle. Strange as it sounds, neither the feds, to the extent they tried, nor the press, could track down the hulking Dr. Morben or any of his diminutive charges. It was determined that castrations had not actually occurred, and there was no record of other cruelties that might have generated a more prosecutorial mindset. The existence of so many conflicting accounts even within the BioSpore email network had an equally deflating effect on any investigative ardor. In particular, the rumor about genetically altered humans scuttling about on dozens of legs gained enough traction to infuse the whole affair with an air of silliness. In my mind, that contributed as much as anything to its ultimate dismissal.

It was StopValve that got most of the attention and generated the most fallout. In the end, even that didn't produce as much outrage as I expected. BioSpore let three people go — my former supervisor and two Senior Science Officers — each of them with a presumably sufficient severance package. By the terms of the civil settlement, a handful of homeless people, the ones they could track down and identify, were suddenly wealthy enough to house themselves and a good number of their fellow indigents, in style and for as long as they chose, if they chose, which by and large they did not. But the larger homeless fund that emerged from the settlement did get some fifteen hundred people off the streets, at least for a time, which made for something of a feel-good ending. Nobody did any jail time, which was a relief to me personally, given how things looked for a while there. They didn't have enough on me to merit an extradition, and I wasn't going back for hearings on my own volition. I was pre-emptive, and apparently just convincing enough, in explaining my position to my current employers. So while all the bad press I got, first in the States and then here, has pretty much ruled out meaningful workplace advancement, I was at least able to keep the job I have. And that, unfortunately, is nothing to sniff at, with my BioSpore annuities brought to a sudden halt. If I ever run into Dmitri, I mean to give him an earful.

49. Richie

Dawn in the jacaranda. At first it's just patches of pink poking through the ferny cover, but I've learned to lie still through a couple rounds of kookaburra calls and to watch as the cover itself comes alive, brightening from colorless shadow to a brilliant back-lit yellow-green. Individual fronds come into focus, no bigger than my fingers, in two neat rows of twenty or more on single delicate stems. I reach for my stash of lerp and start right in. I find a certain satisfaction in chewing through the stuff, but the birds in easy earshot are often annoyed with my early-morning crunching. A few of them express that now with sharp little clicks.

Lerp is fast-acting stuff. Already I feel the warmth building in my belly, and soon I'll be able to peel back my blankets and strip off a layer of night clothing. It's a pretty nice platform I've built up here. I would never call it a nest – I don't have nearly the workmanship, or the saliva, to pull off something like that. And I wouldn't call it a shelter or a tree house either, since there's no roof and no walls. It's just a platform of sticks, tied for stability, with a lot of covering material and a bit of a lip to keep me from rolling off, not that I move much when I sleep. Like the nests, it's not possum-proof, but these days I'm thinking that at least one possum equates my scent with a sharp poker in the backside and won't bother us up here anymore. The birds may or may not appreciate this. They have a name for my platform I can't translate to English, but it conveys, among other things, that they don't much like the look. I'll admit that it's a bit of a blight on the tree, but it's solid enough and plenty comfortable. It takes a hell of a storm to get much water in here with all those leafy layers overhead, and when that does happen I just curl up in a bark roll.

The light in the leaves makes for a stained glass effect, similar to what I'd always imagined in the European cathedrals. It's both peaceful and magnificent. I hardly ever go back in the old house. It's stuffy in there, and I finally figured out something the butchers had been saying for quite some time, that attacks were less likely on established tree-dwellers. What seems obvious to me now was a life-altering revelation. None of them come after me in the trees. And I've discovered that beyond quick trips to the orchard every day or two I don't have much reason to be on the ground. If you'll pardon my vulgarity, I've taken to defecating from the branches. That's been another revelation -- it's much simpler and safer that way. I keep my food in the rucksack, which hangs on a branch just near me, joined by the blade and scabbard when I'm sleeping. I still carry the blade during all waking hours, not so much for protection – I don't bother with the pirouette any longer – but because it's such a part of how the birds perceive me, a point of respect. I've had a couple of isolated swoops on my way to the orchard, but on at least one of those occasions the attacker himself took a good bit of punishment from his peers.

I've gotten agile enough in the trees that you probably wouldn't even call it climbing any more. It's more like bounding. I rarely miss a jump, and my decision-making has become automatic, just below the level of conscious thought. You might be surprised that this newfound prowess hasn't taken me further afoot. But there's a whole network of trees I can access here without touching ground. Add the orchard and it's plenty to cover. There's a feeling that I'm here with the flock that'll have me, and that's brought a corresponding reduction in my wanderlust.

Surviving the Staffie has given me a second life, and I do value the extra time. I never did identify the lead bird from the attacking squadron. Logic would have one of the miners, the most explosive fliers, in that role. But you never know – the butchers can rip it too. The fact is, I never confirmed a single individual from that whole episode, though I'm pretty sure it was the preener who was singing in that tree. In my mind it was all the stuff of legend, but birds just don't revisit things. I doled out as much general praise and gratitude as was admissible, and that was that.

My grasp of the birdsong has improved as much as my climbing. It finally occurred to me to stop trying to jam every snippet of song through the processor in my head. Every time I overthought one bit, others would slip by, unheard and irretrievable. Now I try to stay more in the moment. I hear what I hear and take the meaning in tone. It all works for the better.

With the birdsong so fixed on the here and now, I might have wished for a slightly more philosophical company. But the more I listen the more I think our outlooks are not so very different. All of us occupy a continuum of chance and volition. Our contentment levels hover well within our pre-set ranges. And in the best case, our time just peters out.

Jill hasn't been here in ages, so I don't have access to pomegranate, or dried fruits or meats. But I've kept my handouts going on the sill. It's not the production it once was. I just put out quiet little spreads when the orchard's in surplus mode. I can't spare any lerp, and most of these birds don't love the fruits and nuts I have to offer. But they partake now and then. And on some level, they seem to appreciate the effort.

THE AUTHOR

M. Reese Kennedy was born and raised in Omaha, Nebraska, during its heyday as the world's largest livestock market, slaughterhouse, and meatpacking center. He is the author of three novels and lives in Queensland, Australia.

ACKNOWLEDGEMENTS

Thanks to Champ Cudahy, whose musings prompted my imagining this book, and whose thoughtful comments helped me make some sense of it. Thanks also to Bill Scheft for his encouragements and suggestions at a time of great personal stress. And to John Riley, the closer. Thanks to Zoe and Elisabeth Lawrence, mother and daughter Audubons, for the avian artwork. And special thanks to Louisa and Connor – together we keep a keen eye on the birdlife.